THE EYE OF THE ABYSS

Marshall Browne

Thomas Dunne Books
St. Martin's Minotaur ❧ New York

THOMAS DUNNE BOOKS.
An imprint of St. Martin's Press.

www.minotaurbooks.com

ISBN 0-312-31156-7

First published in Australia by Duffy & Snellgrove

First U.S. Edition: October 2003

10 9 8 7 6 5 4 3 2 1

In memory of my father
Leigh Browne
also a banker

He who fights with monsters might take care
lest he thereby become a monster.
And if you gaze for long into an abyss, the abyss
gazes also into you.

Friedrich Nietzsche

THE EYE OF THE ABYSS

PRELUDE

T
HE WHEEL HAD begun to turn. On a Sunday in September, 1935, in a south German city, it was moving, slowly and subtly, as if some sinister hand had caressed it into motion. The platz was full of uniforms, ill-fitting earth-coloured Sturmabteilung ones, red and black Nazi banners, and pinch-faced civilians. The crowd was dispersing from the rally. The raucous speeches were over and forgotten, the bands had marched away, the public address system was being dismantled. Already the streetlights were on. Clouds were scudding in low from the west, promising rain and a premature nightfall.

A small man in a black overcoat and hat hurried along against a wall, trying to be inconspicuous. Why was he out? Had he misjudged the duration of the rally? Was medicine or a doctor needed so urgently in his household? A party of jack-booted toughs, gripping their standards, marching away to their beer hall, spotted him and the cry went up. They broke ranks and cornered him in a moment. The leader shouted questions. The man had shrunk back against the wall. The leader began to beat him about the head. He went down on his back with a thud. The leader kicked him in the privates; the boots of the others began to kick him like a sack of potatoes.

A slight, blond, well-dressed man appeared from nowhere,

sprang astride the fallen man, raising his hands in protest or supplication. The SA toughs fell back, amazed. But the leader seized his flagstaff and jabbed its brass-pointed eagle into the face of the interventionist.

Blood spurted.

The toughs turned and ran; everyone seemed to be running – streaming away to the exit streets, boots crashing in a cacophony on the cobbles. At the corner, the police detail of a detective and six men, rifles slung, at first had turned away from the fracas. Then, cautiously, they began to approach, the giant plain-clothes officer at their head. The small dark man lay inert, one leg drawn up to his chest. The blond interventionist was reeling across the cobbles, hands clutched over his left eye. But it was lower, on his cheek below the hands: a surprised fish's eye, staring out from a new position. Blood pattered on the stones like water from a tap.

The detective gestured to a uniformed colleague. 'Get an ambulance!'

1

AT ONE MINUTE to eight, Franz Schmidt, chief internal auditor of Bankhaus Wertheim & Co., boarded the tramcar standing in Bamberg Platz. His wife, Helga, a tall, full-figured woman with thoughtful eyes, waited beside the line with their four-year-old daughter, Trudi, to wave him goodbye. In the sunlight penetrating the thinning mist, the uplifted faces and hair of his family glowed gold. What a picture! Schmidt thought. Smiling, he gave his self-conscious wave.

The conductor rang the bell, and the tram shuddered along its length. Helga smiled back, Trudi waved vigorously, and called out. He heard only: 'Papa!' The two dear faces passed from his vision. Precisely, he folded his paper into a narrow strip. For Schmidt, Tuesday, October 4, 1938, had begun like any other work day.

'Good morning, Herr Schmidt!' The conductor, green-uniformed, leaned heavily over the auditor.

Schmidt looked up at the Viennese. 'Good morning, Herr Dorf.' He gave the correct fare.

'A real nip in the air, sir.' Schmidt admitted it. 'On the wireless, the Wetteramt says it'll be a hard winter. Well, all the news can't be good.'

Schmidt concurred again. He wasn't a morning wireless listener himself. The conductor shrugged, swayed on down the car, agile despite his age and weight.

Schmidt eyed the headlines: still rapturous about the Munich Agreement. He pursed his lips, and scanned the columns. It did appear that the Fuehrer had gained a bloodless victory, not only over Czechoslovakia but over Great Britain and France. Had war been averted? Despite the euphoria in the streets, Schmidt couldn't quite believe that. He turned to the finance pages. Certainly business was booming, humming in the air like electricity being generated. He had it carefully under observation, as though it were a suspect loan in the bank's books. A new section of autobahn had been opened. The National Socialist government was pressing forward. Ever forward.

A tooth, lower left-hand side, had an unhealthy tingle. He checked it with his tongue. Damn! He wondered if Dr Bernstein was still in practice.

He alighted at Potsdamerstrasse. Unaccountably, under his shoes glass crunched. Unaccountable only for a second. He looked aside. A brick had been put through the window of the corner shop. A haggard, fearful face glanced at him from the doorway, on which a Star of David had been crudely chalked. Averting his eye, he walked into a narrow street. These days there was more to worry about than weather. Still, this chilly breeze was a tribulation; it smacked into his face, and blew between rows of stone buildings whose bombastic façades, dripping with architectural embellishment, reminded the auditor of overweight burghers. Behind its glass, his eyesocket began to weep. As he walked he gave it dabs with a handkerchief.

Thinking of the Jew's fear, he entered a building under its carved granite lintel. A brass plate said in small letters: Bankhaus Wertheim & Co AG, Private Bankers.

'Good morning, Herr Chief Auditor. The post's gone up.' Respectfully the head messenger nodded his head. Then, gasping for breath, he bustled to the lift, and flung open its door.

Sympathetically the auditor recalled: Asthma. Touch of mustard gas, too. 'Thank you, Herr Berger,' he said. How many men had this mild and responsible servant killed in the war?

Once in his small office on the second floor, Schmidt opened sixty or so letters with precise slits of his ivory-handled knife, a gift from his late father, noted the nature of the business, and put each into its departmental pouch. Nothing to draw his professional attention ... except *this*. He took up the letter from Berlin for Herr General-Director Wertheim stamped *Confidential* and examined the seal. After a moment, he inserted it unopened into a special leather pouch, pushed a buzzer, and a junior messenger hurried in and took it away.

He resumed work left off yesterday, but the image of that seal – an eagle rampant on the swastika – remained in his mind's eye. Why on earth would Wertheims be receiving a letter from that organisation?

The first dislocation to Schmidt's routine came at 9.55: a knock at his door, and Fräulein Dressler entered. Surprised, he stood up. The general-director's private secretary had never visited his office before. She advanced into his room and stopped, her arms crossed over her abdomen, her hands splayed, cupping her elbows. She regarded him, his room, with considering eyes: brown, flecked with gold. A trick of the light? He regarded her: his surprise had turned to politeness. She seemed curious to see him in his domain.

'Good morning, Herr Schmidt. The General-Director wishes to see you at 10.30.' She paused. 'Please come to his office at that time.'

'Of course.' Schmidt nodded gravely.

She paused, smiled. 'Always so serious, Herr Schmidt! It's not the end of the world.' Her eyes were glinting.

Schmidt doubted that it would be. He bowed gravely;

he couldn't help his nature.

She had the reputation of being a humorist; she could afford to be in her rarefied position. Though today, was there an atmosphere of strain behind her remarks?

'Herr Schmidt.' With a slight, enigmatic curve of the lips she turned to go. In a rush, unexpectedly, Schmidt found himself registering impressions: darkish down above her upper lip, subtle heaviness in the hips, exaggerated shapeliness of her legs: hard-packed, swelling calves, thin ankles. Dancers' legs? But the suggestion of thick thighs. About thirty, the raven-black hair cut severely, symmetrically, just below her ears. That flicker of a smile ... he stopped, startled at himself. Certainly enigmatic, but highly efficient, otherwise she wouldn't have lasted with Herr Wertheim. Her husky yet melodic voice lingered in his head. So did her perfume – as discreet as the bank. He shook his head, sat down again, and turned back to familiar territory: his monthly report to the board.

At 10.30, in the general-director's anteroom, the mystique of the first floor bore down on him, aided by wood-panelled walls on which hung the varnished, dead-pale faces of the founding Wertheims. Schmidt was a calm person but he felt his nerves quicken. Only once before had he been summoned to the inner sanctum: in 1934, he'd uncovered a client's convoluted fraud. Herr Wertheim had seen fit to personally commend him. Occasionally, he did come to the boardroom to explain an abstruse point. Otherwise ... The double doors at the end of the anteroom sprang open, revealing a briskly efficient Fräulein Dressler, with no trace of humour now. That letter with its thought-provoking seal flashed back into his mind.

'Herr Chief Auditor!'

Herr Wertheim, fifty years a private banker, smiling benevolently, offered his recognition, his slender white hand, to the auditor, ushered him to a seat, and sat down himself in a high-backed chair padded with cushions. All wonderfully urbane. For a hundred years, the Wertheims had received royalty, statesmen, an affluent clientele – and sometimes valued employees – with such super-refined courtesy. 'Quite bloodless,' according to Schmidt's friend, deputy foreign manager Wagner. 'They get it with their mother's milk.' Also deceptive. Like Wagner, Schmidt knew Herr Wertheim had destroyed many men. However, no-one could doubt the bank's nationwide reputation for discretion and probity, domiciled though it was in this provincial city of 400,000.

'Herr Schmidt.' The general-director flicked a piece of lint from his sleeve as casually as he'd flicked competitors, enemies, and ex-lovers, into the abyss. 'Herr Schmidt! *Excellent* news this morning. In fact, it passed through your hands!' He bobbed his silver head, and let his pince-nez in its tortoiseshell frame drop to the end of its black ribbon. 'The National Socialist German Workers' Party is to entrust its business to Wertheims! What do you think of that?'

The Nazis coming to Wertheims! Schmidt absorbed the surprising news, along with the note of triumph. '*All* of their business, Herr General-Director?'

'Not their clearing business. Their investment business only.'

Schmidt stared at the G-D's face. He'd never before seen it flushed with excitement. 'A very important acquisition,' he said carefully.

'And a great honour, Herr Schmidt! An arduous and special responsibility.' With a matching seriousness, Schmidt agreed. 'Well, well, what more can one say?' Wertheim leaned back as though needing a respite from this phenomenon. His gaze left the auditor's face and went like an arrow to a large painting on the wall: a statuesque woman posed against a gold-leafed background of intricately painted devices: wheels, cogs … Beauty astride Commerce and Industry. The brave new world! Purchased recently, it was the bank's only artistic acquisition for thirty years, and its selection had been widely commented on.

Schmidt politely turned in his chair to examine it. More change.

Herr Wertheim thought the purchase had the same risk-taking character as their step into the Nazi Party's ambit. Could an old private bank withstand *that* shock? His deceased brother would've thought not. Too political by far. He'd been a milky kind of man. A distinct contrast to himself. As head of the family he'd gazed into the perennially murky future of money and politics, weighed them up. Now he gazed into himself, too, wondered at the new tide he felt running there.

It had happened like this: a Nazi Party functionary had phoned Wertheim. The Party was dissatisfied with the management of its investments. Would Wertheim & Co like to put forward a proposal to take over the business? Overnight, Herr Wertheim had considered the matter. The next day he'd travelled to Berlin. At Party headquarters, he'd met the man who'd phoned him. A man called von Streck. Alone, they'd discussed and agreed the arrangements. Von Streck would refer it to a committee for decision. Wertheim was left in no doubt that the fellow was high up in the Party; how high he couldn't tell; he used no title, and was one of those Nazis who didn't wear a uniform. The G-D had returned home confident that he'd handled the matter skilfully. However, he didn't overrate himself. Instinctively, he'd felt that the Party, perhaps the man he'd met, had a secondary agenda. He'd not penetrated what it was. In the fullness of time, he would. He trusted that it wouldn't be incompatible with his own.

Schmidt wondered: What's this all about? He felt he was being put to some kind of test. Wertheim was thin of face and body; even of voice. But his natural cunning and intellect were definitely not thin.

Abruptly, Wertheim returned to the present. 'I *am sorry* Herr Schmidt. And – what do you think of *that*?'

Schmidt, uncertain and slightly puzzled, had reached no conclusion about the picture. 'Very interesting, sir.'

'Like our lives today?'

'Too true, sir.' Our lives? The Nazi Party in Wertheims! The auditor couldn't get his mind away from it, but his face remained impassive.

'Back to business.' Wertheim steepled slender fingers. Where would a trusted employee like Schmidt stand on the NSDAP? He recalled the auditor had lost an eye. A wretched incident. Which one was it? Both watched him with an identical blue stare. What an act of courage! Hard to believe when you looked at this mild, correct fellow.

'Do forgive me, Herr Schmidt. I keep drifting off. My mind's so full. Now … we will take it over on the thirteenth from their Berlin bank.' He smiled as he visualised the consternation there. 'Of course, Herr Schloss and his department will manage it. However, we can't afford the slightest problem. I want you to maintain a special overview. You'll report to me directly. Is this all clear, my dear Schmidt?'

'Yes, Herr General-Director.' It was clear if unprecedented. Despite Herr Wertheim's smooth confidence and excitement, Schmidt had picked up another undercurrent. Nerves? If it was so – natural enough. What a step it was! Schmidt's mind did range into remote corners, but in a million years wouldn't have anticipated this.

Wertheim, uniformed in his boiled, white cuffs and collar, black suiting, silver necktie, gold watch-chain and rings, smiled at this future. 'A patriotic responsibility, my dear Schmidt. And, only a beginning.'

Returning up the rear stairway to his office, passing the three large stone knights upright in their embrasures, Schmidt, a user of back ways ('Where will he strike next?' the staff said), felt the first presentiment of an invasion. Hitherto, he'd observed the rise of the Nazis circumspectly, and generally guarded his opinions. Herr Wertheim had said with a deceptive blandness: 'One of their people will join us as a director.' A Nazi functionary actually working *in* Wertheims! The filter of distance was about to be whipped away.

Fräulein Dressler had given him a cryptic smile when she'd seen him out. Had it suggested pessimism?

Whatever it was, it had vanished behind her professional aura when, soon after Schmidt's departure, she took an instruction from Herr Wertheim: 'Fräulein, please have the directors assemble in the boardroom at five. We'll serve champagne. And, I think caviar. Not too much of that.'

'And only one glass of champagne as usual, Herr Wertheim?' He was mean with small expenditures, and she teased him about it sometimes.

He grinned. 'Now, Fräulein!'

But when she went out her smile faded and there was a deepening chill in her heart.

2

SCHMIDT FOUND HE was unable to resume work. Throughout the afternoon, as the news circulated, a decorous excitement bubbled in the bank. Leaving at five with Wagner, he was impatient to learn his colleague's reaction. But as they walked to their café Wagner kept quiet. In one of his moods, Schmidt decided. Not till they were sitting in the fading sunlight did he open up.

'God Almighty! Can you believe it? Our esteemed directors are up in the boardroom opening champagne. The damned fools! It should be ditchwater!' Violently, he slapped his pockets for cigarettes, and looked his colleague in his good eye at last. Schmidt took the outburst, the look, calmly. Classic Wagner. He broke the eye contact, and gazed at the Lutheran church across the small platz. He was waiting for the rest: the second barrel. Wagner, an idiosyncratic character at Wertheims, always had someone, something, in his sights. Schmidt turned his auditing eye back to his colleague, who with tics and grimaces was still searching his pockets.

Wagner was single and forty-eight, and had been deputy foreign manager since 1933. His face was narrow and white, his lank, fair hair always seemed to need cutting. His clothes were expensive, but stained and sloppily worn. Most Wertheim men were capable of becoming inebriated in the correct environment, but Wagner didn't differentiate. The directors averted their eyes, as if from a nasty traffic accident, when they encountered him staggering homewards. Helga had called him an aesthete. If so, a brooding and intelligent one. But also a numbers man, and a deal-doer. Chain-smoking stained his fingers; the state of his nails reflected an indifference to hygiene. Left well-off by his parents, there was a worm of discontent feeding away in him. What had saved him at Wertheims were his banking skills and international contacts, and his father's service. Insiders understood that he'd reached his promotional limit.

Cigarette alight at last, Wagner carelessly tossed the packet on the table, took a deep swallow of beer, and gave Schmidt an annoyed, yet acute, glance.

'Well, my silent friend. I think we can say old Wertheim's finally lost his marbles. Something's cracked. My father said our esteemed General-Director was two-faced in his financial philosophy. That he'd dual identities. Those cautionary speeches of his inside the bank: "Dear colleagues, our prime duty to our clients is to maintain the *real* value of their capital. It's excellent to increase it, however, never forget the prime duty."' Schmidt smiled. Wagner had caught the G-D's precise tenor. 'In his private finances he's frequently been reckless, but it's been well concealed. You must have an idea of this, Franz?'

'What's your point?' Schmidt asked, evenly. He was thinking: Yes, I do have. But even with Wagner he wasn't accustomed to speak of Herr Werthein with such familiarity.

'The point, my dear, is today he rubbed out that borderline.' Wagner drew on his cigarette, and stared at his colleague. Sensing an interlude a waiter, knowing his customer, brought more beer.

Schmidt thought: Yes, but why? What's behind it? He was uneasy but at a different level from Wagner.

'Well, what *does* our iced-water-for-blood auditor think?' Wagner's wide mouth drooped into a lopsided grin, and the flesh of his face became flaccid. Suddenly he looked aged. He was clearly irritated and worried. Schmidt recalled how his colleague had said to him several times: Jesus Christ! Look at you, never drunk, nails always immaculate − were, even as a junior clerk when the Chief Clerk lined us up for inspection each morning. You're a bloody *cameo* of a man, not a gram of frivolity, do you ever open up even to your wife? Now Wagner drew on his cigarette, smiled sceptically, possibly at the fate which had dealt him this anonymous, cipher-like friend.

'Heinrich, I'm not ready to talk,' said Schmidt. 'Let's keep it under observation. As a nation we've been brought out of difficult times on to a new course. Obviously there've been negative events. Will the progress wash them away? We'll see. You're quick, I'm slower, and I'm reserving my position.'

'Jesus, you speak like this while that *madman* rants away in Berlin! While he hoodwinks the stupid British and French leaders!'

Schmidt turned his head quickly and put a hand up to his false eye. 'Take care,' he said quietly.

Wagner shrugged, swallowed a draught of beer, lifted his strained face to the church steeple. He said tersely: 'Why don't you look up from that damned underworld of green ink, have a look at the real world? Listen, if I take your remarks at face value, I say: Hurry up. Decide where you stand. It shouldn't be too hard, should it, after what the bastards did to you?'

Schmidt thought: Why did I make that weak-kneed little speech? Better to have said nothing, as usual. Yet he'd felt impelled to speak along those lines. A kind of camouflage? In aid of what?

It was chilly, and this would be the last time they'd sit outside. An inner voice told him: 'Go home to your wife and daughter, forget the auditing life, today's events − at least for tonight.'

They finished their beer.

Wagner said, 'I'm going to listen to Mozart, my maid'll have soup ready. Two consolations to end an unnerving day. Going home sober.' He grinned at his colleague. Schmidt was more the good servant of the bank than he was. Nonetheless, something wasn't ringing true about him tonight.

A spindle-legged man in a long black overcoat and a black hat with a whitish face hurried past, dived into the gloom – an impressionistic blur. The Wertheim men were gripped by his tension. Instantly Schmidt recalled the haggard face of the shopkeeper he'd seen that morning.

Wagner shook his head. 'Like a rat into a drainpipe.'

The auditor took the tram out to his suburb, watching the streets, frowning over Wagner. His colleague claimed he was a follower of Calvinist doctrines, but he wasn't the calm type. From now on he must curb his tongue. Herr Wertheim might or mightn't have 'lost his marbles' but he'd selected this new route and thus Wagner was going to take it – as were they all. In a kind of metallic wardance exaggerated by its emptiness, the tramcar rattled from the shut-down finance district into the city's heart, which was blazing with electric light. Café life unrolled in a procession of animated showcases thronged with patrons. The cinemas were full. A huge billboard advertised the idolised Hans Albers, in *Gold*. Helga kept up with the latest cinema. They'd agreed they both preferred foreign films, even the B-grade Hollywoods, to the monotonous, propagandist offerings of the Third Reich. Surprising his wife, Schmidt liked the Westerns.

He brooded on the scene, and a memory of the district in 1934 came: dead-spirited as a strike-bound town. No strikes these days, secure jobs everywhere.

'It's been an interesting day,' Schmidt said to his wife. He spoke with a formality he sometimes regretted, but couldn't

break. The maid had cleared the dinner table. He told Helga of
the day's momentous event. He rarely discussed bank business,
ran his life in compartments. She listened, blonde hair falling in
a loose wave over her face, dark-blue eyes brilliant and intense,
her lips making continuous small flexing movements.

You are beautiful tonight, he wanted to tell her, but the
world went on and he said, 'A Nazi is to come in.'

'Oh? I suppose it's a great coup for Herr Wertheim?'

'It can be looked at like that.'

'How else?'

He gave her a look. 'Wertheims has always kept out of
politics. This is a radically new direction. According to Wagner
a radically wrong direction.'

She pondered this. By upbringing she was thoroughly
domesticated, thrived in the role, though her parents had sent
her to Heidelberg to study the arts. She did read the *Berliner
Tageblatt*, listened to the wireless, knew more than her husband
about the reported affairs of the nation, and passed him pieces
of information.

He was feasting his eye on her. The loss of his other eye
had shocked her. She'd been embittered, but seemed to have
come to terms with it now. Out of the blue, he remembered
the women in the crowd as the Fuehrer rode through the city
in September: yearning faces. To shock him, Wagner had said:
'Not a woman there with a dry pussy.' Had he forgotten Helga
was present?

He sipped his coffee, put down his cup. She'd been watching him as though charting his thoughts. Her eyes were fond,
but questioning.

'Politics, Franz? Surely it's banking business? Where's the
dilemma?'

'You may be right. Though Wagner's very upset.'

'Oh, not Wagner again.'

She found Wagner too complex, too volatile for analysis

– an irritating subject. She didn't approve of his bachelorhood. Nor would the Nazis. Schmidt smiled slightly. In contrast, she had this unworldly husband to face up to. He did live too much of an inner life, he knew, without any intention of changing it.

After the meal he went to his small study, which was mainly furnished with pieces of his father's, those his mother had so far released from her large apartment in an inner suburb. On the wall above his desk was a very old print of Dürer's *Knight, Death and the Devil* – a wedding gift from his father. He'd felt there'd been a special motive behind the gift. Grimly, watchfully, the knight rode through perilous times, a dangerous landscape. Had his father's ancestor knight of the Teutonic Order resembled Dürer's? Engulfed by the silence, he dropped into meditation, and didn't pick up his Municipal Library research trails on the Teutonic Order, as this afternoon he'd not picked up those of his audits.

He left the study. He stood in Trudi's doorway listening for the tiny, efficient breathing. The darkish shapes of an orchestra of toys surrounded her. Could a dream transport her to anywhere more perfect than her everyday dominion?

All quiet on the Western Front … he knew his colleagues, even his loyal Helga, considered he'd no sense of humour. He went on to the dressing room, and heard Helga moving in their bedroom. He'd told her of the new painting on Herr Wertheim's wall. 'Possibly Klimt, from Vienna,' she'd murmured.

Now for it. He took a glass and a bottle to the bathroom and mixed a salt solution. He bent his head, and expelled the glass eye into his palm. It shot out like a musket ball, he caught it adroitly. Better at this now. Carefully, holding his head back, he dribbled the solution into the socket, dabbed it with cottonwool. In a fresh glass of solution he washed the prosthesis. 'A perfect match,' Professor Hesse had said. He did this each week, and hadn't let Trudi into the secret. He concentrated on the tricky bit of getting it back in straight.

Changed into pyjamas, he stood at the bedroom window hearing Helga now in the bathroom. The window was open onto the tiny, iron-railed balcony. The full-grown chestnut trees whispered in the breeze. In a month there'd be only a restless dry scraping. Through a gap in the foliage he could see the street corner. A motor car drifted past, its headlights reflected on the canopy of dying leaves. The corner was deserted.

He must have blinked; now several uniformed men stood there. It was as though a film image had been thrown on the stone wall. Others came around the corner, and heel-clicking and heiling broke out — low-key, like a kind of sinister shadow-play.

They were gone.

He got into bed and lay staring at the ceiling. Yes, the filter of distance was going to be removed at work as swiftly as when they'd whipped his eye out. Fräulein Dressler stepped into his mind, the finest details of her face, her figure, her aura of total control and efficiency; the penetrative, gold-flecked eyes. The last, strange look as he'd left Herr Wertheim's room.

3

ON OCTOBER 13 on the 7.30 am express, Director Schloss, Otto Wertheim, the general-director's nephew, and two senior clerks from the trust department travelled to Berlin. A pair of the bank's uniformed messengers, carrying revolvers, were in attendance – as was Schmidt. The express sped across a black and white checked landscape emitting urgent wails, and the auditor felt that the solemn party, the whole enterprise, had a tone of melodrama; it seemed unreal that these ordinary people with whom he was so familiar were engaged in a mission of national importance.

From the station, they went in two taxis to the famous commercial bank on the Unter den Linden. They gathered beneath a high stone portal encrusted with an ornate clock. Schloss consulted his pocket-watch: ten o'clock precisely. He nodded, and they filed through the revolving door. Uniformed officials with scrutinising eyes were waiting. The visitors were conducted across an expanse of marble suddenly resonant with their footsteps, then by a lift down to a subterranean forest of gleaming steel. Another silent group, sober-suited, stony-faced, with tight white lips, stood guard around a long table upon which were ranked stacks of Reich bonds. Director Schloss inclined his massive, silvered head in a formal bow, shook hands with his opposite number, and presented his credentials.

The reception was frosty yet correct. The Berliners were

still in shock. Schmidt imagined the bitter recriminations flying back and forth in the famous bank. However, they'd retained the clearing accounts and probably management had told the board that these provincials would botch it, and they'd have the lot back. Even so, it was humiliating. And unnerving – to the extent that no-one knew what the NSDAP was up to.

The Wertheim men began ticking off the bonds against their lists. Even Otto Wertheim kept quiet, taking on himself the verification of the payment warrants for the investment cash accounts. Schmidt had noted the bulge under the young director's right arm, the same as the messengers'. He smiled to himself. It would've drawn Wagner's caustic wit: he loathed Otto.

In less than an hour the procedures were completed, and leather satchels packed with the bonds were chained to the messengers' wrists. The Wertheim party route-marched back across the marble. To Schmidt's ears, their footfalls had a triumphant ring.

They returned to the station. In their reserved compartment, Schloss, whose manner was normally as frozen as his Baltic homeland in winter, cracked a joke. This unprecedented event caused an outburst of hilarity; even Schmidt smiled at the witticism. It had crystallised their relief. Schloss went up a notch in his opinion.

Otto sneered, 'We've cooked their goose!'

'Quite,' Schloss said drily. He consulted his watch. 'I will go to telephone the General-Director before we depart.'

§ § §

A stranger waited in Herr Wertheim's anteroom with an air of impatience and nerves, a tall, wide-shouldered, handsome man with penetrative yet restless eyes. He ignored the pristine newspapers on a side table as he paced up and down. The

Wertheim case clock showed a few minutes to noon. Frowning, he consulted his watch. He was in his mid-thirties, and wore an expensive suit shaped modishly at the waist, with the Nazi badge in the high-cut lapel. He exuded physical power plus the authoritative, brash confidence of the Party – a heady mix in the evolving Third Reich. Yet in part it was a façade; like many of his colleagues he was less confident, more subtle than he appeared.

When Fräulein Dressler informed the Nazi the general-director would be only a few minutes more, he stopped his pacing, and turned his eyes on her, as if his thoughts, his air of impatience, had been suspended. He appeared to recognise something in her which surprised him. His gaze intensified, taking in her every centimetre.

Fräulein Dressler didn't blush easily, but under this iron-hard appraisal her face reddened. A buzzer sounded, breaking the spell. *Thank God!* she thought. The Nazi nodded to himself, turned about and entered the inner sanctum.

'Welcome to Wertheims, Herr Dietrich.' The general-director smiled urbanely as they shook hands. 'I've heard from Berlin. Our party is on its way back. Everything is in order.'

Dietrich also smiled, revealing large, yellow teeth. 'Very good, Herr General-Director.' He regarded Wertheim with polite curiosity. Here was the doyen of bankers in this city, but he'd never heard of him until his briefing in Berlin yesterday. He added, 'May it be a fruitful partnership.'

Wertheim nodded pleasantly. He perfectly understood the young Party functionary's situation: he was vested with power and authority, but needed to fit it into this unique situation with some delicacy. Quite difficult for a Nazi. He thought: curious, the way his eyes move.

'A room is ready for you. I hope it's satisfactory' – said with a flutter of bluish fingers.

The Nazi bowed cautiously. A few moments in Herr

Wertheim's presence and he'd begun to wonder what he was getting into; he'd had a brief experience of directors in the commercial bank in Berlin, but this refined man seemed out of another mould entirely.

The Nazi was to be an ex-officio director of the bank; the Party required one of their own on the scene to oversee its interests. This was an unprecedented arrangement for Wertheims. Interlopers of any kind were not welcome here, and Wertheim had drawn deeply on his pragmatism to accept it. He said, 'Doubtless, you have your instructions. I won't detain you. Please join me here at five to meet our directors and receive a more formal welcome.'

Dietrich left, passing Fräulein Dressler without a glance.

Herr Wertheim sat quite still, savouring the occasion.

§ § §

A few minutes after 3.00 pm, Schmidt's first meeting with the Nazi director took place. He returned from Berlin somewhat chilled, and entered his warm office. A messenger appeared to warn him that a Herr Dietrich was on his way to see him. Fortunately, the auditor had just read the memorandum waiting on his desk notifying senior staff of Dietrich's existence.

Moments later the Nazi functionary arrived in the doorway, filling it. He shot a glance into the room, then concentrated on Schmidt, who'd stood up. The Nazi inspected the respectful auditor's face – seemingly every pore and blemish – as he had Fräulein Dressler's.

Schmidt calmly met the interrogative eyes, though a feeling akin to vertigo had come upon him.

'I am Dietrich.'

The Nazi stepped forward and a big hand shot out, and gripped the auditor's.

'Sir, I'm Herr Schmidt, chief auditor.'

'Well, Schmidt, we're to work together. The Party requires everything to run smoothly, I'm here to make sure it does.'

Abruptly he hoisted his haunch on to the edge of the desk, and casually commenced swinging a heavy leg back and forth. Schmidt was startled; it was as though the man had staked a claim. However, he looked at the functionary as though such behaviour was quite normal at Wertheims.

Dietrich's blond hair was slicked straight back from his broad forehead. Two thin metallic-looking strands, sharp as scissor blades, had escaped the smooth surface, suggesting a vigorous, impetuous individual. From his auditor's perspective, Schmidt found the notion unsettling. The large muscular figure, shoulders hunched forward, had fallen into an intent study. The blue eyes stared fixedly, then blinked quickly.

Snaps of a camera shutter, Schmidt thought. And that was close to how the Nazi was operating as he inventoried this backroom banker in this provincial bank: *Snap:* short, small-boned and compact. Handsome. Very. *Snap:* blond, very regular features, skin smooth as a woman's, vague little moustache hardly worth the trouble. *Snap:* a soft man ... yet, an air of self-reliance. Something about the eyes ...

The Nazi suddenly ceased his camera work, produced a silver cigarette case and held it aloft in thick, nicotine-stained fingers, as though displaying it to an admiring circle. Schmidt thought: this is an experience!

'A word of warning, Herr Schmidt. No unpleasant surprises. Keep me informed of relevant matters at all times, please.' He offered the auditor a cigarette. Schmidt, a very occasional smoker, took one; surprises were an anathema to him too. The Nazi clicked the case shut. 'All right, don't look so worried. We'll get along fine. You'll do your job, I'll do mine.'

They lit up.

'I'm not worried, Herr Dietrich.' Schmidt exhaled, spoke quietly. 'We auditors are the serious type.' Some impulse told him that he'd be best served by this kind of reply.

Dietrich assessed the remark, his blue eyes hard but otherwise expressionless. Suddenly, he laughed uproariously. In another display of athleticism he hoisted himself off the desk.

'You don't have a monopoly on that. We in the Party are serious types, too. Serious and dedicated.' His eyes slipped away. He scrutinised the plain room. More photography. It was as though he'd determined to mentally photograph the whole Wertheim province: Schmidt's safe, hatstand, filing cabinet, the only picture: a monochrome photograph of the bank in a heavy wooden frame, taken in 1890, a study in stone – not a shred of flesh and blood.

Dietrich frowned at the picture. Up-and-coming Party officials were developing an eye for architecture: this taste came from the Fuehrer. He switched his gaze back to the auditor ... he would get this small banker into his pocket.

'All right. I'll speak to you again soon.'

He left abruptly, like a man going to a string of crucial appointments. Schmidt sat down. What a character! He'd observed middle-level Party functionaries in the streets, restaurants, at the cinema. Only a few had the prescribed Aryan-look; they came in all shapes and sizes, apparently from diverse backgrounds – criminal ones, according to Wagner. But Dietrich's appearance *did* fit the ideal; only two jarring notes: yellowed teeth and fingers. A piece of pumice stone would work wonders with the latter, Doctor Bernstein, the dentist, with the former. However, the Nazi wouldn't patronise a dentist named Bernstein. With his tongue, Schmidt touched the tooth which was troubling him. For him, such a visit was still possible. He speculated on the Nazi's origins. Behind the poses he'd felt an undercurrent of experience. Perhaps the man had been amusing himself, though a sense of humour hadn't been evident. Schmidt wondered what the G–D thought of him. He glanced at the G–D's memorandum: Dietrich was a lawyer. Did he know anything about banking, auditing?

He'd smoked the cigarette through to the finish. It gave off an aromatic odour which he found quite pleasant. He turned back to his work. In one crowded day a new, unsubtle spirit had impregnated the bank. Were they going to be transfused with the Nazi ethos? Thus far, Wertheims had been insulated from politics by a century of tradition and conservative banking practice. It'd seen political parties come and go like the seasons – except with more racket and stink. It had ridden out the storms of the Great War, the Inflation, the Depression. And its loyal employees had been sheltered from the worst; several had served in the Great War and carried the scars, but no-one at the bank had gone hungry, or had their gas or electricity cut off during the hard years that followed. In a speech at the staff Christmas party in 1935, the G–D had referred to the bank as 'a sound ship in any storm'. He'd likened the clients to first-class passengers, the employees to valiant crew. The metaphor had been admiringly adopted in the bank.

At five, Fräulein Dressler entered his room. Quickly Schmidt rose to his feet. Darkness had fallen and his window reflected his lighted domain. On these nights at the edge of winter, the world outside Wertheims was obliterated. She laid a manila file stamped *Confidential* in large type precisely on the desk. 'Here's the list of the accounts and bonds transferred from Berlin.'

Schmidt thought she had more to say. Again he smelled that enticing scent. His heart was beating faster. He assembled, rejected, words, remembered the look in her eyes the morning they'd had the news about the NSDAP.

She nodded, turned, and left. His head tilted, he reconsidered her eyes. Tonight they'd held him with a pondering melancholy. Then he thought of her face, her neck, her hands. 'Fräulein ...?' he'd nearly said. But it was too late; another exit, leaving him with the notion that he'd failed a test.

4

'WELL, MY DEAR Franz, back from Berlin, what do you think about it now?'

Six pm. Their café. Wagner had been obdurately silent, eyes downcast, until he'd got a cigarette going and taken his first swallow of beer. He flicked froth from his lips. 'Before you tell me, I'm going to tell you what I think. Listen carefully.' He laughed softly, now deliberately lining up his colleague in his gaze. 'A black day for the bank – for all of us. A resident Nazi! Look at the fool striding down the corridors chock-full of his rotten politics, his twisted ideals, his lousy ambition – as though after five minutes he owns the place. Simple-minded, we might think. But remember the damned iceberg. One can only take a pessimistic view of his past. Listen, old Wertheim's not only grabbed the tiger by the tail, he's invited it into the dining-room! *That's* simple-minded.'

He grinned quickly, nervously. Involuntarily, Schmidt had twisted around to check the room.

'For God's sake, Heinrich!' he said in a low voice. He inclined his head sharply at the room. It was filling up, getting noisy: pairs of women in tweed suits, pert hats, tête-à-tête; voluble businessmen, unwinding, resorting to cigars; no uniforms or Nazi badges, but that shouldn't lull anyone into feeling secure. Informers were multiplying.

'For God's sake?' Wagner snapped his fingers at the waiter.

Suddenly Schmidt felt unwell. In a flash the nightmare of the eye had returned. An iron band encircled his chest. He'd had these attacks before, although their timing was inexplicable – like asthma. Fighting to appear normal he said, 'On such brief acquaintance ... you've decided an extraordinary amount ... about our new director.' It was difficult to speak.

Wagner raised his eyes to the heavens. He drained his glass, smacked his lips. 'Unlike you, my auditing friend, I make decisions on the run. However, I don't need to tell a careful fellow like you to watch out, do I? Look how your head just whipped around.'

The pain receded, Schmidt sighed inwardly. He watched his nervy colleague scratching another match alight. He smelt the reek of tobacco from his clothes, the body odour. All day Wagner'd been dealing with banks from Paris to Prague, remitting funds, filling out myriad forms, negotiating with the Reichsbank on exchange control – skating on the foreign exchange thin ice; solving the problems of their moneyed clients whose interests crossed national boundaries. Living on adrenalin, tobacco and caffeine, as he triumphantly reported. Add beer and Mozart. In contrast, Schmidt's world revolved around his careful audit trails.

He said, 'Take your own advice, Heinrich. You're passably discreet in the bank, dangerously careless in public.'

'More careful than you think. Observe the tables I select.'

Schmidt shrugged, unimpressed.

Wagner grinned, nursing an edgy amusement. 'Will you join the Party? That's what they'll be after. If you can pass the test.'

Schmidt was surprised; Wagner seemed to be accelerating everything. He must say more, nail down the imperative for discipline. 'Heinrich, I understand your disquiet. But forgive me, paranoia's hard to disguise. Therefore it's dangerous. One way or another, bit by bit, Wertheims was going to be invaded. When we arrive at the bank it might seem we step out of our private lives, but who totally does? The quarantine's never complete.'

He'd spoken quietly, reasonably, part of his camouflage; part of his cautious character, of trying to help the deputy foreign manager survive; part of buying time to work out his position.

Wagner brooded into his beer. 'So, you're not dumb on the subject. There's a difference between that, and throwing the door wide open. One thing we're going to have trouble with, my friend, is keeping that Nazi's nose out of the business of our other clients.'

'I know that. And the G-D will, too. There's nothing to be done except remain calm, do our jobs.'

'Good God!' Wagner laughed sarcastically, shook his head. 'The auditors' institute did a good job on you, Franz. After your demise, maybe they'll have you stuffed and mounted, put in a glass case in their meeting hall.'

Schmidt nodded slowly, as if considering the proposition. A woman wearing a dark overcoat, which almost swept the ground, crossed an illuminated patch of pavement. Tension clung to her figure. Schmidt sat up, feeling his heart lift. Wagner followed his gaze. His piece of black humour had fizzled out like a damp cracker. They watched Fräulein Dressler disappear.

Wagner said, 'After today, she won't be cracking her little jokes. She'll be as worried as hell.'

Schmidt looked at him sharply. Wagner mused: 'She's often in here. Great eater of cream cakes. That ample, seductively trembling derrière, my friend, is all due to cream cakes.'

Schmidt pursed his lips. 'So? Why should she be worried?'

'Don't you know? She's half-Jewish.'

Schmidt sat frozen, fixated on his colleague's face. That was it! Why hadn't he known this? Her face, features were instantly in his mind's eye: the long, thin-bridged nose, the cast of the lips, the darkish hair, those eyes. Suddenly, her dilemma flowed into his consciousness like molten steel pouring into a mould. He felt stupid and cold, though the café was overheated. He looked up into Wagner's curious gaze. 'Except for old Wertheim I don't know who in the bank knows or has guessed. I haven't heard a whisper. Surprising isn't it? Our venerable institution's usually a hotbed of gossip. Of course, he thinks she's a wonder.'

'And you?' Schmidt's thoughts had narrowed to the specific, as if he'd isolated a suspicious transaction. 'How do you know this, Heinrich?'

'Well, that's a story.' He downed more beer and smacked his lips thoughtfully. 'Two years ago I accompanied her home from the annual concert, was invited in for coffee. Things were around which made it quite plain ... In another sense, it was an interesting evening.' The auditor waited. 'In the bank, she has that aura ... the mysterious humorist. Out of the blue, I found out another Fräulein Dressler.' He paused. 'One a man could drown in.'

Schmidt didn't like this. Repressed women, lonely women abounded in the Reich. A legacy of the war. But Fräulein Dressler?

'Listen, my dear friend, I fucked her standing up in her hall. All over in a minute – I'm not at my best on my feet.'

Schmidt was stunned. It turned to distaste. He said, 'I don't think you should've told me – or anyone – either of those facts.'

Wagner glanced at him with amusement, 'We're not the source of danger.'

But it wasn't only danger that the auditor had in mind.

Schmidt rode the tram out to see his mother, consumed by Wagner's revelations. Fräulein Dressler's particular situation had hit him hard. He contemplated the ink-blue passing streetscape, the dense aggregation of silhouetted steeples, cupolas. Asleep under varnishes of history. He could hardly believe she was one with those black-bearded men slipping through the streets with their cat-like caution. They seemed to exist on a different planet.

In his inner-ear the roar: *Sieg heil!* arose, reverberated like a shockwave, as it had in September over the suburbs from the massed rallies. Tonight, in his room, *had* she been on the brink of appealing for help? He stared at the darkness and in his head the voracious *Sieg heil*-ing seemed to rise to a crescendo.

5

S EVEN PM. NUMBER 178 Friedrichstrasse. A monumental apartment building of the type erected in the 1860s for the middle-class. Entering the hall, the auditor smelt floor-wax, and was immediately mindful of the hazard: you could skid here like an out-of-control skater. Giving the lift a sceptical look, he flexed his body in his thick black overcoat, and, careful of his footing, climbed the freezing stairs to the first floor. He was admitted by Frau Bertha, sixtyish, thin, starch whispering from cuffs and collar, who took his coat and hat, and conducted him to the front room.

Trailing in the wake of her hoarse coughing he sighed: 'Thursday again.' It seemed an age since he'd left in the grey dawn to catch the Berlin express.

The mausoleum, Helga called it. The ambience, the odour of thickly-carpeted rooms dignified with mirrored and columned mahogany pieces in which a Gothic design was worked, were common in this suburb. As was the collection of family memorabilia: portraits, photographs, pieces of silver floridly engraved, ranged in places of honour unchanged since his childhood.

His mother's famous ancestor was represented only by a smallish marble bust in the hall. She never spoke of him by name, only as 'the composer', as if it were a family secret.

Her connection to Johann Sebastian Bach was well known in cultural circles.

A *district* of mausoleums. He was amusing himself to lighten the moment. Lives backed into corners. A flock of aged, single ladies resided here: one might surmise that the male population had been wiped out by a disease particular to their sex. The disease was the Great War, and the subsequent economic catastrophe.

He brought these joyless thoughts into the semi-darkness of the salon. She sat in her elegant wing chair, and he leant over the tall, emaciated figure to kiss her on each cheek: usual whiff of lavender, usual quick eagle's glance above her pince-nez. Each week at this moment he recalled half a lifetime of Thursday evenings. Here was old age held at bay, pessimism, steely single-mindedness, fastidious dressing – her clothes never seemed to wear out: she had oak chests packed with gowns, shoes, from the 1920s. Her fine grey hair rigidly braided across her head was doubtless one source of Frau Bertha's nerves.

'Always on time, Franz. What a burden these little visits are for you.'

'Not at all, mother. Are you well?'

She was. Eighty-six. Indestructible. He went to pour schnapps: two precise measures. He handed her a small glass etched with laurel leaves.

'Your wife and dear Trudi are well?'

They were. Her relationship with Helga was correct. They each tolerated the monthly family lunch. Standing, holding his drink, he prepared to break new Thursday ground. She was interested in Herr Wertheim and his dynastic bank. In joining it all those years ago, he'd made a correct move for once.

'Wertheims has turned in a new direction …'

She listened, and sipped her drink, gazing down the room at shadowy portraits of the dead. When he was finished she said in her light dry tone, 'So, you've been to Berlin and back today. How remarkable.'

He was surprised at what seemed most remarkable to her. She smiled, enigmatically. 'Herr Hitler is much admired here. Frau Webber on the second floor thinks he is wonderful, but lacks the influence of a good woman. Frau Hoffman on the third is, she says, intensely drawn to his artistic persona. I believe their feelings are quite sexual.'

This time, Schmidt was startled. 'What do you think of him, mother?'

'I? I know nothing of the man. Except from their talk, which I must put up with. I don't read the newspapers, on the wireless I listen only to classical music.'

He thought: Yes, by tradition her family abhorred politicians. An article of faith to be kept. Tonight with their talk taking a different path, should he make another attempt …?

'Mother, the Salzburg cantatas. Won't you allow me to put the manuscripts in the bank's vault? I'm thinking only of their historical value.' He would have preferred to send them to a cousin in Zurich who was a musicologist, who would know what to do with them, but she'd never entertain that.

She regarded him with her sceptical eyes, as if his mind was freely accessible to her. 'No, my dear Franz, they're to stay here with the family archives. Once you start a dispersal it's the beginning of the end. No doubt you recall that disgraceful Mendelssohn farrago in 1852.'

He did. She'd engraved it on his mind. Unpublished works released by the composer's widow had resulted in an unsavoury controversy. He studied the patrician face. In other company he might have allowed himself a shrug. These six unpublished cantatas by Bach had come down in the family, been sedulously protected from the world by Frau Schmidt and her forebears. The composer hadn't seen fit to publish, yet for some reason had not wanted them destroyed: therefore a sacred duty remained in perpetuity. Another 'article of faith'.

He drank his schnapps. A picture of his father came to him: departing each morning for the consulting rooms and the operating table, kissing his wife goodbye. A dry kiss; a momentary intersection of their variant orbits; his father's Junkers line had been the antithesis of his mother's cultured heritage. Had a brief incandescent passion enticed her into the marriage?

'Well, mother, I must be home to dinner.'

He put down his empty glass, and went to kiss her.

'My love to your family.'

He stood poised, handsome head tilted, spectacles glinting, waiting for a connection, as if tonight was a night for a breakthrough.

She said, 'I will reserve my opinion on Herr Wertheim's new endeavour.'

And that, Schmidt knew, was that. In the hall, pulling on his gloves, he glanced at the door to his father's study. In this room books about the Teutonic Order, and his family's history, crowded the shelves. A solitary, studious child, it was where he'd begun a lifelong journey. Holidays, weekends, he'd immersed himself in the old records. Even now, it thrilled him to think of his descent from a knight of the Order. He reminded himself that there was a book he wished to consult. Next time.

Speechless, Frau Bertha showed him out past the composer's bust.

'Goodnight,' he said as he went through the door.

These late-autumn evenings Schmidt didn't have time with Trudi. Kissing the small sleeping head on the pillow, a feeling of omniscience came over him. But it was like a false dawn. He could see nothing of the future – and didn't want his forebodings in this room. Back on track, he whispered, in his head: 'Sunday's the time when our worlds overlap. Do you wait for Sunday as I do, my little one?'

At the dinner table, Helga listened to his brief report on the Thursday visit. He gave her an edited version of the takeover of the Nazi Party's business, his introduction to Herr Dietrich. They'd not spoken on the subject since the night he'd broken the news; they'd both chosen to keep quiet. Face cradled in hand, she watched him finish.

He hadn't mentioned Wagner's revelations about Fräulein Dressler; the less said there the better. Suddenly he was alert to her tension.

He said, 'So there you have it.'

He knew she understood that he hadn't made up his mind about the Nazis; was watching it all. Nor had she, though her concern was more pragmatic. He'd decided that the incident of the eye had been an aberration. But the Party's arrival in Wertheims had brought it all back into close range.

She spoke softly: 'Franz, Wertheims couldn't stand aside forever. Sooner or later they'd have been pulled in. Herr Wertheim has stepped towards the future, to sail with the tide, rather than be swept away with it. Isn't this the way you all talk? If Wertheims weren't to do it, another bank would snap it up.'

Schmidt considered her earnest reasonableness, her metaphor. She smoothed her hair back, tried to smile. What she wished to say was: I think I know what you'll decide. But for God's sake don't be too idealistic. Don't rock the boat. If you must put on armour, let it be only for defence. Don't bring us into danger.

She said, 'Dearest Franz, be careful, be on guard. Take nothing on trust. Especially this Dietrich.' She touched the back of his hand. 'If anyone has a right to doubts, you have.'

He said, 'It's my nature and profession to be a doubter.'

She nodded abruptly, hardly hearing him, reliving that horror. Why had he done it? Had the quixotic, futile act been the impulse of a second? Or – and a coldness closed around her heart – had it been a compulsive response grounded in him by his family heritage, his obsessive studies of the history of the Teutonic Order? Would he ever open up to her about his work on it?

The food queues gone; six million unemployed found jobs, the economy surging. New hope, faith in the future humming in the air. Millions were taking it in with their breathing, their morning milk. But personal freedom had vanished like the sun sinking behind a mountain. It was all a gigantic lie. He stood up abruptly.

She looked at him urgently, and said in a low voice, 'Franz you will put your family before everything?'

He looked at her with deep concern. 'Helga, you and Trudi are in the forefront of my thoughts. Always.'

She thought: Oh God! Nothing could be trusted.

6

DABBING AT HIS eye, Schmidt walked through the early morning mist to the bank. In his head, his birthplace was playing a sad adagio. The streets were thick with the melancholy of autumn. He thought: Witnesses to the Great War, the Inflation, the Depression, the Weimar Republic – and Nazi parades.

On the dot of 11.00 am, Dietrich strode into his room, and claimed his position on the desk-edge. The hard blue eyes scrutinised Schmidt's face as if searching for shaving nicks or blemishes.

'Everything in order, Schmidt?'

'Yes, Herr Director.'

'Good. I'm reading your weekly report. I'm one of those individuals who even reads between the lines. Keep that in mind.'

The tempo in the bank had lifted. Each day donations to the Party flooded in, and each day the bank invested the funds. Fascinated, Schmidt was being given an insider's view of the financial underbelly of the NSDAP.

Dietrich produced his cigarette case, and offered it. They lit up, and regarded each other, like opponents at the start of a chess match. The auditor was acclimatising to these stimulating moments. Also to the scent of the lotion which the Nazi apparently rubbed on his skin daily.

Dietrich's face creased into a frown. 'I'm putting together facts about your bank. But you, Schmidt, never talk to me, except to answer questions.'

Schmidt considered this. What was it leading up to?

'Your questions always ably cover our business, sir. I'm a person of few words.'

'Except on paper, eh? You've nearly drowned me in memoranda.'

That was true. Schmidt had bombarded him with briefings on the bank's auditing procedures. He wished to keep him at arm's length, while he got to grips with the Party's business.

Dietrich grinned. 'Never mind. Another matter. You and I have an onerous duty. The Party understands that, wishes to reward special efforts. This is what we'll do: Five hundred marks a month for myself, three hundred for yourself. Pay it out of the Number Four cash account the first of each month. Give me mine in an envelope. Take yours in cash, also. Special expenses, just record that. Your colleagues don't need to know any details. Got that straight?'

He spoke with a negligent air, swinging his dangling leg back and forth. Schmidt had heard surreptitious reports about Party corruption. But this kind of nonchalant, small-scale pilfering!

'Naturally, Herr Director, you'll provide the authority in writing?' The auditor knew that would never happen.

The Nazi frowned. 'Unnecessary, Schmidt. My oral instruction's enough. The same arrangement was in place in Berlin.'

Schmidt laid his cigarette in the ashtray. 'With respect, Wertheims has its own regulations.'

Dietrich drummed his finger on the desk in an irritated tattoo. 'Get that look off your face. We Party officials are modern in our outlook – and decisive! When red tape needs to be cut we know how to cut it. I speak, that's your authority. You need to broaden your horizons, open your mind, my friend. It'll assist you professionally.'

Wagner's words almost exactly. Schmidt analysed the desktop as though it were a recalcitrant trial-balance. What look? And what an amazing speech. Was Dietrich putting his honesty to some bizarre test? No, he decided. This Nazi was in dead earnest. He cleared his throat, not from nerves, but to make his enunciation absolutely precise.

'I'm afraid I can't accept a payment myself. For Wertheims it would be highly irregular.' He'd not looked up.

The Nazi gazed at him – as though at a new vista which had suddenly appeared. 'I suggest you give it further thought. The Party doesn't flaunt its generosity, nor is it accustomed to ungraceful responses. All right! Never mind. One more matter.' He hoisted himself off the desk, fixed Schmidt with another intense stare. 'I presume you're familiar with the Nuremberg Laws?'

A chill came over the auditor. 'Up to a point.'

'*Up to a point.*' Dietrich mimicked the response. 'You must pay attention to such matters, Schmidt. It's every citizen's duty to do so.' He paced across the room. '*All right!* Since 1935, Jews have no citizenship – they're merely subjects. You must know that! Several subsequent decrees have put other restrictions on them. For example, and this is the pertinent point, it's against the law for a Jew to be employed in a firm such as Wertheims. I trust it's now coming back to you.'

Schmidt was hearing the competent lawyer giving a briefing, and taking in the sarcastic tone. The Nazi returned to the desk, flicked his ash neatly into a tray. 'They're required to identify themselves. Many don't. Suspect individuals are everywhere amongst us. The Party's determined to track them down, bring them under the law.' He ceased pacing, stared at the auditor, and thought: What is going on behind that bland, respectful exterior? He probed it, but no cracks. His eyes side-slipped ... 'The Reich will draw its strength, build the future on the purity of the Nordic race. The impure don't fit into this picture. We in the Party are trained to identify such examples.' He peered at the auditor and suddenly grinned. 'Lesson completed! There's the dogma, my forgetful friend.'

Below in the street the traffic was muttering like a sleepy congregation at prayers. Schmidt absorbed the speech and felt the chill spread in him. He knew its impending conclusion. But with his last off-hand remark the Nazi'd again surprised him. Was it possible that the man was a cynic about Party dogma? He looked up from his desk-top as the Nazi spoke again.

'My dear fellow, I suspect that Fräulein Dressler may be a case in point.' Schmidt gazed at Dietrich's face. 'So it's a very delicate situation. Herr Wertheim will be horrified. Though, we're all human. His emotions might be involved.'

So there it was. Though Schmidt had immediately guessed that the destination of the Nazi's remarks was Fräulein Dressler, it was still a shock to hear him speak her name. Herr Wertheim wasn't ignorant of her situation, common sense and Wagner vouched for that. Despite his prevaricating words, the Nazi would've assumed the G-D knew. Was he deviously, patronizingly, planning a way out for the old banker?

'You'll go to the staff department and examine her dossier. If correct procedures are being followed her birth certificate will be there. Take down the details. I'm going to Berlin this afternoon for a few days. Report to me when I return.'

'Very well, Herr Director.'

'Be alert, Schmidt. Dangerous games are being played all around us.' Dietrich nodded, turned on his heel, and took his austere thoughts out to the frigid corridor: Wertheims didn't heat the hallways.

Schmidt listened to the assured but curiously unbalanced

footsteps (one hitting the ground harder than the other?) until they faded away, leaving him with his thoughts. What dangerous games did Dietrich have in mind? Grimly he regarded his powerlessness.

He took out his official diary and recorded the Nazi functionary's instructions concerning the 'special expenses', dated and timed it. Fräulein Dressler's image materialised in his mind's eye. Three weeks ago she'd hardly figured in his thoughts. Now she seemed to be dominating them.

He discovered her very much in the flesh that afternoon when he turned a corner on the first floor. She was pinned to the wall within the stubby arms of Otto Wertheim. A second before he'd overheard: 'You're so strong and masterful, Herr Otto.'

Clearly, Otto had accepted the remark at face value. Schmidt drew in a breath. Otto was trying to combine aggression and charm, a feat well beyond his ability. Hastily he stepped back, and glared at the auditor. Schmidt passed by, his eye fixedly ahead, felt their eyes on his back in the sudden silence. However, he'd caught the mordant humour in the twist of her red lips.

Out of sight he paused, considered afresh Wagner's portrait of a passionate woman, and marvelled at sighting her like this, given the mission he was on. Otto'd been steaming with lust. *A coolish location for a tryst.*

The bank seemed to be awaking from a long hibernation!

Schmidt unlocked a door and entered a room. He found the ten-year-old dossier, and read the birth certificate. It was clear-cut. Coming into the room he'd felt keyed-up but now he was calm. He removed the certificate, put it in his pocket, returned to his room, and burnt the document to ash in his metal wastepaper basket.

'What fascinating developments do you report today from your end of the good ship *Wertheim?*' Wagner demanded. He'd had his first mouthful of beer.

Schmidt raised a shoulder, as if to deflect the inquiry. He inspected the café, the patronage. Five thirty pm. Outside, the streets were as black as a Rhine coal-barge's hold. Dark at 4.30 pm. In a month it would be 4.00 pm. He'd decided to keep both of Dietrich's instructions quiet, for the present.

He turned to Wagner. His colleague's unkempt hair draggled over his collar. Wertheim men wore hats to the bank, mostly homburgs, though not Wagner. 'Herr Dietrich's gone to Berlin. He returns in a few days.'

'Not fascinating, but interesting.' The deputy foreign manager exhaled a stream of smoke. 'Doubtless he hastens to his masters to report on our bank.'

'In that sense, all seems to be going well.'

Wagner assessed the remark. 'Do I pick up a doubt? By any chance, has our new director already unearthed the taint of Jewishness nourished and harboured by our eccentric General-Director?'

Schmidt stared at his colleague. It was hard to keep Wagner out of any picture. But tonight he was implacably resistant to the deputy manager. Depression had come down on him. And worry. His thoughts moved away from the café, from Wagner. Where was she at this moment? What was her state of mind? More to the point, what was he going to do with his particular knowledge of her peril? He felt hemmed in by much more than the early nightfall.

Wagner shrugged, not put off. 'I see one-point-five million came in today for our esteemed client from Ruhr industrialists.'

Schmidt came back, nodded. 'They can afford it. Business is booming.'

'And the more the Nazis push to rearm the higher the

profits, eh? A nice little cycle.' Wagner paused, glass half-raised.
'Thank God the summer's over! It's an end for a while to
those vile rallies. Those obscene flags. You couldn't see the
buildings for their damned swastikas.' All summer this had
infuriated him. 'It's a wonder old Wertheim in his new mani-
festation isn't after the account of that damned flag-making
company!' He drank beer. 'I've been watching him for thirty
years and I tell you, his brain's jumped the points. Take it from
your troublesome friend.' Schmidt smiled despite himself. 'Ah,
my dear Franz, a smile at my expense? You don't believe me?
Listen. The G–D's placed the bank like a high-value chip on
the roulette table. From now on, he's going to unravel like a
piece of thread being pulled. And Christ, look at the succession! Otto, the bank's pervert and ace-farter. Even more insane!
The only hope is Schloss.'

Schmidt turned aside from his colleague. Herr Wertheim
mad? Tonight, Wagner was laying out his own paranoia. He'd
seen nothing in his meetings with the G–D to match what the
deputy manager was claiming. Though there was a change. The
new art on his wall, for example. That gilded woman must be
on the borderline of the Fuehrer's edicts on acceptable art. But
he was inclined to think that if a little eccentricity was in play,
there'd be method in it.

Wagner leaned back, and said flatly, quietly now, 'They've
been watching my flat this last week. Dressed in the stand-
ard black leather coats. The clichés of fear, purveyors of
doom. That's what they're becoming. D'you know our people
call you the Doomsayer?' Schmidt did know. He regarded
his voluble colleague with fresh concern. Threats seemed to
be multiplying around them, and Wagner's face was set with
strain. 'They watch from doorways, sometimes a car. So there
we are.'

'For God's sake, Heinrich, you must mend your ways. Keep
your mouth shut.' Schmidt barely spoke above a whisper.

Wagner sucked at his cigarette, savouring the tobacco. He laughed and a nerve jumped under his eye. 'I'm afraid it's much more than my mouth.'

Schmidt was to meet Helga in half an hour at a restaurant. *More than my mouth.* What was Wagner talking about? If they weren't watching him because of his indiscreet and traitorous remarks? Mentally, he framed a question –.

Wagner cleared his throat. Schmidt swung around. Fräulein Dressler, her overcoat skimming the floor, was going with her precise walk to a table in a far corner. A huge man followed her closely, as though paying court. He removed an old military-style greatcoat, passing it to a waitress, who staggered under its weight. Schmidt noted the luxuriant moustache. A delicate pink necktie added a strange touch to the gigantic, muscled figure.

'Our dear fräulein,' Wagner said tersely, 'and her father, Senior Detective Dressler of the Municipal Police. They'll have plenty to consider tonight. You might say a prayer on their behalf.'

7

AT 6.30 PM SCHMIDT walked to the city centre. Around him buildings soared up like stony cliffs. His shoe-leather smacked down sharply in the empty streets of the financial district. Streetlamps swung in the wind. He turned a corner, and was assaulted by electric light and crowded streets. It was the sensation he imagined an actor might have stepping from the wings onto a bright stage. Stage? Actor? Were these notions presentiments? Or, was everything down to chance? Wagner, the Calvinist, would sneer at that.

The few dim figures he'd spotted on his way suggested covert forces closing in. Closing in on individuals and groups throughout the Reich. Overt forces, too. His own case. Beaten down in the street and his eye whipped out in a second. The terse official apology acknowledging his 'cooperation'. The bureaucratic cover-up of heedless animalistic violence, with the euphemism 'mistaken Party fervour'.

A night for sad and nervy recollections.

Helga was waiting at their favourite restaurant. She was bare-armed, and he'd an illusion that summer hadn't gone. Her pale skin, the blonde permed hair, was set aglow by the shaded wall lights. For the thousandth time, he admired the freckles across the tops of her breasts. This was very much better. He kissed her hand, thinking her in the full flood of her existence.

'Franz, so serious. Even for you. What's wrong? The bank?'

He smiled. 'Nothing is wrong on your birthday.'

'You don't deceive me,' she said.

'Is Trudi better tonight?'

'She ate her supper, and we read a book together. She'll go to school tomorrow.'

He nodded pleasantly, checked the room. He'd been a patron for twenty years. The owners, the chefs, the waiters, the décor, hadn't changed; they were all gracefully ageing together. He'd never seen a brown or a black uniform or a Nazi badge here. Far too staid a place.

He chose a sparkling Rhine wine, and the waiter with a discreet, congratulatory flourish filled the long-stemmed glasses. Helga had turned thirty-eight.

He raised his glass. 'Dearest! My warmest congratulations. You look more beautiful than ever.'

She flashed him a smile, a look. He wondered if these days his compliments bored her; she never dwelt on them. They were totally sincere. Immediately she was serious. 'Franz, a letter from mother. She must have an operation. Her gall bladder. I should be with her when she comes out of hospital.' She spoke dates.

'Of course.' He showed his concern; her mother was seventy. He was fond of her, and his sister-in-law. As the only man in the family he felt a responsibility. 'Will you take Trudi?'

'Yes. It will be the holidays.'

He said, smiling, 'You'll miss the concert.' The bank's concert had never been a star event even in their limited social calendar. Speaking of stars: his mother had mentioned that Frau Webber had said that Herr Hitler 'was following his star'. She was an avid horoscopist. He told Helga.

He found it strange that his pragmatic wife was also a believer. She reminded him that she was a Sagittarian, he a Pisces. Where would his star take him?

'The Fuehrer is an Aries, I think, though on the cusp of Taurus,' she said.

He shrugged. How did she know this? He regretted raising that name. They ate Essigbratlein, the speciality of the house.

'Can Wagner survive?'

He was startled. The question matched his own preoccupation. What was her idea of 'survive'? He recovered himself. 'He's needed more than ever at the bank. A brilliant international man. I've warned him to watch his tongue.' Schmidt spoke quietly. 'He knows they've got watchers everywhere.'

Tonight his suspicion had strengthened that something more was going on with Wagner than his loose mouth. Hadn't he almost admitted it? They ate their dinner.

Helga regarded him thoughtfully. 'If he'd a wife and family he'd be more reliable.' Her favourite hazelnut torte had been brought.

'Do you think so? He has his beer, his cigarettes, his housekeeper, his international trips – and Mozart. No love-life, these days, that I know of.'

'Like all of you he has the bank.'

Schmidt smiled slightly. He wouldn't worry her with the dangerous turn in Wagner's affairs. Nor would he confide his even deeper worry at the clearer peril of Fräulein Dressler. He gazed into the glinting, greenish-golden wine. What action could he take there, beyond his minor act of arson? He shook his shoulders.

'Be careful yourself, Franz.'

That jolted him out of his momentary introspection. Helga with her sharp mind and her intuition was certainly watching him, worrying about his naive, romantic nature. As she saw it. She would never understand that he was super-alert, was tuning in rapidly to the hazards of their times. Sharp as a trumpet call a resolution came: *Helga, Trudi, his extended family, must never be put at risk.*

Into the silence in which so much was shared, so much not, he said, 'I'm always careful.' The stooped waiter held Helga's fur coat. It had been her thirty-sixth birthday present, the year he'd become chief auditor.

He didn't count the occasion a success, though she seemed happy enough, was humming to herself as they came upstairs to a side-street. Bitterly cold air and a dearth of light greeted them. Dried leaves skirled across the road, scraping like metal foil. Odours of sausage and sauerkraut wafted past their faces. They huddled into their coats.

Kraang! Kraang! Their heads whipped around in unison. A column of Brownshirts was bearing down, sparks dancing under their iron-nailed boots. Raucous commands rang out. At the last moment the SA troopers swung out to pass the well-dressed blond couple. The leader saluted. They pounded on, roaring a slogan. The wind hurled back the odour of sweat, the hard-edged words.

Helga had tightened her grip on his upper arm. Now they walked in the other direction. That salute? Could it be that his photograph was posted at every SA branch office as a person for special treatment? Impossible. Already the incident would be submerged in their files. More likely an edict had gone out: Salute obviously Nordic citizens!

'Forget them,' Helga said, 'let's hurry home and look in on Trudi.'

The Brownshirts had finished off her birthday. In his jaw, the toothache flared up.

§ § §

Fräulein Dressler and her father walked through the windy

night to her flat, the guarded conversation they'd had over the meal in their minds. Dressler's head was lowered on his massive chest, huge hands buried in his coat pockets. Beside her erect carriage and precise steps he went with a swaying motion, transferring his weight from side to side. His breathing was laborious. His daughter, a tall, well-made woman, didn't reach his shoulder.

It had come. Senior Detective Dressler told himself that the change at the bank had been just one of the potential catalysts to her situation. Day by day, patrolling his patch, he'd observed the government closing in on Jews, dissidents. It'd been a nagging fear in his mind. Now it was out in the open. To be dealt with.

They reached the shabby building where she'd lived for five years. Entering the foyer she thought: What a carefree time that seems now. This morning the Nazi director had come to the door of the anteroom and stared at her. She felt sick with fear as she relived it. Her father remained on the steps. Massively immobile, he gazed at doorways one by one.

'Papa, will you have wine?'

'No thank you, Lilli. Perhaps coffee?' He was still wheezing from the walk. Once inside, he removed his overcoat and sat down, uncomfortably wedging himself into her largest armchair. She took his coat, saying, 'What a weight! It must be giving piles to waitresses all over town.' Nervously, she laughed her throaty laugh.

'I've had it since the war,' he muttered. 'I don't usually eat at restaurants.' A stool at a zinc bar, with a plate of the day, his coat hung up by himself, was his normal routine.

His large blue eyes had gone first to the silver-framed photograph of his late wife. How his daughter resembled her. The features, eyes, hair. Even the same languorous movements. More the pity. No, he couldn't say that. He'd not been here for six months. She was playing it safe. Some of the distinctive family silver was no longer on display.

She brought in a tray with coffee and his favourite biscuits, then sat down and watched him sip the coffee.

'Herr Wertheim's known that important fact from the first. He's always treated me with great consideration. I was a *particular* favourite of his in the past, not in the present. But we won't go into that. It's the way of the world, papa.'

He knew what she was telling him. Years ago, he'd suspected the relationship they'd had.

'He'll do what he can, should it become necessary.'

Dressler studied the rug. He remembered the day his wife had chosen it. He didn't wish to frighten his daughter, but it was already necessary. This new Nazi director staring at her with his hard suspicion had made that clear.

He said, 'Herr Wertheim can't be totally relied on. In the end, his interests, those of the bank, may be placed first.' He spoke in his usual dolorous tone, tinged now with deep affection. He looked into her intelligent eyes. 'That's the way of these matters.'

She thought: Yes. The bank's been a haven these past ten years. But she must forget that now. Not to do so would be a paralysing self-deception. Everything was changing. And these days, there was something new about Herr Wertheim.

In the grip of his own paralysis, Dressler felt as if he were up against a hopelessly difficult investigation. As a fall-back, they must look elsewhere for a solution. But where? She might go to his sisters in Hamburg or Berlin, but that was no guarantee of safety. Each day the Nazis were becoming more adept at ferreting out. On duty he'd witnessed several painful incidents. The frontiers were now walls of steel. By paying massive bribes a few were still getting out. Even that would finish soon if he was any judge. *They* couldn't raise twenty thousand marks between them.

'I know I can't stay at Wertheims.'

He was silent. He, of course, was not Jewish. He wished he were. He could hardly stand it that they were divided into separate worlds. His heart felt heavier than any time in his life.

'I do have an idea, papa.' He looked at her. 'At the Prague branch they're putting in a new management system. I'm familiar with it. If I suggest to Herr Wertheim that I go there to help, he might agree. With the bank's new influence, he might be able to have a passport issued.' The building was as silent as a cemetery at night. She listened, and ran a hand through her hair. 'I wouldn't return. He would know.'

The detective frowned. *If* it could be done, it would rebound dangerously on Wertheim. He might be able to deal with that. How did the mind of such a man work?

He said, 'It depends on Herr Wertheim.'

She nodded.

He added: 'I doubt Prague will be safe for long.'

'I would not stay there.'

He still held his coffee cup, almost invisible in his great hands.

'Don't worry, papa. Drink your coffee.'

He drank the coffee, and worried on. If only she could have found a good man, married, and migrated. The USA. They'd missed that chance. She was a beautiful girl.

'Yes, Lilli, you should do it. Carefully, the way I know you will. However, we must have another plan in reserve. We mustn't allow things to drift along with false hopes.'

He was putting more vigour into his speech than usual; regret − and fear − in him as sharp as the pain in his head. The failure to act in time. He was perspiring, he wiped his brow with his handkerchief.

'Papa, *please* don't worry.'

Clumsily, he embraced her, held her head against his chest, looking down with his inarticulate love.

From the doorway he examined the street. Quiet. Distant car lights. The icy air scarified his weathered face. He was watching his front as he had in the war. Even in circumstances like this she could make her little jokes. He shook his head. Since childhood she'd been like that. He'd been wounded three times in the war. And gassed. He kept an oxygen cylinder beside his bed for bad winter nights. He was a holder of the Iron Cross First Class. In the 'twenties he'd been a dead-minded man walking his police beat, a piece of steel in his head. Obviously, in the Third Reich, none of that made the slightest difference to their case.

8

A BLACK-SUITED MAN holding a camera stepped directly in front of Schmidt and snapped his photograph. The auditor was startled, but he walked past before stopping and turning. The black suit had disappeared in the office-bound crowd. A street-photographer? But no ticket had been handed out. People were bumping into him. Considering the incident, he continued on, arriving at the bank at 8.45 am. From a flagpole on its pediment, a brand-new swastika snapped in the breeze. He paused to gaze at it. Alongside the Nazi flag, the blue, worn Wertheim flag fluttered like a washed-out rag. Hitherto, the house flag had been flown, absent-mindedly, on a few notable days each year. Obviously no longer: the new affiliation was to be advertised.

He continued to gaze up, his face showing nothing, but his nerves had sharpened at the irritating snapping. Wagner'd have a fit! Then he remembered: Tomorrow was Memorial Day – 'blood witness' to the Hitler putsch of 1923.

He rubbed the wet from his shoes on the mat, and stamped his feet. His eye socket was weeping. He dabbed it. Herr Berger watching with patient sympathy said, 'The post's in your room, Herr Schmidt.'

Schmidt nodded politely, and was ushered to the lift. This foyer's as chilly as a meat-packing factory, he thought. He'd found a small oil heater for Berger, which he kept in his booth.

Entering his room a stronger sense of pressure came down on him. A week had elapsed since Helga's birthday. He'd not seen the general-director's secretary during it, but her face kept appearing in his mind. A week had passed, too, since Herr Dietrich had disappeared to Berlin. The Nazi had been absent longer than expected. Why? This uncertainty was part of the pressure.

And at 7.30 am, he'd farewelled his family at the station. He could tell Helga was reluctant to leave him alone in this situation, though she didn't know its extent. He'd felt sick and dull as he'd watched the two ghost faces at the misted carriage window being carried away. However, as the last carriage was claimed by the foggy day, his determination had risen: He was free to act. And Dresden wasn't the moon.

Dealing with the post, he was surprised at the Wednesday morning bonanza of half a million for the Party. He registered the details, donors' identities: today no household names, just medium-sized firms from the length and breadth of the Reich. Sending the post on its way, he began to check the typing of his current report, then suddenly put it aside. He must act! No more delays.

But at that moment a summons arrived from Herr Wertheim.

He entered the general-director's warm and spacious anteroom. Fräulein Dressler looked up from her work. His heart turned over.

'Herr Wertheim's waiting.'

'Thank you, fräulein.' He bowed slightly and moved past. Definitely, something special in that look. He entered the inner sanctum.

Though it seemed like only yesterday, it was four weeks since his previous attendance here. At rest in his cushions, Herr Wertheim regarded Schmidt amiably, and raised a languid hand. 'Sit down Herr Schmidt, tell me how you are getting on with our new client.'

'Everything is under control, Herr General-Director.' Calmly he reported some details. Herr Wertheim listened, and nodded.

'And Herr Dietrich? You're able to cooperate with him, and meet his reasonable requirements?'

Schmidt regarded the silver-haired banker: 'Silverfox', two generations of the staff had dubbed him. Was it a fox-like question? He thought not. However, was Dietrich's instruction on the special payment a 'reasonable' requirement? He doubted the G-D would welcome him raising it. In money terms it was small beer.

'I believe Herr Dietrich is satisfied to date.'

The general-director smiled enigmatically. 'Very good. All of that is interesting. Actually, I wished to speak about something else.'

He smoothed the empty desk-top with his gold-ringed hand. Schmidt watched with a loyal sympathy. He knew Herr Wertheim saw himself as the guardian of their clients' assets and secrets – and of the bank's hallowed tradition. A terrific weight, especially these days.

Herr Wertheim was considering how Schmidt would react to the new task which he was about to be assigned. Such a handsome, compact man, so respectful and serious. He thought: The shutters are always up – though, isn't that part of our culture? Is it the right one, or the left? I *must* ask Fräulein Dressler.

'Herr Schmidt, as you know the Prague branch is being reorganised. I would like you to go there for two weeks to keep an eye on this. Will you do that?'

Schmidt was surprised. The Prague branch had its own competent auditor. 'Of course, at your service Herr General-Director.' He waited. This couldn't be the full picture.

'Fräulein Dressler,' Herr Wertheim said quietly, 'will accompany you to put in the head office reporting system.'

The auditor blinked. A much stronger surge of surprise, and hope, went through him. That was what had been in the air in the anteroom!

'She'll need a passport. In today's conditions, therein lies a complication. Schmidt, I trust your discretion completely. What I say next is strictly confidential ... Our dear fräulein had a Jewish mother.' Eyes narrowed, the G–D watched Schmidt. His experienced scrutiny often learnt a lot from a person's reactions, helped him decide the next move. He smiled. This auditor was a hard nut to crack.

'I understand, Herr General-Director.' Schmidt's intelligence, hyper-acute in the G–D's presence, was engaged in an inner monologue: 'It's a pretext, she's not needed in Prague. I'm not needed there. He's trying to get her out. Has Dietrich talked to him already? Or, has he realised he can't continue to protect her?' That she had initiated the proposal didn't occur to him. Involuntarily, he leaned forward.

This interested Herr Wertheim. 'It's not an easy time for travelling. The fräulein will need your protection. I put the preparation of her passport application into your hands. I'll lodge it through a special channel. You'll have access to her personal records, birth certificate.' Ah, the birth certificate! 'Please prepare a supporting letter from the bank.' The general-director's gaze left Schmidt's face, and travelled down the room. The auditor followed it.

Another new work of art hung on the wall. A huge painted eye, Prussian blue, set at the apex of a geometric pattern which depicted a kind of corridor. His single-eye vision had kept it from him. Also, he'd been concentrating on Herr Wertheim.

Schmidt turned his own eye back; Wertheim's face was bland.

'It's entitled *The Eye*.'The G-D smiled. 'One finds one-self watching it.'While Commerce and the Future might just scrape by, this work must be categorised as degenerate art. Schmidt waited. 'It was in the Fuehrer's exhibition of unsuit-able art in Munich last year, much of which finished up with an art dealer in Switzerland.' Schmidt remained silent.Why was Herr Wertheim telling him this? 'My dear Schmidt, you should plan to depart the last week of November.Thank you.Always a pleasure.'

As Schmidt went out he imagined the gaze of *The Eye* on his back. It was amazing! Such a picture in the bank − given their new direction. Conundrums were circling the good ship *Wertheim* like sharks. He remembered a recent Wagner asser-tion: 'Just when old Wertheim thinks he has this tiger by the tail, it'll have its teeth in his arse.'

But perhaps something was going on in Herr Wertheim's mind which was outranging them all. Or was there something in Wagner's wild claims of insanity? One thing was clear: He was to play a part in getting Fräulein Dressler out! The weight of indecision − the pressure to act − had come off him.

She looked up quickly at the sound of the door. He walked towards her, past the table of newspapers, black head-lines blazing up. It seemed matters were in hand; no longer any need for him to warn her against Dietrich. Immediately, he doubted that.A vision came to him of the Nazi, restless, intrusive − back again − striding down the corridors; that man wouldn't remain inactive until the last week in November. He must leave nothing to chance.

She was smiling, the first real smile he'd seen from her.A light touch of relief was in the air. Close to her, he smelt a scent reminiscent of a flower he couldn't identify. She sorted papers efficiently, stood up, handed him a folder. He knew it would be the passport forms.

'Fräulein, could we meet this evening for a private talk?'

She gave him a look. 'Good Heavens, Herr Schmidt! You haven't forgotten the bank's concert's tonight? The night of the year!'

Schmidt was taken aback. Momentarily he had. 'Of course. After that?'

She was smiling broadly now. 'It'll be late – but, yes, if you wish.'

He named a place, and felt the strangeness of doing this given his married state. He went out, wondering what Wagner would think of this. He'd not seen him for a week, but his friend wouldn't miss the concert.

He paced the corridors, locked in thought. 'Doing the corridors', Wertheim people called it.

At 12.15, Herr Dietrich swept into Schmidt's room, as though borne from Berlin by powerful winds. The visit had apparently given him a booster-injection of vitality, quite unneeded in Schmidt's view. The Nazi had become a semi-permanent appendage to his desk: even when he wasn't there Schmidt visualised him on its edge, leg swinging, hair gleaming, hard blue eyes probing, a cocktail of tobacco and face-scent in the air.

'Well, Schmidt, there you are. The Party needed my services longer than anticipated. All in order here, I trust?'

'Yes, Herr Director. This week's report is on your desk.'

'You can rely on me studying it. By the way, I presume our little arrangement's in place?'

'For the first of the month.'

'Good. Including yourself?'

'Herr Director, as I said ...'

'A pity. However, I'll send you to Berlin soon, to talk to the Party's finance people. You will enjoy that. It will widen your horizons. The energy, the sense of purpose in Berlin, is boundless. You might bring some of it back here.' He laughed softly.

Schmidt nodded.

'Your report on Fräulein Dressler?'

The auditor blinked. No 'By the way' for this – just the question fired like a torpedo out of its tube. The Nazi's eyes were drilling into him with a similar precision. He took a shallow breath. 'I have to report there was no birth certificate on the fräulein's file.'

The Nazi's leg ceased swinging. He held a cigarette in a hand which had frozen halfway to his lips. In an eye-blink, the big handsome face clouded with suspicion. He stared at the auditor, disbelievingly.

Abruptly, the cigarette's passage recommenced. 'You see how it is, Schmidt? How cunning they are? What we're up against even at this low level? Some enemy has stripped the file of the evidence. Never mind. I'll obtain the certificate through a special channel. This virtually proves what I suspected.'

Schmidt was silent. 'Special channel' – that phrase again. He, also, would have to rectify the deficiency. How much time did he have?

'So, it's all quiet my friend. When it's like this I'm suspicious. The Party's focused on the rebuilding of the Reich, the welfare of our legitimate people – on a wonderful future. It has little time to worry about its own interests. *We* have that heavy responsibility, you and I, Schmidt! Don't relax your guard for a moment. Perhaps, even in Wertheim & Co, there's a fifth column biding its time to strike a treacherous blow.' He stubbed out his cigarette. 'Don't look surprised, Herr Auditor.'

Schmidt was, genuinely.

Grinning to himself, his manner suddenly a contradiction to the dire warning, Dietrich quit the desk with his usual athleticism. 'Just remain vigilant!'

Schmidt listened to the self-important footsteps depart. That slight unevenness of impact again. Did the man's left hand know what the right was up to? Did he really believe the cant about the fifth column? Why was he allowing a trace of irony about Nazi dogma to show? Schmidt shook his head. He felt in need of a short recovery period.

Dietrich's absence and the missing birth certificate had bought a little time. Presumably, Herr Wertheim believed he could quarantine himself and his auditor from the repercussions that would follow her escape – if that was intended. He was ninety-nine per cent certain it was. Yet, if the G-D had misjudged the situation, the outcome for Franz Schmidt – and his family – could be disastrous. It chilled his heart. He opened the file which she'd handed him. Getting the scheme into play under the eyes of Dietrich was going to be not only challenging but dangerous. That was a one hundred per cent certainty.

9

SENIOR DETECTIVE DRESSLER was out on a case – his own. With his rolling, nearly silent walk, he entered a maze of eighteenth-century streets in the city's inner eastern district. Fifteen years he'd pounded this beat, patrolled it as a detective for the past ten. Efficiently he observed black beards, black clothing, intense confidential conversations, figures floating in the opaque afternoon. He smelled soup; absorbed the foreignness and watchfulness. Light cords were being pulled; the lights barely illuminated the brandy-coloured interiors.

He was a human almanac on local petty crime: safe-breakers, burglars, pickpockets. He knew the faces of many of the small-traders who watched his giant figure pass by, some of their names. They knew him, and every public official who went that way. Behind his back, their children imitated his walk. His wife's people, working, and watching. For many years, he'd been a near insider; involved in family gatherings. In the early 'thirties, her family had left, scattering across Europe like chaff in a wind.

He proceeded under an archway into a narrow defile, dank as a sewer. He couldn't help wheezing. His damned damaged lungs. He wondered if the sunlight ever got down here even in summer. The more he thought about it the less confidence he had in Herr Wertheim. Now, at this late hour, he

was consumed by the need to find an alternative plan. In the
war he'd never panicked; he'd studied the terrain behind him
as painstakingly as that in front, plotting a line of withdrawal.
Several times it had saved him, and his men. He peered at the
houses, looking for a number.

They were waiting for him. He'd telephoned a man, and
it'd been arranged. Perspiring, breathless in a phone booth, he'd
had to bear down with all his desperation to overcome the
man's reluctance.

'Here we are,' he said, as though she was by his side.
He turned, scrutinised the street, and entered a building. He
climbed a stone stairway to the third floor, his body brushing
the walls. What a hole! The Propaganda Ministry was cunning,
with its films of rats swarming in narrow spaces. The room
smelt rotten with damp. The three men waiting for him had
kept their overcoats and hats on. The smell of body odour was
strong; their brows sparkled with beads of sweat.

Dressler felt pity. He nodded and took the vacant chair
facing them and said in his dolorous voice, 'I'm sorry to bring
you here. Thank you for agreeing to see me. I have a problem.
I understand it has been explained.'

Collectively, they studied this minor official of the Third
Reich who'd stepped from one existence into another. They
understood his deadly dilemma. He'd called in several favours
to be here. They knew all of this. Their fear and uncertainty
were palpable. It would be up to Rubinstein, the man in the
centre, who stared at the detective, squinting – as though he
was trying to see into his soul. Behind his gold–rimmed spectacles Rubinstein's face was not always this serious; he was
well known for his mordant wit. At that moment, in his own
mind, he was playing the Devil's Advocate. Or was it Russian
roulette? He released one of his tight smiles. He'd been a judge
until 1933.

The policeman's credentials were good. An honest, reasonable, humane man. Fifteen years – they'd no cause for complaint of him. However, was that record about to be debased? For example, had he done a deal with his masters to get his girl out? Was their network the quid pro quo?

Rubinstein said, 'What is it, specifically, that you wish from us?'

Dressler blinked quickly at the end of the delicately balanced silence. 'Mein Herr, my daughter has a plan to leave which, if it eventuates, should be safe. I fear it may not eventuate. If it does not, time will be a crucial factor. I wish to find another way. Some Jewish people are getting out.' He meshed his giant fingers together. 'I request your assistance.'

He took a deep breath, breathed in their fear, and let it go in a sigh. All he could do was be himself. Why should they help? The risks were too great.

Rubinstein absorbed the man's honesty, and pain, his constrained breathing. His own breathing seemed quick and refined in comparison. He said, 'Thirty per cent of our people in this city have left Germany. Most under conditions which were difficult, though far easier than today.' He shrugged. 'Last month, the Government demanded the surrender of all Jewish passports. Two ways exist, which might be acceptable to you in terms of the risk. We can forget the others. Firstly, certain Nazi officials are prepared to arrange exit papers for a price. A very high price. Very few can pay it.' He looked at Dressler.

'Secondly, false papers can be prepared – these are expensive – but the expense is more manageable. However, the danger is much greater. Day by day, the authorities become more vigilant. To be detected is … one chance in five.'

The rickety chair had creaked under Dressler's weight, though he had not moved his body.

'Would you arrange an introduction? For the real papers.'

Rubinstein nodded slowly. 'Nothing is safe or sure in these dealings. I would recommend them only as a last resort.'

Back outside, Herr Dressler surveyed the gloom. The slit-like street had two low-powered lights at either end; between was a black gulch. Fortunately, the Gestapo were short-handed in this city. He knew their exact number. Informers were the worry.

He began to retrace his steps, hands plunged into his pockets. Tears were in his eyes, he realised. He felt gratitude towards these men, admiration. They were traders used to sizing up persons, taking risks; nonetheless, this was a deadly game. Today, whom could anyone trust? He couldn't trust his colleagues, they observed each other with embarrassment. The orders coming down from Himmler's office were accepted with feigned indifference.

He recalled an incident. Two years ago after a Party rally, SA thugs had suddenly identified a dark man, chased and cornered him; kicked him to a bloody pulp. A citizen had remonstrated. Amazed at this temerity, the Nazis had turned on him, one had speared him in the face with the eagle-head of his flagstaff. The man had staggered back, his eye hanging on his cheekbone. Like a flock of pigeons taking off, the crowd had scattered. Standing with uniformed colleagues, Dressler had witnessed it. Almost in a drill movement, they'd looked away. He'd felt sick to his stomach, dishonoured, and had stepped forward to summon medical assistance. The dark man was gurgling in his death throes. The other had gone off to hospital following his futile act belonging to another age, or the Great War. Dressler had understood that kind of heroic, reflex act; that it owed little to logic, or the way the world was. It was just the way certain men were. Like these he'd just met.

He let it go, and padded on through the darkness. Shadowy human forms slipped past him in the murk. Optical illusions? His brain couldn't always quite cope. A tiny splinter of steel was still lodged there. Blinding headaches came frequently, the triggers of his war memories.

'God help us,' he whispered. He turned a corner and was gazing at the city centre's electric lights.

§ § §

Three pm: coming into Dresden. Juddering over junctions of points, each increasingly complex, Helga watched the familiar suburbanscape rolling out through the window: the minutiae of domestic and commercial life, unaffected by the structures of the Third Reich. Trudi, absorbed in endless plaiting of her doll's blonde locks, kept her tiny face as serious as her father's so often was.

Helga had been going over and over the same questions. The Order was at the heart of his 'other world'. Throughout their marriage it had aroused in her various emotions: curiosity, exasperation … She'd resented the interminable hours of research at the Municipal Library special reading room. Following in his father's footsteps. And, his unwillingness to discuss it. As far as she knew he hadn't discussed it with a single soul; he even kept himself anonymous from its mysterious headquarters in Vienna. She couldn't understand these things.

In the early days, half teasingly, she'd asked him what part of the cosmos he went away to. Clandestinely, she'd dipped into certain books, searching for a point of entry. She'd entered a labyrinth. She'd roamed blindly, knowing he was mining at much deeper levels.

She'd chided him: 'What does it say about our marriage, your love for our child?' He'd come from these bouts of study in a daze. 'Returning from the cosmos?' she'd ask.

She'd been putting behind her the eye. He'd seemed quiescent. But that had changed in the past month; she could sense it. Was it conscious or unconscious? Would his thraldom to the Order's fantastic ideals, archaic lore, bring them all into deadly danger?

God! What was he doing, what was he considering at this moment? The concert was tonight. Her lips tightened, making her pretty face severe. 'Forget the Nazis, Franz,' she whispered. 'Let them do what they must.'

She must quieten down. Be her usual pragmatic self. She took deep, steady breaths.

Trudi stood at the window, the doll clasped to her heart, watching Dresden's platform drift by, looking for her grandmother, her aunt. There they were!

A few years ago Helga's mother's friends had still called the mother and her daughters the three sisters. Now she took in at first glance the new frailty in the woman who stood arm-in-arm with her elder sister, and thought: No longer. Everything's changing.

§ § §

Schmidt gave it a look: a nondescript building wedged between two small streets looking like a mean slice of cake. He had left work early due to the pain in his mouth. He went up the narrow stairs to the first floor, aware of why the dentist had been reluctant to accept the appointment. But his jaw had settled into a throbbing ache, and he'd been Dr Bernstein's patient for many years.

The waiting room was empty and the door to the surgery open, and the auditor heard the clatter of instruments on marble. 'Come in, Herr Schmidt,' the doctor called.

Schmidt removed his hat and coat and went into the surgery. The nurse was absent. 'Good evening, Herr Doctor. Herr Wagner sends his regards.'

The Jew smiled slightly. 'I'm glad to have them.' He gestured at the chair. In a moment, he was gazing into the auditor's mouth. He probed the tooth, causing Schmidt to flinch. 'Aha,' he sighed. 'A wisdom tooth. Decay. It should come out.'

'Do it,' Schmidt mumbled. In turn, he was gazing up into Dr Bernstein's pebble-thick glasses, his puffy white face, black slicked-down hair. Wagner had once said the doctor was also a skilled financier; Schmidt didn't know what that meant.

With sure movements the doctor made an injection. 'We'll wait a few moments,' he said. 'I'm to cease practice.' Standing back, he shrugged.

The odour of corruption filled the air as the tooth came out. Then Schmidt was rinsing and spitting, and a small dressing was inserted. 'Bite on it for half an hour. The bleeding will stop by then. Rinse well with salt and water tonight.'

Just like the eye, Schmidt thought, putting on his coat and hat. Dr Bernstein waited at the door, a card in hand. 'Here is the name of a good dentist – for the future.' He smiled thinly, and gave an expressive shrug.

They shook hands with mutual regret, and Schmidt went down the stairs to the street. He stood on the pavement in the dusk: More, and more, change ... a man wrapped in a greatcoat walked away into the black mystery of a dilapidated alley. His attention caught for a moment, the auditor wondered why anyone would be going that way. He stared after the figure. Momentarily, he'd felt a cold breeze on his face. The breath of danger? He turned to hasten from the locality.

10

A T HIS NEXT destination, Schmidt looked up from his reading. Had the person sitting across the table spoken to him? Apparently not. The man's face was lowered to his book. Schmidt noticed a prominent mole on his right cheek.

The auditor lifted his head more, scanned further: shaded reading lamps daubed the special reading room of the Municipal Library with green light. He glanced at the man again: an unearthly pallor. Like himself, no doubt. A homburg rested on the table near his elbow. He wore black leather gloves. Curious … Schmidt was sure he hadn't been sitting there when he'd come in.

He returned to Felix de Sales' *Annales de l'order teutonique*. He was rereading the Order's conquest of Prussia in 1233. It'd been a highwater mark for the knights. After that, slowly but intractably, their power and wealth had declined. They'd begun the descent to oblivion. He gazed at the page without seeing it. Thoughts of the end had taken him back to the beginning; the twelfth century in Palestine during the Third Crusade. In 1188, with crusading forces besieging Acre, some German merchants from Bremen and Lubeck had formed a fraternity to nurse the sick. They'd become known as the House of the Hospitalers of Saint Mary of the Teutons in Jerusalem. As a boy he'd thought the long name had a marvellous sound to it. He smiled at the memory of his enthusiasm.

'Herr Schmidt!'

He had been right. He stared across the table in expectation, and the man slowly raised his eyes. A slight smile played on his lips. Warily, Schmidt studied him. A mass of tiny black curls flowed back from a large domed forehead. The dark eyes appraising him were sardonic. What was going on here? Why hadn't the man spoken when he'd looked up the first time?

'I beg your pardon, mein herr. Did you speak?' Talk was forbidden, but they were the only people in the room.

The man nodded. 'Yes, I spoke your name.'

'I'm sorry, have we met?' Was he an acquaintance he'd forgotten? Schmidt felt disorientated. When he did his research he entered this other world unreservedly, and came out in a daze. He wasn't yet back on terra firma.

'I've not had that pleasure. This will serve to introduce me.'

An object lay on the table before the man. He flicked it with the black-gloved index finger of his right hand; it slid across, and came to rest before Schmidt. The auditor gazed at the leather identity-holder, at the gold, embossed eagle and swastika.

'Please open it.'

Schmidt glanced at him, did so, and looked down at a photo of the man's face, at the Party seal. On the facing page he read: Manfred von Streck. In the space for rank/title had been typed: Special Plenipotentiary. It reeked of the Third Reich at the highest bureaucratic level.

Schmidt returned to the man in person. A chill had come over him, and he blinked quickly, to better focus his eye. This Nazi was short in stature but immensely broad and thick-set; on his feet he might look grotesque. On the other hand, good clothes and grooming gave him a stylish air. Now Schmidt was being watched meditatively; the man's hands were joined under his chin. He motioned for the document to be returned.

Employing the Nazi's method, Schmidt sent it back. He said, 'I don't understand.'

'It's quite a simple matter.'

Smoking was also forbidden, but von Streck produced a cigar and scratched a match alight. 'I wished to meet because of your responsibility for the Party's banking affairs at Wertheim & Co. Your unique position in relation to matters of special interest to me.' The cigar-end glowed red. 'Within the Party, I've a parallel duty, amongst others.'

Schmidt's mind clicked into focus; he'd alighted on terra firma: the NSDAP accounts were illuminated in his mind, and on the margin, winking like a warning light, was Herr Dietrich's instruction about the monthly special payment. But, such small beer?

'I see the official reports from your famous bank, and from the Party functionary seconded there, but an *unofficial* channel could be most useful. Sometimes the most important information, the *real* situation, comes along such a route. Regardless of that, it's also in place for emergencies.' An ironic smile. Schmidt watched the slight movement of the thick, mobile lips, and wondered at the terse identification of Dietrich. 'An escape road off a steep mountain descent, a way out should the brakes fail.' He dropped ash on the pristine floor.

Schmidt listened, his nerves strangely quiescent. Perhaps dealing with Dietrich was conditioning them. He wondered what 'special plenipotentiary' meant. Of course, there'd be massive distrust and suspicion within the Party, given the type of people the Nazis were, the rampant ambition, the scramble for power. Checks and balances would be imperative.

'Therefore, Herr Chief Auditor' – a note of authoritative formality – 'I want you to report to me if you find any special irregularity, or anything noteworthy. You may never need to make a report. I hope that's so. However, here's my card.'

A card came across the table.

Schmidt didn't touch it, didn't move.

'You're in doubt, Herr Schmidt?'

'I must say I am.'

'In what direction does this doubt lie? The basis of my authority? The irregular nature of what I propose?'

Schmidt had passed through his surprise, and was thinking fluently. He didn't doubt this Nazi's authority, though he would check it as far as possible. There was a logic to the approach which he understood. And there could be an advantage to himself in having special access to the Party: though he'd be closer to the fire.

He leaned forward. A certain polite reticence always worked well for him. He said earnestly, 'Mein herr, with the greatest respect what you ask puts me in an invidious situation. Already I report directly to Herr Wertheim – also to Herr Dietrich. From the tenor of your remarks, I assume those gentleman are not to be informed of this additional reporting line.'

'Correct. You won't mention our arrangement to anyone. That's a strict requirement.'

'I'm not comfortable with such a deceit.'

The Nazi official puffed away at his cigar, and pondered the pleasant-looking, correct man. 'I respect your professional ethics, but you should look at it this way: it's simply that escape road, purely for emergencies. The decision to use it will be yours. You're an intelligent man, Schmidt. I'm certain you'd know if and when it should be used.' Escape road, Schmidt thought. Intelligent? How does he know? 'We live and work in complicated times. For instance, in the past year, there've been five assassination attempts against the Fuehrer.' Schmidt was startled. The Nazi smiled. 'When you've thought about it you'll see no insurmountable difficulties, only advantages. I'm going to count on that. There's something else.'

He slid another small object across the table. Schmidt gazed down at a photograph of himself. It was embossed on a stiff card, a swastika next to his head, his personal details type-written on it.

The morning street photo! Now in amazement he stared up at the Nazi.

'A good likeness? I think so. That will enable you to obtain prompt access to me.' He appeared to be memorising Schmidt's face. He reclaimed his homburg, and nodded at the large tome before the auditor. 'I must go. I see you read French. I'll leave you with your research. There's a paragraph which I, personally, find of particular interest.' He mentioned a page number. 'Good reading!' He glanced at his watch. 'Though I trust you've not forgotten the concert begins at eight?'

Schmidt watched the Nazi depart. His powerful figure seemed almost as wide as it was high. Yes, grotesque in a way – yet, that air of being above the ordinary. The homburg was placed squarely on the mass of small curls. Despite his bulk, he walked panther-like through the green-hued semi-darkness, as if the special reading room was his home away from home, and not the arcane jungle that it was.

What did a man like that know of the *Annales de l'order teutonique*? How had he known he was reading this book? Schmidt turned over the pages, and ran his finger down the close-printed columns until he found, unmistakably, what von Streck was referring to. He read it carefully, twice, then closed the book and stared at the room of medieval knowledge, won-dering what new territory he'd entered tonight. The section he'd just read concerned a knight of the Order called Erik Streck, who had gone with the Grand Master to Marien-berg, the new headquarters of the Order's feudal state which included not only Prussia but the eastern Baltic lands. A man who'd lived in the fourteenth century.

11

'A STRAUSS OVERTURE to begin,' Wagner muttered
sarcastically, nudging Schmidt's elbow. 'Offenbach's
next. It's beyond their imagination to leave him out.
I speak only of the quality of the music.' He puffed steadily
away at his cigarette, and stared stonily at the conductor who
stood, baton raised.

Schmidt thought: But Mozart later, so be patient.

For over thirty years, Wertheim & Co had subsidised the
symphony orchestra and this annual concert for the bank's
staff and families, three hundred of whom were gathered that
evening in the gilded hall situated beside a Lutheran church,
was a major event in the bank's calendar.

Wagner was even nervier than usual, the cigarette grafted
to his fingers. They sat in the dress circle overlooking the two
rows of directors and their families. Schmidt had picked out
Dietrich immediately. The Nazi's hair gleamed in the light
like a gold coin as he sat erect between Herr Wertheim and
the ultra-thin Frau Wertheim – identified by Wagner as Frau
Thistledown.

'Offenbach?' Dietrich said to the general-director, lifting
his hard eyes from the program also to the conductor. 'Isn't the
fellow French – and Jewish?'

'Yes, but born in Germany,' Herr Wertheim replied, smiling urbanely. He'd especially requested Offenbach.

The concert began and Schmidt kept on with his thinking. He'd caught a glimpse of Fräulein Dressler as they'd entered; she was sitting somewhere behind them. It wouldn't take long to give her the warning, for all that was needed was privacy.

Submerged in the music, sniffles and coughs, he pondered the encounter in the Municipal Library. A chilling question came. God! Could it be that this Nazi was a fanatic involved in the Order Castles? Rumours had been circulating about the schools for the Party's élite, grounded in the heritage and traditions exappropriated from the Teutonic Knights. He sat like a statue now, completely oblivious to the music.

Wagner leaned close: 'They're playing tonight like an old dog dragging its belly up the street.' He laughed contemptuously, nudged Schmidt at some further transgression of conductor or orchestra ...

Why had the Nazi revealed that he knew of Schmidt's connection to the Order – perhaps his obsession with it? He hadn't needed to; the reason given for approaching him had been plausible. He shook himself out of this, looked around, and saw faces again. The hall was poorly heated, but inside his overcoat he'd begun to perspire.

By interval he'd recovered. He stood with Wagner stoically enduring the deputy foreign manager's foul cigarette, and the overpowering odour of mothballs. They were sipping a sparkling Rhine wine, the same one Herr Wertheim had served the past two years. Following Dr Bernstein's instructions, he'd gone to the lavatory to rinse his mouth out; his jaw was aching formidably.

'Filthy taste. It's the same as last year,' Wagner complained, holding his glass up to the light. 'The really bad news might be that our esteemed General-Director's cornered the vintage.'

Schmidt smiled vaguely. Same conversation as last year. Wagner knew Helga and Trudi were away, and he'd want to go out drinking beer afterwards to remove the taste of the wine. Wagner's story of how he'd escorted Fräulein Dressler home from the concert two years ago was in his mind. A Wagner exaggeration? He'd been nearly drunk the night he'd spoken of it. Schmidt framed an excuse to give his colleague the slip.

'Look at that,' Wagner hissed.

Dietrich, his athletic body bending efficiently at the hips, was saluting the directors' wives. His tight-lipped mouth side-slipped over the back of each raised hand, his heels clicked, his eyes shot here and there. His baritone boomed pleasantries above the din.

Schmidt thought: Party manners tonight. Smooth as the new machines with their steel ball-bearings, lifeblood of the Reich's reindustrialisation. He watched the small play of insincere formalities, aware that his calm observation of the Nazi was infuriating Wagner.

His heart stopped. Through the haze of tobacco smoke, Dietrich, a strange look on his face, had *him* under observation. The Nazi looked away quickly.

Wagner blurted out, 'Doesn't all that make your blood run cold?'

Uneasily, Schmidt said, 'Is it so remarkable?'

Wagner stared at him. 'My God! Are you becoming immune too? Careful, my dear …' He turned abruptly to push his way back into the auditorium. He spoke to Schmidt only once more during the performance, out of the corner of his mouth, 'Listen! He shakes a hand, kisses a hand. Close-up, he gazes into a face searching for a hint of the Semitic. That is what it's about.'

Schmidt knew that was only a part of it. The pursuit of ambition was also in play, a series of poses being employed, each calculated for effect. A conviction was forming in him that Dietrich was not a straightforward Nazi, if such an animal existed.

Wagner was overexcited tonight even by his standards. Schmidt regretfully decided to measure off some distance between them. With a shock he realised that he'd done the same with his family. Like the good ship *Wertheim* he'd changed to a new course. It made him sad-hearted. Yet he felt a slow-burn of excitement

After the concert, Fräulein Dressler was waiting for him. He was slightly embarrassed at not having accompanied her from the hall. She'd understood his reason: as much influenced by his married state as the presence of Dietrich. Even so, who might they encounter at this café? They shook hands, briefly, firmly. Her hand out of its glove was warm and smooth. His first touch of her. Zither music throbbed from a cellar. He hesitated. Under the hard streetlight her face was stark-white, sculpted. The languorous look was obliterated. He was reminded of the shining purity of enamel. Her eyes seemed larger, iridescent.

She said, 'If you wish privacy, my flat is within a ten-minute walk.'

He nodded, under a spell. Side by side they set off. Though it wasn't Jewish, it was a neighbourhood he knew only slightly. His mother's district evoked for him an image of multi-tiered wedding cakes on gilded plates; this, boiled beef on a tin plate. And, tonight, it seemed depopulated. She spoke only once. 'Did you drink that wine? Isn't it terrible? A cousin of Herr Wertheim makes it. He thinks it's marvellous. And he gets it free.'

The shabby building they arrived at had several lighted windows. Wagner, also, had climbed these same stairs after the 1936 concert – according to Wagner. The flat was of modest size, but freshly painted and furnished with solid chairs and cabinets. In an armchair he took the cup of black coffee which she offered. At the same instant, as though a chemical release had occurred in his brain, his interest in her took yet another stride forward: it was intriguing to see this woman from the bank's hallowed first floor in her private domain. He took a spoon of sugar, and looked up into her expectant face.

'I suppose you're surprised ...' He paused. She sat opposite, watching him. In the shadowed interior her face had lost substance. He thought: No, *not* surprised. He looked down, studied the carpet. 'Fräulein, I'll come straight to the point. You may already know this, but, in case not, Herr Dietrich's investigating your parentage. Like many of these Nazis he's an authority on the Nuremberg Laws. He hasn't verified his suspicions yet, but I fear it'll only be a day or two.' He paused, reluctant to be communicating this, yet certain it was necessary. 'Your birth certificate's disappeared from your dossier, which has delayed his inquiries.' Her eyes widened. He went on quietly. 'I hope to have a replacement by noon tomorrow for the passport application. I expect Herr Dietrich to take your situation to the General-Director when he's ready to do so. What will happen at that point ...' His voice had faded out.

She sat totally still, watching him as if he were telling an absorbing story. He'd not expected an emotional response, but this didn't meet his expectations either. He realised he was breathing quickly, though lightly. Abruptly, heavy footsteps crossed the floor above. In a quick reflex, he glanced up. She started, as though coming out of meditation. He sensed something like an inner sigh.

'My heartfelt thanks for your concern. Herr Dietrich's intentions have been crystal clear. Herr Wertheim is doing his best for me, I'm sure, but if the obstacles are too great – even for him – then I'll look in another direction.'

Schmidt sat back slowly, and felt a sense of reassurance. His admiration, also, was rising to a fresh level. What a remarkable woman! She spoke with calmness and fortitude – almost as if she were fully in control of her destiny. Then he thought: What other direction? The choices were few and dangerous. Bravery, intelligence and competency breathed across the room at him. That these might not prevail seemed a travesty, but that was what they were facing. He came back to earth – hard, autumn earth – and said, 'We'll hope for the best result with Prague. I trust we'll be on that train together.'

He'd forgotten his coffee; it was only warm as he drank it now. When he'd made his excuses earlier, Wagner had stared at him critically, shrugged, and slouched moodily off. Two years before, on this anniversary, he presumed Wagner had been in this same chair. What words had been spoken, moves made?

He should leave. He stood up. Unexpectedly, she helped him into his overcoat in the tiny hall, that flower-like perfume again. As they moved awkwardly in the tiny space, like strangers avoiding each other on the back platform of a tram, her hair brushed his face.

Suddenly he'd the notion of being a detached observer, taking notes. Had this been the way of it with Wagner? No, Wagner didn't think like that. She was in front of him now. He took a small step forward and without the slightest misjudgement their bodies met, and then their lips. Instantly, the mouth moving under his own was passionate, at first yielding then pressing forward, yielding again in a kind of desperation. His right hand was on her breast. They staggered, broke apart – breathless. Later, he held no detail in his head of the moment of connection, only of that disconnection.

He'd no memory of coming down the stairs, either. He stood in the dark doorway vaguely conscious of a cold breeze. He was not in a state of equilibrium – a rare experience for him. But it was returning.

Hardly believable! He'd been where Wagner had been after the 1936 concert! Not *quite* where Wagner'd been. Not that far – thank God. The dark neighbourhood seemed neutral, reluctant to bear witness to anything concerning him. Car lights undulated down a street. A sense of horror swept over him. A miscellany of considerations – foremost, the images of his wife's and daughter's faces. For the chief auditor of Wertheim & Co, what had occurred was not trivial. For Franz Schmidt – likewise. That embrace had taken him from the margin into the heart of her life. Now he remembered the flashed expression in her eyes – of trust? Of hopes aroused? 'We must get to Prague!' Had she whispered that in the tiny hall, or had he received it by a kind of mental telepathy?

He didn't know. But he felt a new man was standing in his shoes. He squared his shoulders, as though to meet the great challenge of his life.

12

HAD IT REALLY happened? A rhetorical question expressing his amazement that it had. Schmidt switched on the bedside light. Last night's scene in the tiny hall was stark in his mind. He shook his head: it was hard for a man of his profession and upbringing to believe. In the middle of this wonder, by a kind of osmosis, he became conscious of a sullen atmosphere. A spongy silence. Quite eerie. He lifted his head to listen better. A memory of the curfews of the Weimar Republic came.

Shaving and washing, eating his breakfast prepared by Maria, with his family absent, Schmidt felt a stranger in his own house, and regretted it. However, he put this regret into store as he had, yesterday, at the station. He rose from the breakfast table and went to the window. A few pedestrians were treading the footpaths; no motor traffic yet. But the significant silence intensified, and insistently began to sing in his inner ear like an edgy kettle on the hob. He returned to his coffee. What obscure anthem was the city playing today?

At 8.00 am, he boarded the tramcar in the platz. He paused before taking his seat, and glanced around; the kettle was still singing. The few faces, most known to him by sight, were pale and considering. No chatty little conversations today, just dead quiet. 'What is it?' he asked himself. 'Has something momentous occurred?' He should listen to the wireless.

The platz, a tonal study in greys and blacks, had suc-
cumbed to the depressing season. Streetlights, yellowish blurry
orbs, stood in the gloom like mourning-candles. A deathbed
feel. How could the human spirit cope? Was that it this morning? Bouts of general depression did wax and wane during
winter ... he unfolded his newspaper.

They started off. Herr Dorf, sombre-faced, came along.
Ignoring his fare-collecting he went to the front of the tram,
and spoke confidentially to the driver. Even his agility seemed
constrained. He merely nodded to Schmidt.

Schmidt opened his paper. *Dastardly Murder in Paris:
German Envoy Shot by Jew.* He read the headlines, the first
paragraph. The tram started down Bonnerstrasse. A sharp
intake of breath came from across the aisle. Schmidt looked at
the man, past him to the outside world. *Good God!* Smashed
shop windows, destroyed displays, merchandise littering the
streets. God in Heaven! Unaccountably, had a flood surged
through in the night? The thought shot to the surface. He
stared at the panorama of destruction rolling by the tram
window like a grainy black-and-white film, and held his
breath. Here, depicted in the flashes of his single vision, was a
fouled-up world. In the fastness of his apartment, his suburb,
he'd heard nothing!

'You're *not* dreaming my friend' – Wagner's voice in
his head. As though a switch had been flicked in his brain,
enlightenment came. Some of his fellow passengers were
screwed around in their seats, gaping, others had had his flash
of insight, and were averting their eyes. People stepped forward
at the stops, their faces strange, their shoes crunching glass. His
right hand gripped the backrest. Then he was breathing again.
Hitherto the thugs of the SA had perpetrated random acts
of terror while the authorities turned a blind eye. Here was
stark evidence of the full weight and connivance of the Reich.
Insidiously, the cold travelled up his limbs to bring a dull

ache to his chest. His mind shifted urgently. What did it mean for her? For the Prague plan?

They rattled across another platz. A synagogue sat like a ship ablaze and dead in the water. Deep in its heart pulsed an incandescent glow. Obscene smoke alive with sparks boiled from its high orifices into an overcast, aglow as from a mistimed sunset. To the auditor's horrified eye, the whole sky seemed to sag like a great overindulged belly. Several fire carts and groups of firemen stood idly by.

This particular spectacle animated four or five well-dressed men and women in the front of the tram. They pointed excitedly, laughed amongst themselves. 'This'll show them!' a man cried. Defiantly he caught Schmidt's eye.

The tramcar shuddered over points, glided into the city centre. No change here. He hurried to the bank, anxious to get within its walls. Once inside, he sorted rapidly through the pile of letters on his desk, found the envelope from the Registrar of Births. He extracted the document, scrutinised it, then going to his safe took out the manila folder containing the passport application, attached the birth certificate to it, and put the folder in his desk drawer.

At 9.30 am, he retrieved the folder and went to the first floor.

He hesitated outside the anteroom. Going through that door was another crucial step. Instantly, the spontaneous embrace returned, as fresh as though it had happened minutes ago. In the ten years of his marriage, he'd never broken his marriage vows. Not once. Then, last night, precipitately and dramatically, the ground had shifted under him. The incident, insignificant to others perhaps, was for him a metamorphosis sharpened by the brutish chaos viewed this morning ... He remembered Wagner's words about drowning. He entered the anteroom, wearing his professional mask. She glanced up, and watched him approach, equally well grounded in her

Wertheim character. The eyes that met his were calm, her air of superiority unchanged. He found that he wanted to say her name. 'Fräulein Dressler ... here's the submission for Herr Wertheim.'

She nodded, and gave him a smile, an almost indecipherable curve of her lips, which he drank in. She had on a crisp white blouse and her lips, which had been without colour last night, were reddened with a bright lipstick. What was in her mind this morning? How did he seem in her eyes, what motives did she find in him? He left without another word.

Herr Wertheim would have to move fast, tap into that special channel before Dietrich acted. Schmidt walked and thought. Analysis in these corridors was a chilly business, but according to the G-D, didn't the brain work better in the cold?

§ § §

The new painting had shocked, then amused Dietrich. In Munich in the summer of 1937, the Fuehrer had been absolutely clear about which art was degenerate. The grotesque eye at his back, as he faced Herr Wertheim across his desk, was a cut and dried case; patently a chancre in the general-director's make-up. What a paradox the old banker was presenting! With such interesting exploitative possibilities! But should he accept it at face value? It seemed so crazy.

Turning his handsome face, his brilliant blue eyes downward to regard his cigaretteless hands, he thought: Could the general-director be playing a game where he, Dietrich, had missed the commencing whistle? Perhaps a convoluted duplicity was at work here which required unravelling. If one could ever crack this porcelain-like shell of urbanity!

However, he'd no doubts on the subject he was about to raise. Decisively, he cleared his throat, and looked up. 'Herr

Wertheim, I'm obliged to draw your attention to the situation of Fräulein Dressler.' He paused, checking his tone for the appropriate delicacy. 'The rather *unfortunate* situation ...' Herr Wertheim watched the Nazi. This wasn't unexpected. With a pang, he wondered whether he'd left it too late. It had been long in the back of his mind: might've still been, but for her request to go to Prague. '... and to the Nuremberg Laws, and the subsequent supporting decrees. With respect, Herr General-Director, she should not be employed here. Of course, mein herr, with your great burdens I understand how easily this might've been overlooked.'

Dietrich's tone was insistent but respectful – he was confident of his mastery of the diplomacy required, sure of his ground – the dramatic events overnight had given him that edge. He spoke in the dogmatic yet respectful cadences of a hundred lawyers the banker had listened to. How far would Dietrich go? Wertheim wondered. Could he be bought, or was the situation too close to home for the Nazi to run such a risk? And the vital question: had Dietrich the power to neutralise the strings which he hoped to pull in the higher echelons of the Party?

Dietrich was experienced in situations of this type. No need to refer to certificates of descent, or birth certificates. Each party was fully conversant with the issues: if not on the table, they were in the air. He watched the banker's face, and confidently guessed his deliberations. They could have only one conclusion; no need to unduly force the pace. Nonetheless, for the record, it was necessary to play his next, entirely predictable, card.

'I must say, that when the Party entrusted its investments to your fine bank it had certain expectations.' No need to say more, but he did add: 'The Party's steadfast on this question – as are the people. One has only to look at a certain district this morning.'

Herr Wertheim pondered, as though analysing the yield

on an investment. After a moment, he said: 'Yes, indeed!'

Dietrich leaned forward, a trifle impatiently. He was dying for a smoke. This old banker used silences as effectively as an experienced preacher in a pulpit. He wanted to get on now. Nail him down. The momentous overnight events were staggering; he was astonished his colleagues hadn't forewarned him, and was anxious to phone Berlin.

'You know, Herr Dietrich, she's a greatly valued employee. Of immense use to me, her father's of good Aryan stock ... a war hero.' Herr Wertheim was thinking quickly.

The Nazi shrugged his heavy shoulders in a minimum show of sympathy. 'I'm afraid such considerations don't change the law.'

'Of course – of course!' Herr Wertheim instantly was avuncular, decisive, pragmatic. 'Leave it in my hands, my dear colleague.'

Surprised, the Nazi hesitated, then, seeing his departure was required, rose, bowed stiffly, and left. He strode past Fräulein Dressler, genuinely not seeing her.

Watching him go, she thought: I've ceased to exist.

Two grey-suited men, each with a matching pallor, sat in the anteroom conversing in tense whispers. For once the newspapers had been disarranged, as the visitors had scanned headlines. Directors of an insurance company, the bank's client for fifty years, they were facing disastrous claims, an outcome which the Nazi bosses apparently had overlooked when they'd set last night's madness in train.

From his door, Herr Wertheim watched them. He expected it might be easier to solve their problem than the one remaining from his previous interview. But he never failed to solve problems – was famous for that. The thornier the better. Suddenly he frowned with pain. He'd been getting these sudden fierce headaches recently. He must ask the fräulein for aspirin.

13

AT 11.00 AM, Schmidt took the lift to the basement and entered the bank's vault. Wagner was waiting, ashen-faced, badly shaven. The deputy foreign manager raised a cryptic eyebrow, plainly harking back to last night and his being left to drink alone. The acerbic remark on his lips was cut off by the arrival of Herr Otto.

Without a salutation, Otto growled, 'I have clients coming in. Get this over Schmidt, without your boring delays.'

Schmidt took in the brand-new Nazi Party badge. Politely deferring to seniority, he invited the general-director's nephew to take off his combination-lock from the safe reserved for the NSDAP. Otto had his usual trouble remembering his numbers. Goddammit! His fleshy face flushed a bright pink. Angry and embarrassed he consulted a scrap of paper, and made another attempt.

Wagner watched with undisguised contempt, Schmidt patiently. Was the embarrassment due to yesterday's encounter in the corridor when he'd had Fräulein Dressler against the wall? What had that been about? Schmidt had sensed more in the air than Otto's infamous lust. Then he recalled his own encounter.

Otto got his combination off, and stood back staring moodily while the deputy foreign manager twirled the dial with disparaging aplomb, and the chief auditor followed with his usual care and precision. The working stock of bearer bonds which the investment department used in their trading activities was due for Schmidt's first audit. About once a week the trio attended in the vault with investment staff while bonds were lodged or withdrawn, but this was a different procedure. He took the opened packet to a table together with the register which recorded the ins and outs, the running balance. He proceeded to count and examine each certificate held in the working stock, comparing its number with that recorded.

Wagner lit one of his offensive cigarettes, and leant against a wall.

'God save us!' Otto complained. He moved away, paced up and down, weighty matters on his mind. Schmidt balanced the face value of the certificates against the running total.

The young director pulled up, swung around on them. 'I trust you're meeting *all* of Herr Dietrich's requirements?'

Wagner shrugged carelessly. Schmidt intervened quickly, 'Herr Dietrich's watching everything with great care. He tells me he's satisfied thus far.'

Otto grunted and resumed his moody patrol. Schmidt verified the seal and notation on a second large expandable envelope. He replaced the two in the safe, locked up, and they went their ways. Doubtless, Otto would retape the scrap of paper with its secret combination numbers to the side of his left-hand desk drawer, where Schmidt had once observed it. Strictly against the bank's regulations, but the heir apparent had already begun to make his own. *No political affiliations* was the unwritten Wertheim dictum; predictable, that Otto now saw that as obsolescent.

'Christ!' Wagner said to Schmidt as they parted on the landing.

Herr Dietrich was waiting in Schmidt's office, an air of impending action about him. Standing in the door, Schmidt felt a surge of adrenalin; this reaction was becoming chronic. At one point, as he'd checked the bonds, he'd had the uncongenial notion the Nazi was double-checking over his shoulder.

'There you are, Schmidt.' With an amused expression, the Nazi regarded the auditor. 'Busy as a beaver, as the Americans say.'

Schmidt nodded.

Dietrich laughed. Clearly, he was in an ebullient mood. 'I have visited the United States, you know. An interesting place. Never mind. I wished to tell you that I've settled the Dressler matter. Not quite settled yet, but it *will* run its course to a satisfactory conclusion. She's Jewish. The birth certificate provides the clinching evidence. We lawyers are meticulous with the facts. I've spoken with Herr Wertheim, and I've no doubt he'll take the correct action. So there we are!' He paused and silently added: 'And how do you like that, my little friend?'

Schmidt regained his chair, and held his composure together. As he'd listened to the Nazi his thoughts had run a kind of parallel race. Wertheim, the old silver fox, playing for time, might've deceived the Nazi about his intentions, might've fobbed him off while he sorted the matter out at a higher level. On the other hand, the banker might have capitulated, and sunk his good intentions. Unfailing urbanity was the G-D's only predictable characteristic, especially these days.

Dietrich watched the auditor. 'Another matter. Have you ever considered joining the Party? ... *I* invite you to do so. The Party needs competent people of sound stock. Naturally, membership brings arduous responsibilities. As the Americans say: There're no free lunches ... what do *you* say?'

Schmidt gazed into the hard but avuncular blue eyes. This morning the Americans were really to the fore. He considered his desktop, the spot where the manila folder with Fräulein Dressler's passport application had lain an hour ago. Sound stock? Could von Streck's knowledge of his heritage extend to Dietrich? Another nerve-stirring idea. Nothing could be counted out.

'A great honour, Herr Dietrich. Not to be taken lightly. Of course, the bank's regulations –'

'Would not stand in the way. Look at Herr Otto. You're such a serious fellow, Schmidt. And you don't have to tell me again it's a professional characteristic. But think about it. Each of us must plan our future. I know about the unfortunate business with your eye. I trust no bitterness lingers there. We've eliminated undisciplined elements, people are now reliable.' If it had happened to him he would've been bitter and revengeful. Why not this auditor? This correct little man had courage to do what he'd done. No doubt about that. He moved easily off the desk. 'You've seen the streets this morning. The selected streets. This is a watershed, Schmidt. It's time for us to become more rigorous about the question of the Jews. It's all gathering momentum, all under control.'

He grinned, showing his regular, though nicotine-stained teeth. 'They're calling it Kristallnacht.'

He went off, to ring Berlin for the latest news.

The auditor remained immobile, heedless of his stacked in-tray. He wished he knew what was in Fräulein Dressler's mind this morning. What of Prague now? He hoped she was staying calm. He hoped, also, that Herr Wertheim was still seeking a path through the thicket of complexities.

The teasing, probing character of the Nazi was a worry. He felt he was only half a move ahead of him, if he was ahead at all.

§ § §

Herr Wertheim had been fifteen minutes on his call to Berlin. Fräulein Dressler felt a pain in her heart as she glanced at the light on his private line. *God grant him aid!* She was breathing lightly, quickly. He was talking to a man he knew well at the Party's headquarters. Aid for her from that source seemed an unlikely proposition. However, in the past she'd seen him manufacture miracles out of thin air.

She couldn't concentrate on her work. The minutes ticked by and her thoughts became more intense. More worried. She'd neither seen nor heard the overnight outrages, but the banner headlines, deadly smoke-trails and stench of burned material drifting over the city told the story; had begun the day-long constriction of nerves in her throat.

Herr Schmidt's appearance in the anteroom at nine-thirty had been reassuring. He moved about the bank like a shadow. She'd concluded that he was honest and principled and compassionate. It would have surprised him to know the depth and longevity of her scrutiny.

That spontaneous embrace! For him to step out of character like that – how remarkable! What a woman she must be! She smiled a tight, self-mocking smile.

Herr Dietrich had passed through the anteroom like the stale wind which blew in summer off the city's industrial fringe. At 11.00 am, the insurance company directors had departed and she'd received instructions from Herr Wertheim to convey to the director of lending. She'd rearranged the papers; they'd felt sticky and repulsive. Then Herr Wertheim had placed the call to Berlin.

The light on the private line went out.

For nearly an hour, Herr Wertheim remained incommunicado. She resumed her duties, glancing frequently at a bulb which, when lit, would summon her to the inner sanctum. He often sat immobile for long periods these days gazing down his room at that painting. 'Repositioning the furniture,' she'd named these interludes. Today her situation was the furniture. And the delay wasn't a good sign. She stopped her work, put her hands to her face.

The light on his private line winked on again. He was

making another call. This lasted about ten minutes. Her heart was pounding. The bulb to summon her lit up, making her catch her breath.

'My dear fräulein ... sit down, won't you?' Wertheim stared across his desk into the eyes which, despite his interpretative skills, had always baffled him, even during their intimate moments years ago. As though turning over the pages of a photo album, he remembered passionate afternoons at a little flat he kept. She'd been slimmer in those days ... For ten years, she'd efficiently administered the first floor, absorbed without trace the bank's secrets, his own. Made her little jokes. What a pity, he thought. No! What a tragedy!

'I'm afraid I don't have good news. In recent weeks, there's been a change. A high official who had discretionary power, no longer has it.' In a tone, polite but deadly, it had been pointed out to him by the high-ranking Nazi that she was a lawbreaker, as were Wertheims; that this made the case extremely difficult, and with Herr Dietrich's already-documented interest – the Nazi had wasted no time – it could hardly be glossed over. Further, that policy was less fluid by the day, instance the major overnight initiative, which, the high official ventured, was going to cost the nation a packet in repairs.

A hard case, his contact had sighed. However ...

Usually, Wertheim was absolutely straight with her, as though amid all the shifting sands of his affairs he needed one mind as bedrock. Today, he didn't communicate what the Berlin functionary, finally, had suggested: that if an apartment building or a factory was available to transfer to the Party, a passport might still be feasible. Sitting there after the call, he'd thought of von Streck, with whom he'd negotiated the transfer of the Party's business. Could that mysterious man do anything? He'd begun to reach for the phone, and then decided against it. Such an approach might be to the bank's detriment.

He said gently, 'Thus we can't proceed with the Prague

visit.'

On her face, in her eyes, not a hint of disappointment or emotion. It would be a relief to see something. He thought: She is enmeshed with my life. Yet, like all my old loves, a fading echo. He went on. 'Our lives are now overshadowed, in part, by ill-conceived forces. Nonetheless they've the authority of the law.' He watched her keenly. 'My dear fräulein, I had hoped to ride out this storm. Of course a woman of your intellect has read the signs. Having taken the steps we have, it will be dangerous for you to stay at Wertheims.'

'Yes, dangerous,' she murmured. Her face had frozen with shock.

He paused. 'Unfortunately, Herr Dietrich is alert to your case.' He observed she didn't react to this. Obviously, she knew the Nazi's intentions. How much else was going on around him which he was missing? 'It must be faced – and we must be the ones to choose your moment of departure. Within a few days.' He leaned forward, his hands spread on the desk before him.

He spoke for twenty minutes more, laying out the proposition he'd devised. When she came out to her desk she was moving in a daze, but she collected herself, and began to marshal the most urgent matters to be attended to. Prague was dead; now she was going to Saxony.

14

'HERE WE GO again,' Wagner said tensely. 'This time they've a car.' In his pitch-black parlour, he stood back from the window peering down at the street. Behind him, still in his overcoat, Schmidt waited uncomfortably. More Wagner eccentricity. They'd come in from the street and Wagner had steered him past furniture to what seemed like the centre of a black pit, then abandoned him.

'They?' Schmidt inquired. He felt he'd gone totally blind.

Wagner remained absorbed in his counter-surveillance. He said, 'I surmise it's the SD or the Gestapo. Take your pick. Perhaps both.' Abruptly, he stepped back, drew the curtains and switched on a side-light. He added tersely, 'Fucking gangsters.'

Schmidt blinked at the room. He said, 'Why?'

'Come on!' Wagner grinned, and removed his coat. 'Work it out for yourself, my dear. Take off your coat, I must go out and speak to the maid about supper.' He opened an interior door and went down a dark passage towards a light.

While the maid served the meal they talked intermittently about bank matters in the shorthand of insiders. They drank burgundy, a bottle Wagner said he'd brought back from his last visit to Paris. Schmidt had never set foot outside the borders of the Reich. When the maid had cleared the table and left them with coffee, Wagner went to a cabinet and produced a bottle of schnapps. Despite their close association, Schmidt had been here only once before, long ago, and remembered the apartment for the Biedermeier pieces which Wagner had inherited. The furniture of the past, and of the future, Wagner had said then. Happier days.

'Two glasses only of that brilliant burgundy? Even an abstemious fellow like you, Franz, will try this.' He poured small glasses full to the brim. His hand was shaking slightly. 'Well, have you worked it out?' He lit a cigarette, and gustily exhaled smoke.

The auditor shook his head. 'If there's something to tell, say it. Don't waste time.'

'Aha!' Wagner went to a record player, wound it up, and put a record on. In a moment a Mozart sonata began; a sound of heart-gripping pathos. The deputy foreign manager took up his glass, and tossed the schnapps down. 'That makes a nice little fire inside. Listen my friend, it could be a number of things: my business missions to European capitals; my accurate, but possibly intemperate pronouncements on our so-called government; the dislike which I inspire in Herr Health and Sunshine.' Schmidt winced. Wagner had taken to calling Dietrich this. With Schmidt, all nicknames grated. 'But *more* probably, the fact that for five years until the damned thing sunk under me, I was active in the Social Democratic Party. The Nazis've got their dirty hands on the membership records.'

Wagner connected to the SPD! Schmidt was astonished. His mind grappled with it. Wagner had thrown out hints. *More than my mouth,* he'd said. Schmidt cleared his throat. 'But that's all in the past. Forgive me, that party's finished, it'd be raking over dead coals.'

Wagner regarded him indulgently. 'To the Nazis, once an opponent always an opponent. Is a defunct party absolutely defunct? Could there still be danger there? They think like that, the paranoid *arseholes.*'

Schmidt flinched at the obscenity. These days, a few drinks and his colleague was losing control.

Wagner grinned nervously, refilled his glass, tossed it down, still holding the bottle. He suppressed a cough. 'Last night several hundred Jews were murdered or injured. Tens of millions of marks of damage done to their property, and to non-Jewish property. It's a new phase. Everything's speeding up. It's been bad enough so far, but by God, if you're Jewish, or out of step with the government, you'd better watch out from now on.'

Schmidt took a first sip of the suddenly-remembered schnapps. 'I've been telling *you* this, Heinrich,' he said quietly.

'Yes, dear Franz, you have. But what should we do? Go on day to day simple-mindedly trying to fit the routines of our lives into what's evil, immoral – nonsensical? Allow ourselves to be tickled on the stomach and stuffed like the miller's daughter? Dance along in this crazy comic opera?'

Schmidt frowned. Was this what Helga was doing? No, she had its measure; there was nothing simple-minded about his wife; she was just standing cautiously aside.

Wagner laughed roughly. 'I can see you think I trivialise it. Far from my intention. Does Greek tragedy fit better? Our Fräulein Dressler's on stage for that, Franz.'

They were silent, and in his chair Wagner dropping his head on his chest, for a while seemed to drift away with the Mozart; then he looked up and chuckled. 'Hear that fat bastard Otto come down on me for my smokes? *That* from the arch polluter of the corridors, the bank's ace-farter! You can bet he doesn't let it go in his own room. Is it his diet, his guts? The War Ministry should get a sample for analysis … Ha! Already a Party member!' His head dropped again.

Despite himself, Schmidt smiled. Then grimly his thoughts regrouped; the music after those opening moments was as inconsequential to him as it'd been at the concert. Dürer's knight, he imagined, had lived in troubled and opaque times, had negotiated them warily, with what outcome? 'Is that an example for me – for us?' Schmidt silently asked his slumbering colleague. Abruptly, the Nazi von Streck loomed up in his mind.

At 4.00 pm this afternoon, Herr Wertheim had called Schmidt to the first floor, and told him that the Prague mission was cancelled, no explanation – though he knew the reason. Fräulein Dressler hadn't been at her desk. He'd returned to his room struggling with this. He'd not breathed a word to Wagner about the events unfolding around her, of his own part.

The record finished. Wagner woke up, put on a new one, his head dropped again. Unregarded, the music played on uninvolved in the changing, dangerous times, though obviously soothing to Wagner's brain and spirit. Schmidt thought of Helga and Trudi in Dresden, probably already asleep. Was he in little Trudi's dreams? His family life seemed a million miles away.

Wagner woke up again with a start and vigorously cranked the phonograph; he sat there, a new cigarette drooping from his lips, his face slack and meditative, his fear back in its cell in his brain. He looked slyly at his colleague: Still present. Schmidt wasn't a social stayer; he was adept at making excuses and fading away, back to his arcane studies – Helga'd let something slip once. And what else are you up to these days, my clever, reticent friend? Has the delectable Fräulein Dressler found a champion? Franz had the guts for it; that eye business had been nothing but raw courage. He watched the auditor sip the last of his schnapps, and true to form, prepare to depart.

Schmidt said, 'You're not still active in politics, Heinrich?'

'Active? Inactive? Dormant? Inert? My friend, I'm not going to tell you. But take heart, the SPD is banned, disbanded. What did you say about dead coals?'

It was not the answer Schmidt had hoped for.

§ § §

Senior Detective Dressler's giant shadow was cast on the façade of a row of houses. The street was deserted. His footfalls were silent on their thick rubber. Exception: glass crunched occasionally beneath his weight, though most of it had been swept away. Through cracks, lights glimmered here and there. The shop windows were boarded up with new lumber.

An atmosphere of dread and mourning. He'd had a good education, and had disappointed his parents when he'd joined the police. He wasn't a literary-minded man, though some things he'd read stuck in his mind: 'For all guilt is punished on earth.'

'We must live in hope about that,' he said to the darkness.

Against orders he'd been here last night seeing what he could do. Not much. The teletype from Berlin had chattered out its instructions at 6.00 pm: the police were not to intervene. At 8.00 pm, truckloads of Brownshirts had swept into the district. From a doorway, he'd watched its violation; the beating-up, dragging away of citizens, hair, beards streaming, clothing torn, eyes of dumb animals, though some with eyes more calculating. He'd heard screams, frequent explosions of shop-windows, shards of glass clanging onto the cobbles; possessions had rained down from buildings. His beat. The representative of law and order, he'd stood by, backed into the shadows, massive in his overcoat, his pistol strapped to his chest – as helpless as a baby. The only reactive force had been in his brain.

Now, he went on. It remained his beat. He still had to look these people in the eye. How could he? Moreover, how to reason it through? He wished he'd Lilli's brains. 'Though what's the use of brains, these days, Dressler?' he asked himself.

The Party had been out counting, sending excited reports
to Berlin: three synagogues, twenty-two shops and businesses
destroyed, 150 shops and businesses damaged, uncounted
number of dwellings damaged and sacked. Two Jews killed,
twenty-five seriously injured. Not a bad result for a city of
four hundred thousand. Multiply that across the Reich.

He'd been of some use: a Jewish merchant draper whom
he knew slightly had run out to the street screaming of a sexual
assault. The detective had left his doorway, hauled himself up
two long flights of stairs into an apartment. Screams of terror
guided him to a bedroom where two Brownshirts, white bums
pumping in unison, had two women down on a massive bed,
side by side.

Dressler's huge hands had plucked them off the frantic
women like pulling weeds from the earth. The heads of the
SA had cracked together. He'd thrown them down the stairs,
reclaimed them at the bottom, his breath steaming out, vision
blurring with the effort, handcuffed them together, propelled
them, dazedly clutching their trousers, into the street. Other
SA men had run up threateningly, but he'd flourished his
badge and roared: 'Caught raping Jews!' They'd shrunk back
reluctantly, knowing the consequences.

As he walked on, the acrid smell of burnt material came to
him. So Herr Wertheim had failed the test Lilli had set for him.
Not unexpected. Steel barriers were crashing down against
even the most influential. Now this alternative scheme – no
less suspect. And as yet, he'd no fall-back plan. Bleakly he wondered how Herr Rubinstein had fared last night, whether he
was still in a position, of a mind, to help. He'd been waiting for
a call; now it might never come.

§ § §

Ten pm. With an untired eye, Schmidt inspected the street. No
car, no watchers. Perhaps it had become too cold. Or were

Wagner's nerves playing tricks? He stepped into bitter air. In a warm, counter-attacking wave, the single glass of schnapps rallied in him.

Wagner was up there behind that slit of light, drowsing in his fecund atmosphere of Mozart and Biedermeier, his haze of schnapps and cigarette smoke. Fervently, Schmidt hoped his colleague could find a way to modify his behaviour.

Abruptly, as though nudged by his destiny, he turned in the direction of Fräulein Dressler's flat.

She spoke insistently through the door. 'Go away, Herr Otto.'

'It's Franz Schmidt here.'

She opened the door a little on a chain, and they regarded each other. 'I see,' she said.

She wore a silk gown, which allowed a glimpse of deep and creamy breasts, and clung to her abundant hips. This Fräulein Dressler staggered him. Incongruously, he remembered Wagner's description of her as a devotee of cream cakes. Her face was pale – as a white tea rose – but resolute, even defiant.

Staring at her in the gap of the door, her aura of perfect efficiency seemed cracked, like a porcelain plate. He was mesmerised. His brain had stopped functioning, then like a stalled aeroplane at the top of a loop turning its nose down, re-igniting its engine, it cut back in. Suddenly it was distasteful being here on her doorstep, gazing at her like a mournful bailiff.

Last night's passionate embrace overwhelmed him afresh. It had more immediacy than the present moment. He struggled with himself, fighting down his emotion.

'How can I help you, Herr Schmidt?'

'Might I come in?'

She opened the door, and stepped back into the minuscule hall. She motioned him to a chair.

'I hope it's not too much of a shock, Herr Schmidt, to see me minus cosmetics and glamour. But then you're a married man.'

He hardly heard that. Help you? he was pondering. I wish to help *you*, but how can I?

'Well, Herr Schmidt?' – the general-director's secretary back on duty. The hints of intimacy from this morning had evaporated – with the abandoned Prague mission? Did she even remember last night?

'Herr Wertheim informed me this afternoon the Prague trip is cancelled. Herr Dietrich, that –'

'My days at Wertheims are over?'

'Yes.'

'How kind of him. Nearly over. I'll leave this week.'

He considered this. Reluctantly, she came and sat opposite him, and gave a small, dismissive shrug. 'Herr Wertheim did his best, but the problems of people like me worsen each day.'

Schmidt would have sympathised with bitterness, but detected none. He was sitting here on the slenderest of pretexts. How ridiculous it must seem to her: a kind of meddling curiosity. What was going on was rotten and terrifically bad luck, but merely saying, thinking that was worse than useless.

Had the knight ever had such self-doubt, been a host to similar powerlessness? He said: 'I wish to help but I don't know what I can do.'

'Thank you. I've understood that. Herr Wertheim has a new proposal.' She considered how much to say. 'He knows a man, an academic living a reclusive life in a remote place, who he's persuaded to take in a secretary. He believes in this household I'd drop from sight. Until something else can be arranged.'

Silently Schmidt gazed at her. A stop-gap solution. Out of Germany, beyond the reach of the Third Reich was the only safe haven … This was no good. Dietrich's interest in the case wouldn't cease at the point when she left the bank. The dedicated Nazi, the Munich-trained lawyer, would want to see her before the courts. In prison.

It had been a long and eventful day, but Schmidt didn't feel weary, instead more and more keyed up.

She said, 'I've not decided to accept Herr Wertheim's offer. I wish to discuss it with my father.'

He stood up. He'd come here, he realised, to discover what, if anything, was to replace the Prague initiative. At least he'd that answer. Another reason existed, he supposed with a pang of self-disgust. 'Herr Otto ...' she'd said through the door. He had the unpleasant vision of the director and her in the corridor.

She watched him leave. There was to be no repetition of that passionate embrace. He felt he'd been dismissed from her mind as he closed the door. However, when he was gone, Fräulein Dressler remained motionless, staring at the varnished oak. A strange, well-meaning man. That serious, watchful face, his worried concern, awoke her sympathy. Did he realise the danger he might be in? It was far too late in the day to render assistance. They'd all been sleepwalking. A million troubled consciences such as his couldn't make any difference now. She'd felt the sexual pressure upon him, brushing against her spinster's life. It should have been merely a surprising and curious byway, yet the blood had been coursing through her last night, as it did sometimes in her solitary and intimate moments. Eligible men were few, and far between. Affairs had been rare in her life. A generation of mates killed off. Millions of German women shared her predicament. Some nights, she was desperate − less so these days.

Forget that! She had to move quickly and surely now. And stay calm. There'd be no second chance.

15

TWO DAYS HAD elapsed since Schmidt had dined with Wagner, and paid his second visit to Fräulein Dressler's flat. In his office, he stared at the wall as if to project Herr Wertheim's latest plan on it; but it remained a sketchy blueprint in his head. He felt like a tram driver whose hand had frozen on the shut-off lever in an emergency. Abruptly, he smoothed his blotter, made a decision, and went to the G-D's anteroom. She wasn't there. He returned to his office.

At 10.00 am, Dietrich terminated this. The Nazi was a specialist in bringing matters to a head. Schmidt looked up to meet the calculating eyes, and the wolfish smile. He'd no idea how the man had arrived so silently in his doorway.

'What do you have to report, Schmidt?'

Schmidt began to rise. Dietrich waved him down impatiently. 'Listen, Herr Auditor, don't bother to stand up for me. You Wertheim people spend half your time lifting your bums off your chairs when a superior appears. We're now close colleagues with the same aims. Remember that.'

Schmidt watched the Nazi; doubtless he'd the guardianship of the Party's business in mind. He collected himself: Feeding time. 'Herr Director, one million in from Bremen this morning. Herr Schloss's department's already invested it.'

He husbanded these morsels for Dietrich, to deflect his scrutiny. Probably the Nazi had begun to see through it, hopefully saw nothing more than an anxious underling's desire to please.

'Very good.' The cigarette case crossed the desk. Dietrich lit both their cigarettes. The oak of the desk creaked under his weight: a subtle Wertheim & Co protest. He waved his big white hand to disperse the outbreak of smoke, and appraised Schmidt with a speculative yet friendly look. 'The Dressler affair finishes today.' He inhaled luxuriously. Schmidt absorbed this as he did all of the Nazi's utterances, with meticulous attention and outward calm. But his heart beat more quickly. 'It will be tidied up this evening. The Gestapo will pick her up at her flat. That'll be that! Another one of them flushed out, extracted from circulation. Just like the Reichsbank's extraction of dirty banknotes! Very correct, eh Schmidt?' He tapped his thick fingers on the cigarette case in a rapid, valedictory tattoo, and smiled at the ceiling.

Schmidt felt his stomach rise and fall. He nodded slowly, automatically reaching deeper within himself for calm. With that smile the Nazi, too, seemed to have reached inside himself. Did Party members receive a bonus for this kind of thing? Perhaps only a testimonial. Schmidt couldn't interpret the tone, the smile. A hint of irony? Possibly. More one of challenge, he decided.

'Nothing to say? Never mind. Have you thought over joining the Party? No?' Dietrich grinned. 'My dear Schmidt, you're not one to rush into action are you? When are you going to step up to the plate?'

This last question puzzled Schmidt, but the subject was far from his mind. 'It's an important decision. I wish to discuss it with my wife.' He heard himself saying this.

'And she is in Dresden attending to her mother.' The auditor looked hard at the Nazi. How did he know that? 'All right, Schmidt. We'll pursue it another time.' He rocked a little on his perch. 'One picks up many things at the centre of power.

For example, the Social Democratic Party, banned, presumed disbanded, in actual fact survives. Is treacherously running its affairs from Paris. From Paris! Stay alert, Schmidt! Nothing's as safe and sound as we think.'

He grinned again at the auditor. 'By the way, please recommend me your dentist. I wish to have a check-up.'

He departed with Doctor Bernstein's address in his notebook. Schmidt considered what he'd done. For a moment, he'd thought of giving the Nazi the name of the dentist recommended by Bernstein, or of saying that the practice had closed, though he knew it was open till the month-end. But immediately he was certain these subterfuges wouldn't work; he'd sensed that more was involved than Dietrich's teeth. He picked up the phone to warn the doctor.

After the call, Schmidt stared at the photo of the Wertheim building taken that long-ago summer day. His body felt chilled. His brain seemed to be overloaded. The SPD survived! Wagner had been to Paris several times this past year. Coincidence? He shook his head. Intemperate outbursts were one thing. He couldn't believe his friend would run such a deadly risk as this implied.

Dietrich seemed to be fitting Franz Schmidt's life together like one of Trudi's jigsaw puzzles, and what was this new bonhomie? An intimacy being attempted which was ominous. He must maintain his distance; use his polite, circumspect manner to its full effect. He stubbed out the cigarette.

He knew now what Dietrich had put in motion, but remained ignorant of the situation on the first floor: knew only the general steps of their mysterious shadow-dance. Could she get away in time? Dietrich had served the news to him like a delicacy on a plate; it teased him with its danger. He was perspiring. He straightened in his chair. For him the road ahead had opened up.

§ § §

Dietrich left with a brooding expression on his face. He was confident that the Dressler situation would be correctly finalised. His revelation to Schmidt of her imminent detention, before he'd dealt finally with Herr Wertheim on the issue, underlined that. He was becoming intrigued with Schmidt's nature, with penetrating his smokescreens. If they were that. He felt attracted to the man.

He arrived at the first floor, and walked straight into the general-director's office. Herr Wertheim gave the Nazi a quizzical look, and motioned him to a chair.

Dietrich believed that the old banker's negligence and intransigence concerning his secretary, now unmasked, had changed the balance of power between them. However, the hierarchal system should be respected. Up to a point. He began by raising one or two routine matters. The banker listened, patiently receptive. Instead of smoking, the Nazi employed his hand in expansive gestures. He paused ... 'Herr General-Director, I have to inform you the Gestapo will arrest the Dressler woman this evening at her flat. At 6.00 pm, I believe.'

The faded eyes dilated. Wertheim laid a bluish hand on the desk; otherwise he was as inert as the paintings on his walls. After a long moment, he said, 'Mein herr, you surprise me. I understood it was being held in abeyance pending my consideration. Our further discussion.'

The Nazi raised his open hands, palms uppermost. He lied with an easy conviction: 'Unfortunately, the illegality of her position came to the attention of the ever-alert authorities through other channels. It's now out of our hands.'

Herr Wertheim didn't doubt that it was. He stared past the Nazi to the far wall, meditated on the so-called degenerate picture. He sighed to himself. This Nazi was not as subtle as he thought he was. It was distressing to hear the reference to 'the Dressler woman'. They'd accelerate her departure to his cousin in Saxony.

With narrowed eyes, Dietrich watched the Silver Fox. He said, 'It would be a mistake for the fräulein to try to avoid arrest. For example, to attempt to hide in some well-meaning but misguided household – even in a region as remote as say … Saxony.'

Herr Wertheim's gaze broke contact with the unblinking eye on the wall. His face had assumed its most profound urbanity. But he was thunderstruck. So they were tapping his private telephone line! He felt the slightest film of moisture on his hands, a palpitation of his heart. His fertile plan was a frozen ruin. He was stunned. From a controlled defence to defeat, in one move.

Dietrich stared at the banker, wondering how he'd taken it. He still couldn't tell.

The general-director glanced at the big clock on his wall. This was a city of clockmaking and it had been presented to him by a famous manufacturer; it resembled those they suspended above prizefight rings. The innovative sweep-hand seemed to devour time. He smiled. 'Herr Dietrich, I won't detain you any longer from your important work.'

Fräulein Dressler watched the Nazi stride out through the anteroom, as though on parade at a rally. The man seemed to possess a ragbag of poses. All he lacked was a uniform. Herr Wertheim's red light was flashing. She took up her notebook and went in, and sat in the chair still unpleasantly warm from Dietrich's bodyheat. Herr Wertheim was emitting hints of strain. After ten years, she detected what others couldn't; more so than his wife, she liked to believe.

'My dear fräulein … *bad* news. To my deep regret.' To another he might have said, 'Please stay calm.'

The absence of urbanity in his voice froze her heart. Then

he startled her by rising, and coming around the desk to stand
looking down at her, his hands caressing the air. She thought:
My God!

'The authorities intend to detain you for questioning
this evening. Six pm. At your flat. They've discovered our
plan. They're listening to my private line!'

Now Herr Wertheim was speaking in a strange voice. It
seemed as if she'd been watching a moving picture of herself
caught up in a dramatic plot, a climax coming, the interweaved
skeins of the Prague solution, the Saxony solution, her father's
quest for a solution. And a minor thread: the inexplicable
intervention of Chief Auditor Schmidt. On the physical plane,
her life had become unbelievable; yet intellectually it was
as clear-cut as this building on its granite foundations. She
thought: *Please God help me!*

'There's no time to lose.' Wertheim spun around and went
into an alcove. He came back with an envelope, and gave it
to her.

Five thousand: his emergency travel funds.

'Go to one of your father's sisters. I can only recommend
that. You must leave immediately.' He knew she'd three aunts
in different cities. Years ago, he'd sent flowers to one who'd
become widowed. He couldn't recall which cities. 'All else
being equal, go to the largest city.' He paused and lightly
rubbed his cheek with a veined hand, feeling events closing in,
ice freezing around his heart. He became dizzy; his temples had
begun to pound. 'Astonishing, *my* telephone line! Presumably
they can trace calls made to it. To contact me, do so through
Herr Schmidt. But be very careful.' He pursed his lips; the
implications went beyond Fräulein Dressler's case.

She thought: He's breathing rapidly. Someone else will
have to remind him about his pills. But he'd never reveal such
agitation to others.

'We'll get money to you – through your father.' He smiled

painfully, took her hand and formally shook it. She felt his deep sadness; also, his will to deal with this problem and put it behind him. She knew him too well. Suddenly, he lifted her hand to his lips. Ah, yes, she thought, but we do return, briefly, to the old days.

Ten minutes later, Fräulein Dressler, loyal and irreplaceable private secretary to the general-director of Bankhaus Wertheim & Co AG, quit the bank and the life in which she'd hoped to be grounded for the rest of her working days. Departing by the tradesmen's entrance, she thought: Now I must really move fast. *Stay calm.* As she hurried into the street she said to herself: 'Farewell dear Wertheims. I'll leave you my ghost.'

16

HELGA GLANCED AT her watch: 3.00 pm. On a glass skylight, rain rattled. Frau Seibert's operation was in progress somewhere in the bowels of the Dresden hospital. She formulated an image of this, as she sat with Trudi in a waiting room. The child, diverted from her doll by the passing parade of mysterious, white-clad people, the squeak-squeak of trolleys carrying persons of even greater mystery, watched this new world.

Helga was not wholly preoccupied with concern for her mother. She'd spoken by telephone to Franz on two evenings, and had been disturbed by his unusually reserved voice. Was his life-long, seemingly genetically-implanted fascination with the Teutonic Knights moving him to confront the Nazis at the bank? If so, they were in danger. She bit at her lower lip.

'Well! What a delightful little girl!'

A boomed-out remark, followed by a staccato heel-clicking. It smashed her reverie. The beaming, pink face of an officer of the SS bore down on her. He bowed stiffly; creaking black leather, hip-joints, white shirt, black uniform sprinkled with silver insignia. An apparition superimposed on her anxious thoughts.

As though admiring the first flower of spring, he touched Trudi's blonde head. 'This little one would delight the Fuehrer's heart!' Abruptly, he saluted, heel-clicked again and left in a quick-strutting gait. Trudi looked at her. Helga stared after him. An odour of new leather remained, subverting the hospital smells. Each day, like fungi cracking the earth, these people were breaking into their lives. Now totally alert, thoughts of the Order gone, her gaze after the departing Nazi became intense, her eyes slightly dilated, as if she feared his destination was the chief auditor's room on Wertheim & Co's second floor.

§ § §

Schmidt left his office to run the icy gauntlet of the back stairs to the first floor. It was 3.02 pm. Since Dietrich's departure he'd sat immobile, plunged in thought. The anteroom was deserted. Fräulein Dressler's desk was cleared: evidence of an efficient departure. He stared at it, and in a flash had a notion that from the deck of the *Wertheim* he was looking at an abandoned lifeboat on a wide sea.

The case clock bled seconds.

He turned on his heel, and went back to his office for his overcoat and hat. That clock was ticking in his brain.

Hurrying through the grey mid-afternoon, he felt a stranger in the streets at this hour. In ten minutes he reached the gloomy, utilitarian building. He climbed the stairway quietly, holding his tension in check. He hesitated, then rapped lightly on the door with his knuckles. A lingering silence – a suspension of life. Iciness from the concrete floor speared up through the soles of his shoes into his bones. Did this building ever get warm, even in summer? He strained to hear; heard his own breathing.

He said, 'It's Schmidt.'

Immediately the door opened; he stepped back. She'd been behind the door. A gesture to enter, but no sign of panic. He took his resolve past the questioning eyes into the flat. The crisis appeared to have brought her a deeper calm; the flat looked stripped. She closed the door behind him.

'Fräulein, you know?'

'Tonight. Yes.' She stared at him.

'Have you a plan?'

'Yes.'

'Herr Wertheim's plan?'

'No. It can't be used. They've found it out. They listen to his phone.'

Another twist. So the techniques of totalitarianism were invading Wertheims. Quite predictable, though apparently not to the general-director. Technology'd never been his strong-point.

Heavily, someone was coming up the stairs. *God! Too late?* He glanced at his watch: 3.25. They listened, hardly breathing, joined in the danger. The steps trudged past the door, and kept on ascending. Each fading footfall took a weight off his heart.

It was good that she was reticent, but he must test this last-ditch plan. Wertheim & Co had abandoned her! In effect. From the moment he'd gazed at her empty desk, his unfocused concern, his tentative actions, had coalesced into a direct responsibility. His vision had cleared.

'What is your plan now?'

She began to move, continuing with what he'd interrupted. She'd no time to question his presence here. Yet another move by this auditor ... 'I'll go to my father's sister in ... another city. I'll leave tomorrow.' She clearly enunciated the words, the last of which made no sense. He stared, his lips tight. This wasn't calm and collected.

'*Fräulein*, with respect, you must leave this flat immediately. Go to the station. Tomorrow will be too late.'

'I will leave the flat, but I must meet my father. I've not been able to contact him.'

'Your father's flat will be the *next* place they'll go to.

A hotel is out of the question.'

She turned to him with a perplexed but obdurate expression. The telephone shrilled in the hall. She started, hesitated, then went to it. She came back, her eyes suddenly glittering with nerves. 'They hung up.'

Schmidt thought: They're on their way. He glanced around the room. 'Three suitcases?'

'Yes.' She closed the lid of one, and lifted it to where the others waited. 'O God,' she intoned softly. It sounded like an amen.

Schmidt thought: We must go *now*. Get clear of the locality. He visualised a black car on its way from Gestapo headquarters. He had, in the last minute of concentrated mental effort, thought where to take her, where he could bring her father to meet her, if he couldn't persuade her to go direct to the station.

She was putting on her overcoat, her hat. He'd not taken his hat off. The compulsion on him to get out was now tremendous. But were they already waiting? He moved to look down into the street, stopped: learning from Wagner. He stepped back from the panes, black as photographic plates, flecked with raindrops. 'Leave the lights on,' he said. 'Is there a back way out?'

She shook her head.

There was nothing to do but to walk out of the building carrying the suitcases. Commit themselves to the streets. Streets murky as the Fuehrer's mind.

They were out ... his heart seemed to be tapping like a hammer on ice. Perspiration soaked his shirt.

An act of deliverance! A solitary taxi waited at the corner. Once they were in, and away from the area, he began to whisper in her ear, brushing the fragrant hair with his lips.

Frau Bertha was shocked. In the open door, faded blue eyes staring, her mistress's commanding voice at her back, she gazed at Schmidt, the woman and the heap of luggage, as if they'd arrived from a foreign clime.

Warm air flowed out from the apartment to the chilled arrivals; Schmidt had discharged the taxi two blocks away, and was breathing audibly from hauling Fräulein Dressler's packed-up life. He smiled tightly, ushered her into the hall past Frau Bertha, the sightless bust of the Great Man, and returned to bring in the luggage.

In her plush salon, Frau Schmidt, her pince-nez elegantly held aloft, inspected them. Then she concentrated on her son's face. Schmidt drew in a silent breath, and made formal introductions. At first, he'd thought to leave her in the hall while he spoke to his mother. He'd changed his mind. He was now deciding things on the run.

'Mother, Fräulein Dressler, is a colleague at the bank. She's leaving tomorrow, for … another city. She needs your hospitality for tonight.' He went forward, leaned close. 'I'm afraid the fräulein's in some difficulty. She's Herr Wertheim's secretary. Her mother was Jewish, and the situation has changed at the bank.' Would this old patrician lady understand the implications, the danger? Frau Schmidt glanced at her son. A meagre smile played on her age-marked face. She spoke up, a nuance of triumph in her voice, as if gratified to confirm her opinion of what she had once called his 'unstable teutonic romanticism'. 'You are very welcome here, Fräulein.' Her remark, ignoring Schmidt, was woman-to-woman.

'I'm sorry to impose on you, but I seem to have no other choice,' Fräulein Dressler said with a fleeting smile.

What business had his daughter here? Number 178 Frederick-strasse. For Senior Detective Dressler, a single upward glance was enough to transmit the building's history and status. He took it in automatically. Only three kilometres from the district of his patrol but a world away. Yet many decrees issuing from the ministries in Berlin were now falling on each with equal weight.

His rubber soles squeaked on the marble stairs. His breath whined in his throat. Her brief phone call had been guarded, but he knew the blow had fallen. His huge gloved hand reached for the bell-push. Before he could touch it, the door opened. The detective regarded the small, soberly-suited man standing there. Blond hair, bright blue eyes; smooth, almost feminine skin. He didn't recognise Schmidt − an unusual failure of his memory. But he did decide instantly that here was an individual who could blend into the background, like a person fitted for a life of crime.

Schmidt did remember Herr Dressler − from the café a few weeks ago, and a Christmas party five years back; his size. He looked up at the huge, cautious face, and thought he saw a family resemblance. Another vague memory was hazy in his brain.

He said, 'I'm Herr Schmidt, a colleague of your daughter's. Please come in.'

The detective stepped lightly onto the highly-polished parquet floor, full of wonder and confusion. Schmidt closed the door, and led the way into a room on the right.

Fräulein Dressler waited before the fireplace. The Dresslers stared at each other, then she moved to him and was enfolded in the overcoated arms. 'O Papa!' With a shock Schmidt saw that she was trembling. He left the room, closing the door. He settled down to wait in the hall. The room he'd left was his late father's study; his father's cannonade of a reply to his mother's salon. She'd kept it so.

He paced the hall. His mother had retired with a cryptic look, though still tinged with her triumph. He sighed. Frau Bertha, doubtless, was in her room smoking a clandestine cigarette, listening to her wireless, worrying about this singular and dangerous event.

Still pacing, managing his own nerves, it occurred to him that he was face-to-face with his childhood. Here had been the beginning; the first visits to the study, the light turned on in his brain, precursor of his inner life. His father's room was a museum of the Order of the Teutonic Knights. Its entanglements, chronicles – fables. A museum unknown to its mysterious headquarters in Vienna, which over the centuries had shrunk, he understood, to a church and archives.

He'd never divulged his passion to school or university friends – not that he'd had many. In his younger days it'd seemed like a sacred secret. A wonderful one to be held close. And he'd been imitating his father's reticence on the subject. In adulthood, the secrecy had been ingraind in him. He'd told no-one at the bank, not even Wagner. Of course, Helga knew.

Abruptly Fräulein Dressler appeared. He saw that she'd regained her calm. He rejoined father and daughter. Senior Detective Dressler, still in his coat, the electric light gleaming on his massive head, leaned slightly forward, like an oak balanced against a high wind. It struck the auditor thus. He moved efficiently despite his size. Did his mind match his physical competence?

The detective cleared his throat. 'Herr Schmidt, I wish to thank you for the assistance you've rendered my daughter. For the risk you are taking. Your deed, your mother's, allows one a little hope for the future. We've decided which of my sisters she will go to. I will return at 7.00 am with a motor car, and drive her out of town to join the train to her destination.' Schmidt thought: They'll avoid the barrier checkpoint.

'It will be a temporary arrangement. We hope to find a better solution.' Herr Dressler's heavy accents lingered in the wood-panelled room.

Schmidt nodded. He'd nothing to offer these counsels. Yes, he was putting his mother's household in hazard. The degree of it depended on the efficiency of the Reich security agencies. It was strange how sanguine he felt about it.

'I am on duty,' Herr Dressler said. He took his daughter's hand, carried it to his lips, looked down into her fondly watchful eyes. Full of concern for him! He could hardly stand it. Abruptly, looking aside, he offered his other hand to Schmidt in an uncharacteristic, throwaway gesture.

17

OTTO WERTHEIM LOUNGED in a chair in Dietrich's room smoking one of the Nazi's cigarettes. They'd been having quite a session: the room was thick with bluish smoke, the odour of tobacco; a bottle of cognac which Otto had brought was nearly empty. The engines of Wertheims had quietened to a murmur; only a few lights remained on, in the foreign department.

Otto was very satisfied with the atmosphere of this informal little celebration of his Party membership. Dietrich might not be of his class, but he was a superior example of his type, and on the way up in the Reich. One had to move with the times, adjust one's social circle, manage it like a portfolio of investments. As his uncle had so astutely, albeit surprisingly, recognised: a fortune was there for the taking; thousands of businesses were gearing-up to a plethora of exciting opportunities, and Wertheims had entered the traffic!

Enough of business, it'd still be there at 9.00 am tomorrow. Inevitably, a surfeit of brandy, the late hour, had turned his thoughts to women.

Dietrich, equally as relaxed in his disciplined way, watched the young director with a tolerant but sardonic look. The majority of the things that the Nazi did in his life had a specific objective. Sitting here at this hour, drinking brandy, having the kind of conversation that Otto Wertheim was capable of, wasn't a stimulating experience; but it was a correct investment of his time. The sum of Otto wasn't much, but his privileged position in the bank's condensed world counted. A rarefied world, which the Party had sent him into. And tonight he'd gleaned more information on that slippery old fox, Herr Wertheim.

'How about coming on to a club,' Otto said. His eyes shone like glass, his fleshy face, soft as wax, had fallen into lustful anticipation. 'Girls who're plump, juicy, and willing.' He laughed. 'And you don't have to talk to 'em in the morning. Or, at any time.'

He gulped more brandy; a trickle came from the corner of his mouth.

'Not tonight, my dear Otto,' Dietrich said evenly. He'd narrowed his eyes, his handsome face had become brooding, even lustful in its own way. An interesting proposition had occurred to him – a realisation, really. It concerned Franz Schmidt. He sipped his brandy, equably regarded the other's disappointment. He said, 'Fräulein Dressler's no longer with us. The Gestapo are picking her up tonight.' He glanced at his watch. 'Might already have done so, she could be under inter-rogation at this moment.'

Otto sat up. Lights seemed to be spinning before his eyes. He said thickly, 'Did I hear you right?' Amazement was flaring in his brain, dissipating the mist of alcohol.

'You did. Didn't you know she had a Jewish mother?'

Otto frowned heavily, trying to force his mind to take hold of this startling development. A red light was flashing in the mist. He'd known it, but had never thought it through to any kind of a conclusion. That racial stream in her, perhaps, had been the source of his sexual fantasies, of numerous ses-sions of masturbation. He fumbled for his glass, brooded on its emptiness, as though everything had turned inexplicable and threatening … the Gestapo!

'Never mind,' Dietrich said. 'In concealing that fact, in working here, she's been breaking the law for the last three years. She'll certainly go to prison.'

'Interrogation?' Involuntarily, Otto mouthed the word caught by his groping mind. He'd found a track in the mist. 'I'd like to be there for that. I'd like to get my hand up that superior Jewish bitch's cunt, make her squeal and squirm. Hear her begging ...' His voice had risen, cracked, then become thick. Something else was on the rise; he felt it straining at his trouser flies.

Dietrich's wolfish teeth showed. 'My dear Otto! Those are hardly correct sentiments? Strictly criminal sentiments ... never mind.'

The phone on his desk jangled. He casually reached for the receiver, his sardonic look continued to hold the flushed, confused director. He listened for a few moments, not surprised by what he heard. Cunning bitch. 'One minute,' he said, and took a small notebook from his pocket, flicked it open. 'Here are two addresses.' He read them off. 'Heil Hitler,' he responded laconically and put down the phone.

Aha! Probably not *her* cunning. Someone had warned her: was it complicated, stone-walling Auditor Schmidt who'd fallen into his trap? Or the fertile Herr Wertheim? Fascinating! He was going to enjoy finding out which. Perhaps it'd been both!

He smiled patronisingly at Otto, but the young director, his hands hanging over his knees, was gazing at the carpet with his bloodshot, hangdog eyes.

When they entered the corridor Dietrich didn't attempt to support Otto, but, amused by the spectacle, allowed him to weave towards the lift. One by one, the lights behind the pebbled glass doors of the foreign department went out.

Wagner appeared. He watched the two directors approach as he put on his overcoat, interested in their contrasting conditions. Attempting to pass the deputy foreign manager,

Otto's shoulder struck the wall. He cannoned off it towards Wagner who adroitly stepped aside.

Otto came to rest against the wall. He lifted his head, and roughly focused on Wagner's face. Through some chink, the deputy foreign manager's contemptuous scrutiny penetrated Otto's brain. He squinted, trying to bring the face into better focus. The corridor reeked of brandy.

'I know you, Wagner,' he said thickly. 'I can read your damned thoughts. I see you looking at this badge.' He fumbled for the badge on his lapel, but his nerveless fingers couldn't find it. 'You'd better remember ... we're all in the same ship. If you know what's good for you.'

'A ship of fools?' the deputy manager inquired with a succinct offhandedness.

He turned, and walked away along the corridor. Otto peered at the departing figure, as if trying to nail it immobile against the wall with his unreliable eyes. He didn't understand what had been said. A single idea was in his brain. *'No-one here ... turns his back ... while a Wertheim director is talking to them,'* he shouted, seemingly chanting with difficulty from a book of etiquette. *'D'you think ... your father can save you? Dead man, save you?'*

Wagner had gone. Otto's voice trailed away. He was left with the empty Wertheim corridor, the usually solid but now apparently movable Wertheim wall, against which he'd lustfully pinned the aloof, fragrant Fräulein Dressler, now also departed.

Dietrich, standing back, watched this interlude with increasing delight; it might've been a show put on for his entertainment and instruction.

He stepped forward and began to steer the semi-conscious director towards his room, and its leather couch. 'Come on you dull-witted, foolish fellow. The Bavarian maidens will be safe tonight.'

'Thank you, Frederick,' Otto mumbled, 'very good of you ... where are we off to my dear Dietrich?'

§ § §

Schmidt knocked softly on Fräulein Dressler's door, listened, heard the soft 'Come in'.

She sat on the edge of the bed, fully clothed. At first he thought she was looking at the curtain-covered window. Then he realised she was contemplating the future. Like a nervous girl waiting to go to her first dance. The last image was incongruous, but in his mother's apartment she struck him as being stripped of her character, taken out of her life. For him, more regret.

'Excuse me,' he said. 'Do you need coffee, a drink, something to eat?'

She'd turned to him, and the contour of her chin seemed to imply trust. 'Nothing, thank you, Herr Schmidt.'

'Will you sleep?'

She glanced at him as though it hadn't occurred to her. Her suitcases were unopened. 'Herr Schmidt?'

He stood in the room, the light glinting on his spectacles. The weight of matters unknown, unexplored, between them seemed to pulse in the air. Though how could she be thinking of anything but this desperate trouble?

But he underrated her. Fräulein Dressler's brown eyes and organised mind were considering him in a new light. Here in this stranger's room stood a man of action. Amazingly, a different man. Yet there'd been the incident of the eye. It had been a mistake to see that as an aberration in his character. They should have known. She looked down at her hands locked in her lap.

Schmidt found himself mute. His mother's apartment was as silent; nothing penetrated these walls. The city had lain down and died. Four hundred thousand people dead to the world. His brain did get some relief in thinking like this. How to communicate? What to communicate?

Suddenly the memory of them embracing in her hall came. He was aware of that scent of flowers, the smell of musk from a body which had been in haste. In the heated room, it had coalesced into a humid sensuality. Everything which he'd observed Fräulein Dressler to be: proud and dismissive, humorous and ironic, mysterious and alluring, pragmatic and sensuous, rose up in a towering wave in his head. His testicles were aching.

This was absolute madness. And wrong! His mind reeled, yet held him on an unswerving course, and left those thoughts behind in a flash. His eye was locked with hers. Those glints of gold. The realisation transmitting between them.

He turned and in three paces was at the door, had closed it, turned the key. Somehow their hands were together, fingers interlaced, she'd fallen back on the bed, he standing at its edge, leaning over, pinning her down. Their lips met violently, teeth jarring, the unbelievable intimacy of lips and tongue and moisture, and that habitual hint of scepticism melting away. Their mouths broke apart and he was kissing her cheeks, her eyes, her hair. The room seemed resonant with their breathing. Unbelievable pressure! He stood up, frantically threw off his coat, his braces, let his trousers fall to his ankles. Her hips were on the edge of the bed. She'd drawn up her legs, was removing underwear. He threw back her skirt, had a vision of thick white thighs above her stockings, of the darkness between, tucked up his shirt till his penis was free, fell forward on her, their hands interlacing again, felt her hips spread and give under him, the uplift and warmth of her stomach, found the spot, thrust once, was partially in, twice, glided in to his full extent, was rocking on her pelvis, the room filled with lubricous sounds.

Wagner said he'd been here; Otto perhaps had been; by

rumour, Herr Wertheim had – didn't matter. One of her legs had encircled his, he was about to ejaculate – did with a spurting force which made him cry out – just as her body, her pelvis, arched up to grip him.

He lay on her as they seemed to subside into the feather bed. Thirty seconds had passed since that first thrust. His still-hard penis was locked in her. The sensation of release spread though his body and mind. Their lips were pressed together again. Had he heard or imagined that long languorous: 'Oh Franz!'?

He walked home through deserted streets in a daze – not noticing that fog was accumulating, blurring the streetlamps. He couldn't believe what had happened. Yet again! Couldn't believe, that he'd done what he'd done. However, step by step his mind was clearing.

Overwhelmingly came a stark horror which pulled him up: that he'd borne down on a defenceless woman at her most vulnerable. The next second, he saw this wasn't precisely the case. She was stronger than he! What had occurred, had happened because she wished it, had been in control. Briefly in that post-orgasmic state of possession he'd thought she'd laid her character, her mystery, open to him. He saw now that she hadn't: the enigma remained.

He stared at the night, at the future. Images came twisting to the surface: her face, shadowed in the room at the moment of departure, a mixture of affection, something else. The ghostly faces of his family. He began to walk again.

He'd stood in the room, somehow dressed.

She'd said, 'You must go.'

'How can I leave you like this?'

'You must. There's no other way.'

He'd let himself out of her room, out of his mother's front door, half-understanding the well of her strength. Feeling empowered himself, coming out of his dream now, he went along the dark street looking towards the morning and steeling himself for the coming hard realities.

18

THE SMALL BLACK car crawled with a clattering, misfiring motor along Frederickstrasse's kerb, a beetle that had lost is bearings. Six thirty am. A yellowish fog blanketed the city, choking the avenues and narrower streets with swirling clouds of water vapour. The driver gazed at this murky world. His eyes were bloodshot.

His colleague was walking the pavement, searching for number 178; each agent was invisible to the other. They kept in contact by a succession of piercing whistles. With sour, end-of-shift weariness, the driver thought if they'd been Red Indians on the hunting trail it might've been birdcalls. A thumping on the side panel; he braked, and peered at the blurred figure suddenly at his window.

'This is it, better get a move on, we're late,' a disembodied voice said.

'Any wonder?' the driver grunted.

Frau Bertha hurried through the apartment bearing a tray of hot rolls and coffee. The household had been astir for half an hour, and she knew the young woman in the guest bedroom was fully dressed, pacing the room. Her mistress, warm-gowned, already was issuing instructions with her early-morning disdain. What a start to the day!

The doorbell clanged in the hall. Good heavens! What

next? Agitatedly, Frau Bertha put down her tray on a side-table and hurried to the door.

§ § §

The tramcars had not started up because of the fog. Schmidt set out to walk from his flat to his mother's. He was aware of occasional blurry figures on the move in the fog, which almost took shape, only to decompose again. He could see a metre or two. He worried about how Herr Dressler would navigate across the city. At any rate, the trains would be delayed. He breathed lightly, trying to avoid taking in the acrid vapour.

Last night was irradiated in his mind. A marvel. But hopeless, like a corpse on a slab. Now they'd be absorbed with arrangements, racing against time. It must be thus if they were to succeed. As surely as he'd fallen out of his character last night, with this dawn, he'd slotted back into it.

Footsteps sounded, as if they were from an invisible twin. Ahead or behind? He stopped suddenly, so did the twin. The tapping of a blind person's stick passed by to his left: no difference to him this morning. He went on; the twin was back. Echoes. Why was he, a man who loved his wife and daughter, engaged in these perilous events? The dripping silence for an answer.

§ § §

Black-garbed, severe-faced as priests, the two men inspected Frau Bertha. *A pair of crows,* she thought. She'd frozen, as if every last nerve-end had iced up. The pavement-walker held his warrant card, casually, over his heart. The official seal: the black eagle rampant, claws sunk into a swastika, glared at her. Another bird! Frau Bertha was closer to the Reich's streetlife than her mistress. But until now, that menacing world hadn't physically invaded the enclave which harboured No. 178.

They stepped into the hall and the smell of leather and a whiff of foggy air came with them. Frau Bertha, grasping for normality, remembered the same odours at early departures in the household's days of touring motorcars.

'Tell Frau Schmidt we wish to speak to her,' the pavement-walker said. His eyes left Frau Bertha's face, and side-slipped to the hall furnishings, and the Great Man's bust. He sniffed as though testing the upper-middle-class atmosphere. 'Be quick!' A Munich accent; the maid recognised it.

In the corridor which led to the hall, a door opened and Fräulein Dressler appeared. She paused, sizing up the situation, then came forward.

'I am Fräulein Dressler.'

Both the Gestapo agents nodded, as though nebulous suspicions harboured during a long shift were confirmed. They knew nothing of her background; she was a name on a warrant. 'You're under arrest, fräulein,' the walker said. 'You'll come with us, bringing one bag only.' He inclined his head at her, spoke to his partner. 'Keep her under observation.' He turned to Frau Bertha. 'You'll take me to Frau Schmidt.'

The maid led him down the passage to the salon. The driver stepped forward, and selected a hot roll from the side-table. 'Breakfast!' he said heartily to his colleague's departing back.

In her chair, Frau Schmidt waited for the denouement of the commotion. Without the buttressing of her fine clothes and jewellery she appeared as weightless as thistledown. The strict black ribbon dressing her plaited hair, the alert eyes, belied that.

So it appeared to the unshaven man in the leather coat, who'd not removed his soft black hat. He examined this effete vision of the bourgeois, categorised it. With equal contempt,

Frau Schmidt marked his manners.

'By what authority do you enter my household?' The walker sighed. Her fine-boned wrists showed from the gown. He'd snapped similar wrists like chicken-bones. As a means to an end. 'By the authority of the Reich,' he said in a matter-of-fact tone. He held out his identification. 'We've arrested the Jewish fugitive, Dressler. How do you explain her presence here?'

'Explain her presence? She is a guest.'

'She is a colleague of your son's, is she not?'

'Of course.'

'Did he bring her here?'

'Naturally.' Frau Schmidt was unaccustomed to the slightest prevarication.

His stare lifted from her face, and went around the room, taking in the rich collection. Still appraising he said, 'Then, you and your son have committed a crime. The penalty is severe. Get dressed, please.'

Frau Schmidt did not move, continued her unblinking stare at this example of the new Germany.

'Did you hear me?'

The imperious head lifted. 'Do you know who I am? I am the direct descendant of the most famous German in our cultural history.'

The pronouncement, never before uttered by Frau Schmidt, except to herself, wafted in the salon. The agent's face was empty – waiting for more information. She whispered the name, parting with it with extreme reluctance to such a recipient. '*Even* your Herr Hitler pays my ancestor the most profound respect.'

The man of secret orders, of subterranean cells, of the calculated dawn visitation, returned her gaze. Was she mad? Senile? Instructions for cases like this had evolved, but behind the scenes frequently lurked special influence – and purchasing power. Traps for the unwary. Now her body shook for a moment and she was staring at him fixedly. He'd be cautious. Nonetheless ...

'Nonetheless, please do as I say.'

She sat there, immutable. He waited almost a minute, by turn uncertain and impatient. She did not blink.

'Frau!'

But it was too late. Frau Schmidt had died.

Her body remained fixed in its last position, the derisory eyes uplifted to his face.

He took a step forward, looked into those eyes, and lifted a porcelain wrist. 'Shit!' he swore under his breath, and let it drop. He turned, and went out to where Frau Bertha waited. He gestured impatiently to her to go to her mistress.

Fräulein Dressler waited in the hall with the driver who, watching her but not seeing her, was munching a second roll. The stress, agitation, and fear of past weeks had come to a dead-stop. She was dazed. 'Oh Papa, what can I do?' she breathed desperately.

The other man entered the hall. 'Come on,' he said, 'let's move.'

'What about ...?' the driver said, wiping his fingers, nodding to the interior.

'I'll tell you later,' his colleague growled. He took Fräulein Dressler by the arm, and they went out. She'd picked up her suitcase. The driver followed, closing the door precisely. The apartment was deeply silent; then the maid shrieked. He wondered what mistake his colleague had made.

§ § §

Schmidt and Senior Detective Dressler met at Number 178 at 7.10 am, and shook hands in the icy lobby. A minute later, they were confronted by Frau Bertha's tear-stained face.

'Too late,' Dressler whispered, heart-sick in an instant.

A moment later Schmidt stared at his mother. She appeared to be still in command of her salon, almost on the verge of speaking to him. He felt he'd gone out of the world himself — had ducked out a side door, and was looking down on the scene from a high vantage-point.

Dressler, filling the salon doorway, his hat gripped in big fingers, took in the scene, jotting down facts in his mental notebook. It was a side-show to the shock, the deep foreboding for his daughter. His head was throbbing badly.

Schmidt turned to him, more obviously shocked. The detective, intimate with sudden death, squinting his eyes against the pain, framed an interim conclusion: heart attack. The fear for his daughter was ringing in his own heart like an unanswered alarm. Somehow he switched it off. He regarded Schmidt with sympathy. This bank man must feel like he'd entered hell. Welcome.

'Come,' he said. They left the room and he questioned the distraught Frau Bertha, gently but persistently. He said to Schmidt, 'Phone your mother's doctor. He must examine her. He will tell you what to do. The maid — she should sit down, have some coffee.'

'Your daughter?' Schmidt turned slowly towards the detective. 'What's happened?'

'The Gestapo. The clock was running too fast ... we were too slow.'

They walked out to the hall. The detective's voice had trailed away. He halted, frowning, trying to reorganise his thoughts. Droplets of moisture glistened on his brow. He stared grimly at the composer's bust.

'What can we do?' Schmidt said.

Dressler dragged his hand across his jaw. 'I will go to the Gestapo office. Try to ... if you wish, I'll contact you later. You ought to find a good lawyer. Familiar with matters like this.'

Schmidt nodded vaguely. His thoughts had done a circuit, and settled on the main fact: Fräulein Dressler. Here last night ... gone now ... into the abyss. They'd failed. Failed ... His mind seemed to be slipping badly.

'Herr Schmidt!'

Sternly, the detective was staring at him. For a second it surprised Schmidt, then he found himself coming back. Shakily. Suddenly, he was turning over scenarios in the future involving his family, the bank. The detective was correct and helpful to point him towards the defensive. He'd regained stability, his mind was no longer a conveyor belt missing notches ... The policeman had established control over the father, as the situation demanded. A pillar of a man. Have you killed your mother with your good intentions? Or, had her time come by the unknowable clock running for each of us? With your imperfect plan, have you delivered Fräulein Dressler into their hands? He shook his head.

The detective had watched the auditor reassemble himself. Quite a tough one. Pragmatic, at least. Without a handshake, silent on his thick rubber, Herr Dressler walked out of the flat.

Schmidt went back in, told Frau Bertha to sit down, and phoned the doctor. Then, while coffee heated, he returned to the door of the salon. Was her spirit greeting her revered forebears? That would have been her expectation, and this morning no kind of strangeness or mystery seemed improbable. He blinked, and broke the spell. How had the Gestapo known to come here? It was one question he believed he knew the answer to.

It was too early to ring the bank, but not Helga. He'd been due to call this morning anyway.

'Franz?' The familiar voice, up an octave. 'The operation was successful. She's recovering ... Is all well with you?'

He drew in his breath. 'Helga, I'm very sorry to tell you

my mother died this morning.' He listened to the echo of his voice down the trunk-line, her silence.

'Good God! What happened?'

'The doctor's not here yet.' He considered whether to prepare her for what he would need to tell her, what she would hear from Frau Bertha. In the worst case, from the Gestapo. No, not yet. 'Probably a heart attack ...'

A pause. 'Franz, my dear, we'll come home. Will you meet the six o'clock express?' He hesitated. It would be better if she didn't return. But immediately he knew there'd be no stopping her. They discussed a few details.

He hung up. The apprehension which had arisen in her voice saddened him. What had she been thinking these days apart in Dresden? Doubtless, much. In consideration of the path he'd chosen, bills were going to come in from several quarters for payment.

At this point, in his father's study, his mother dead in her salon, there came into his consciousness – not in a flash of light, rather with a steadily increasing glow – the true nature of his purpose and his situation. He stared fixedly at the room, letting it pour into him.

19

AT 8.15 AM Herr Dressler, holder of the Iron Cross First Class, thrice-wounded, gassed in the Great War, strode into the Gestapo office and asked for an officer by name. The black-uniformed, suspicious SS Untersturmfuhrer in a glassed cubicle at the door deliberated on his police identity card, examined a checklist, sized up the giant figure, then brusquely nodded him in. The municipal police fitted into the Reich bureaucracy, albeit at a subordinate level.

He was told to wait. He sat down on a wooden bench and regarded Gestapo clerks working on files at desks behind a counter. They looked like tired shift-workers anywhere, not administrators of terror and deceit. Their replacements were arriving. The detective sat like a statue, his big fingers interlaced in his lap, regarding a huge poster of the Fuehrer flanked by red and black swastikas. Blood and darkness, he thought.

Phones began ringing. He observed what was going on, keeping his feelings strictly under control, used to that. She wouldn't have been brought in through this vestibule; prisoners and suspects for questioning came in at the back. His control slipped. Suddenly he felt sick in his stomach at the fear she must be experiencing. She was a strong, competent person but this would be far too much. Eventually, fear came to all. He gripped his hands together. Deliberately, he turned his head, taking in everything. A vast coir mat emblazoned with a large swastika was spread at the entrance, and the people coming in were conscientiously wiping their shoes on it. The irony of this wasn't lost on him. In the army they would have judged it bad staff-work. The Gestapo was an immature organisation.

'Heil Hitler!'

Said quickly as a formality behind him. Dressler stood up. His army comrade's son had entered through a side door.

'Good morning, Herr Lueger.' They shook hands.

'Please call me Hans, as always. What can I do for you?'

The sallow, intense youth he remembered stood there, still sallow, no longer youthful, analytically watchful now rather than intense. Nervy, too, the detective noted. The Gestapo might stand in the nation as an instrument of terror, but danger roamed its own hierarchal structure. Towering above the Gestapo man, quietly he told him what had befallen his daughter. Plainly, reasonably, he said that he didn't expect to change the course of what was in motion — a lie: one way or another that was his aim, but he asked could he see her, could he have an idea of what lay ahead, could Herr Leuber *advise* whether there was any process of intercession which might ameliorate their difficulty.

The Nazi listened, eyes downcast. Dressler absorbed his reluctance to become involved, his resentment of the old family connection. Had his eyes glazed over at the recital of yet another awkward case? Watching the man's reaction, at the end Dressler slightly increased the energy of his speech.

'Wait here, please, while I make inquiries. It may take some time.'

The giant detective didn't immediately return to the bench. He stood, legs apart, easily balanced on his rubber soles as though on a stake-out. In the yellowish, unnatural light the black figures flitted by, perhaps on hellish errands, perhaps going to the lavatories. The smell of damp clothes moved through the vestibule. Guttural voices faded down corridors.

He didn't expect good news, but implacably willed that the son of the man whose life he'd saved might return with news not wholly disastrous.

§ § §

'What have you been up to, Franz?' Helga said, half insistently, half reluctantly, when they were alone at last. Grimly, she wondered what answers she'd get.

Schmidt thought: Yes, I should be asked that. Trust Helga. He'd met the train at 6.00 pm, and now it was 7.00. Throughout the day the city had been covered with fog. In his head, one of the Great Man's requiems had been playing its monumental cadences.

They'd given Trudi her supper. He'd made the funeral arrangements, and notified by phone or telegram the few relatives and friends of his mother's generation who survived. The doctor, who'd been treating her for a heart condition unbeknown to Schmidt, had no problem with the death certificate. He'd received several callers. Wagner, sounding subdued, had phoned his condolences; otherwise it'd been resoundingly all quiet from Wertheim & Co, and grimly Schmidt pictured the confusion and concern in the bank, over the Fräulein Dressler/Herr Schmidt imbroglio.

And, what had been in the mind of Dietrich this day?

He'd not heard yet from Herr Dressler. And the Gestapo were ominously silent. Trouble *must* be waiting there. He'd obtained the name of a lawyer, but had decided not to speak to him at this stage.

He opened wine and poured two glasses. He wished he'd some of Wagner's schnapps. Schnapps and beer. 'Stimulation, and satisfaction' – Wagner's phrase. Carrying the Dressler suitcases had done something to his back: high in his spinal column a single vertebrae felt like a hot coal.

Obviously, Helga had been delaying this, agonising over the question just asked; but it could be postponed no longer. He'd exposed his family to danger. He'd told himself, he'd told her, that he would never do that. But events had swept him up. He wondered if his face looked as drawn as it felt. His heart seemed to be heavy with so much, and deeply worried at the situation he'd brought upon his loved ones. Deadly sad about Lilli Dressler ...

'Fräulein Dressler,' he began at last. Step by step, in his meticulous way, he told her of what had overtaken the general-director's secretary; of his own part. His ineffectual part. He'd the sensation of being a mourner driving in a funeral motorcade, headlights on. As tomorrow he would be. He did not tell her everything.

His wife listened, tight as a violin string, but with a neutral expression. He kept looking into her eyes, trying to track any flickers of reaction. She was silent when he'd finished, her wine untouched. Her tension, her dead-white complexion, sickened him with regret: in Dresden the golden tan of summer had been lost.

'Did you do it consciously, Franz? Put yourself, our little Trudi, me, into danger?' But she answered herself. 'No, I don't think so. I've feared this. Oh *don't worry*, I share your doubts about our new Germany, of those in power. But what of the *family*? Can there be anything more important? Your mother? God knows, where do you stand there? Do you take the responsibility for that, Franz? *Where do you stand on any of it?*' she cried. He gazed at the pale wine as though its colour fascinated him. Yes. He took that responsibility. Would say so, when she'd finished. 'I've never really spoken of that other world of yours. But I can guess the path your mind might be following. Am I right? Are you trying to mould that code to your life – our lives? In these times?' He thought: Not as simple or as stark as that. Events are pulling on me like a tidal race. She's slicing ideas out of the air. It's wonderfully close. 'You'll never tell me! But if you are – of course you are! Oh, Franz, first your eye – now this unfortunate woman – and your mother! That time can't ever translate to these modern times! What danger are you bringing down on us?'

He regarded her intensely, affectionately.

She burst out, 'All these years, I think you've been waiting for the Nazis! Your Fräulein Dressler!' Her speech had become rapid, distracted, as she tried to enunciate her way through the nightmare, then concluded hopelessly. That final tiredness in her voice was another weight on his heart. There'd been no deliberating process in his involvement with Fräulein Dressler. His sense of justice, and ultimately his emotions, had been the conducting forces. The fantasy of his inner life had prepared the ground, begun the slow movement to where he now stood. And, the flowering of the long, latent attraction …

A rare flash of anger came. The real catalyst was this evil era. He rose, and went to the window. Behind him she waited. The trunks and branches of the trees were visible, shining dully in the streetlamps; the fog at last had lifted. He said, 'I will tell you, Helga …'

§ § §

As they lay in bed he went over what he'd told her. It was as though he'd revealed the intimate details of a love affair about which she'd only a sketchy idea. Still, even then he'd not gone down to the deepest roots of his motivations, of his obsession with the Order, of his feelings for the G–D's secretary. Even to himself, he couldn't fully articulate it.

They made love with a passion which recalled their earliest married life. As though blotted out by some chemical release in his brain he did not, at that moment, recall the previous night. When he awoke in the darkness he was surprised to find her awake.

'I'll take Trudi back to Dresden,' she said, 'this afternoon, after the funeral. We may not return.'

They lay awake together, holding hands as though sealing a bargain, watching for the dawn.

§ § §

In his overcoat and hat, his pistol still strapped to his shoulder, Dressler had sat all day in the vestibule of the Gestapo offices. Once he went out into the foggy streets to phone his station and buy coffee. He continued his relentless watch on the ebb and flow of grim and nervous citizens. He observed these visitors being given forms to fill out, apparently never the information they were seeking on loved ones. The smells of cabbage soup, and sausage, steamed up a stairway.

At 10.30 pm his contact reappeared. He came to where Dressler sat. Watching him approach, rising to his feet, the detective's nerves blazed to life in his stomach. Here, in the dregs of a dispiriting day for all in this city – a terrible one for him – he was to receive his news. Leuber, nearing the end of a 14-hour shift, appeared strained and irritable as he eyed the detective. Then Dressler was listening to the terse apology for the day-long delay, hearing the rest of it.

He went out into the city, which was now clear, cold and livening up with the traffic going to and from dinner and entertainment. *She was still there.*

Walking at a formidable speed he passed the two policemen stationed at the corner, omitting his customary companionable nod. His pace, and the night air, had set up his wheezing. At the close of his report, the Gestapo man had intimated something to him. It had sent him back to his starting point: back to Herr Rubinstein and his Nazi contacts who, for money, might provide a visa out of this hell. But could they do that now? Despairingly, he muttered, *'She's already in their clutches.'*

20

TWO DAYS AFTER his mother's death (*murder*, Wagner categorised it later), Schmidt returned to the bank. He'd heard nothing from the Gestapo. Uneasily, he wondered if they were waiting on his return to the office. Perhaps Dietrich had a hand in that – wanted to be in charge of events. Puffing hoarsely, Herr Berger crossed the ice-box of the foyer to gasp his condolences. Like a last breath, Schmidt thought. Will he survive the winter? Will I? He said, 'Thank you. Is your heater working, Herr Berger?'

'Yes, Herr Schmidt. It's my internal heater that's packing up.'

Schmidt saw that he was regarded with a new respect. It was a similar look to the one he'd received when he'd returned from hospital after the eye. In his room he sat down at his desk, and began to sort the morning's post: away two days, it felt like a month. Had anything run out of control? He'd been on duty in another world. What had been happening here?

He looked at the phone, apprehending its ring, Dietrich's voice booming down the line. That deadly Nazi. He found he'd turned over a page on Dietrich – to a new one, deep-edged in black. He considered this. That page now allocated the Nazi a specific place in Schmidt's universe. 'Public enemy number one' – the Nazi's own phrase.

On his desk, a handwritten letter of condolence from

Herr Wertheim. At the funeral, bitter cold had struck the mourners. Though they'd been rugged up, it'd shocked them into a deeper reflection and reticence than they might've anticipated. A pneumatic drill had been brought in to dig the grave: already the ground was rock-hard.

Afterwards they'd collected Trudi, and taken a taxi to the station for another mournful ceremony, on a smaller scale. Waiting on the platform his socket had wept and he'd been forced to dab it with his handkerchief. But he'd been more conscious of the cold accumulating in his soul.

He dabbed the eye now.

Helga had been preoccupied throughout the day, doubtless dwelling on the events surrounding his mother's death, and the previous night's conversation. She'd not spelt out her intentions and he'd not wished to force the issue. On the platform, with a desperate but determined look, she'd said, 'We must separate – physically. To protect Trudi.' She'd stared into the future and seen the potential outcomes.

In the here and now – thank God for it! – messengers came and went to distribute the post. He was marking time, waiting for Dietrich to make his move – to reveal the motive he'd had in signalling Lilli's impending arrest. The Nazi had set him up. He'd known it as he'd hurried to her flat. When Dietrich appeared would he have the Gestapo in tow?

Much is in hazard when a knight manoeuvres in the face of the opposing force ... The precept rolled through his mind. He brooded on the papers before him. Resolutely, as though nothing of the past days had happened, he turned to take up the thread of an investigation into a deficiency in the head cashier's department.

The morning dragged on. The smell of coffee wafted in the corridor. Despite his absorption, he began to feel a new additive in the air. A morbid expectancy? He phoned a colleague. Wondering at the news, he replaced the receiver.

Field-Marshal Goering was to arrive at noon! Apparently to entrust his personal banking to Wertheim & Co. No wonder Dietrich hadn't appeared.

Schmidt went for a walk through the building. Wertheim employees were steeped in conservatism, but clearly it wasn't proof against the news whirling through the bank. Clerks and typists had congregated at front windows on each floor; they dropped their eyes as the Doomsayer passed by.

He went to the first floor and entered the general-director's anteroom. A tall, blonde, blazingly blue-eyed Amazon stood at attention beside Lilli's desk. He stared at her. She returned his gaze, wide-eyed, plainly ignorant of his function – anxious about his intentions.

The replacement! Hand-picked. The bluish, gold-ringed hands of Herr Wertheim were instantly in his mind. Her appearance was iconic, like the Nazi flag now permanently fluttering from the bank's flagpole.

'How do you do, fräulein?' he said with a slight, formal bow. 'I'm Herr Schmidt, the chief auditor.' He handed her the folder he carried. 'For Herr Wertheim.' It contained his report to the board on last month's audits.

Her hands were shaking, he noticed. A tremulous smile fluttered on her red lips, and her face was coloured with a rose-pink blush. He surveyed, politely, her huge-breasted, statuesque figure. Only twenty or less. A schoolgirl – for *this* position!

'The Field-Marshal will be here in a minute,' she said huskily.

'You are?'

'Fräulein Blum, mein herr.'

'From?'

'Munich.'

He caught her quick puffs of breath. 'Calm down, Fräulein Blum. Herr Wertheim will have everything under control. And he's a considerate man.' For someone like Fräulein Blum he

was, most certainly. He smiled, underlining his authority on
these matters. She slipped him a glance, and seemed to become
calmer.

The double doors to the G-D's room stood open, and
he glimpsed the directors standing about the room, like strangers at a wedding reception awaiting the bridal party. At that
moment klaxons blared in the street.

Two minutes later the Field-Marshal swept through the
anteroom in a chorus of crisp, commanding voices. Herr
Dietrich, his voice ringing out pleasantries, strode beside the
corpulent powder-blue-and-white-uniformed personage,
whose baton was waving in a clockwork-like motion. Dietrich's face shone with confidence and respect. Aides spotted
with silver insignia piled into the anteroom. Following the
Field-Marshal and Dietrich in a gleaming phalanx, they moved
with the clicks and clacks of colliding ball-bearings. Standing
back, Schmidt had the impression he was at the opera.

'Heil Hitler!' Another resounding chorus, arms flashing up like railway signals, as the famous Nazi and Dietrich
entered Herr Wertheim's inner sanctum. Definitely the opera.
Emphatically, the doors were closed.

Their power abruptly switched off, the aides came to
rest. They turned aside to the leather chairs like normal
men, casting glances at the ranks of papers, eyeing Fräulein
Blum. Thoughtfully Schmidt returned to his room.

Dressler phoned after lunch. Schmidt felt his chest tighten
as the detective identified himself.

'I have news, could we talk this evening?'

They agreed to meet in the central platz at 6.30 pm. For
the next few hours, Schmidt waited for Dietrich. But the Nazi
was still attending the Field-Marshal, or tied up in the aftermath of his visit. At last darkness enfolded the city. In contrast,
the Wertheim building was ablaze with electric light, though
quietening down as clerical activity was suspended.

Unmistakable footsteps sounded in the corridor. Dietrich entered, his yellow teeth instantly bared in a grin, and
stood, hands on hips, staring at the auditor. His brain instantly
hyper-active, Schmidt thought the Nazi looked like a hunter
inspecting something in his trap. But he didn't flinch.

Dietrich closed his lips over his wolfish grin. 'My condolences on your bereavement.'

Schmidt nodded, bowed slightly in his chair. The Nazi's
demeanour exhibited full knowledge of that event. The auditor was reminded of the earnest communication he'd had
from the SA following the incident of his eye: not a nuance of
hypocrisy detectable. Yet, Dietrich did seem to be measuring
him in a sympathetic way. 'Never mind,' the Nazi said. 'These
hard facts of life are beyond our control.' He advanced to the
desk, casually hefted himself to his usual position. '*Another* big
day for the bank, Herr Auditor! The Field-Marshal's bestowed
a great honour on us. We'll enjoy additional prestige.'

Schmidt absorbed the 'we' and the 'us'. Apparently, the
Nazi had decided to split his allegiances between the Party
and the bank – nominally, at least. Or did the phrasing bespeak
a new familiarity in their personal relations? More interesting
still, had he picked up the faintest trace of irony?

'My dear Schmidt, I saw you, observing from the side-
lines. Right in character!' He lit two cigarettes. He smiled, lifted
his blond head, the shimmering hair looking more metallic
than ever, exhaled fragrant smoke at the ceiling. The auditor
watched it rise as seriously as if it were a new type of transaction passing through the system. 'Right in character. I read you
like a book, my friend. *Now!* I set my little trap and you walk
straight into it.' Schmidt kept his eye on the Nazi's face. Dietrich shook his head. 'But I do understand. Your sympathy and
your loyalty directed you. Admirable qualities. You'll be gratified to know you share them with the General-Director. *Why*
did I make this small test? Because, my dear Franz, you had to

be brought to your senses. With the great challenges before us, we can't afford to let private emotions sway us from the greater duty. You're a bright man, Schmidt. After what's happened I'm sure you see what a mistake you've made! I'm an emotional man myself. I prize loyalty. But intellect must strictly set the priorities. When you've had my training, they become very clear.'

Schmidt listened to this diatribe, smoked the cigarette, kept a respectful demeanour. Though he could hardly credit his ears. It was amazing. Was the man serious? Dietrich, a student of his character! And that mentor-like cadence! Could it be the preparation for another trap? The Gestapo weren't going to be as forgiving as this.

'Being the person you are, you've considered your position, learned a lesson. I trust that you have. We've seen the cost. My Gestapo colleagues are the rigid type. Necessary people, good at their work. Or, should we say, getting better at it. Even with my influence I've had a job to persuade them to overlook your crime. Yes, crime. But in its way, understandable.'

Schmidt studied his desktop.

Warningly the Nazi shook his head, hardened his eyes. 'One mistake only, my friend. I've had to work very, very hard to get you clear of this.'

Schmidt's mind was racing: Why are you taking this trouble? That's the nub of it. He was staring at that black-bordered page in his mind, carefully suppressing the loathing.

Dietrich, suddenly businesslike, glanced at his watch. 'All right — the Field-Marshal's account will also come under your special supervision. An interesting assignment, isn't it?' Schmidt acknowledged that it was. 'Now. About joining the Party. Have you discussed this with your wife? No? And she's returned quite suddenly to Dresden.' He smiled. 'Never mind, we'll have to let things cool down. Probably for quite a while. By the way, many thanks for introducing your dentist. Very satisfactory. You've interesting contacts, Schmidt.' He grinned.

Schmidt nodded slightly. Whatever service Dr Bernstein had rendered, it hadn't been a clean and polish. But his pulse had quickened again: he was thinking now about the Nazi's knowledge of his family's movements.

Dietrich leaned forward to stub out his cigarette, and Schmidt guessed that his restless brain was on the move again. 'In fact, my dear Schmidt, the more I look into you, the more interesting things I turn up. I find you're a scholar. Medieval history! A long-term devotee of the Municipal Library. Well, well. I'm a scholarly person myself. Obviously we've much in common. I look forward to discussing this with you – but not tonight.'

Schmidt's eye was locked to the Nazi's. He'd frozen, the cigarette still burning in his fingers. Who had he heard it from? Had this Nazi any more surprising stabs of information?

Dietrich lifted himself off the desk and went to the door. Schmidt knew that in the doorway, he'd turn and one of those torpedoes would come. The Nazi grinned as though he perceived he'd been found out.

'One more thing. I strongly advise you to reconsider your relation with Deputy Foreign Manager Wagner. As I said – you can't afford another episode of contamination.'

He left.

The cigarette had burnt to a column of ash in Schmidt's fingers. He stared at the wall. He felt he was barely breathing. The ash dropped to the desk.

21

ANOTHER NIGHT TO MAKE cold bones. Precisely at 6.30 pm Schmidt arrived at the nominated corner. Senior Detective Dressler wasn't there, nor did a quick scan of the platz immediately discover him.

'Herr Schmidt!'

Turning quickly, the auditor saw the huge figure standing in a dark embrasure of the cathedral. He crossed the pavement, and joined the detective in his shadowy hide. They shook hands.

'Unwise to go to a café,' the policeman said. He coughed and struggled for breath. 'Lilli ... was tried at a closed court yesterday, found guilty under the Nuremberg Laws, and committed to Ravensbruck concentration camp for two years. She has been taken there already.' The heavy voice trembled in the dark. Instantly Schmidt felt a fresh heart-sickness. Two years! He stared across the platz to a string of brilliantly lit cafés. He'd nothing to offer but sympathetic silence. 'My Gestapo contact says she will probably be assigned to secretarial work ... I have my doubts about that, and, about the duration of the sentence ... Our justice system is now corrupted.' His strained breathing punctuated the gaps in his speech.

The auditor felt the cold rising up his legs, and the suppressed power of the father's feelings. He said, 'Can an appeal be made? A fine negotiated?'

'No.'

A tramcar crossed the platz, scattering blue sparks as its wheels clashed through points. Schmidt visualised the Field-Marshal's aides, their comparable clatter. It was bound for his own suburb. Better for him if he were on it?

'What do you propose to do, Herr Dressler?'

The policeman stared implacably across the stone-cobbled void at the cafés as though getting their range. 'I'm in contact with a Jew. An activist who's put in place arrangements ... With influential Nazis. God knows how! For substantial sums some Jews are released and given passports. It *might* be done for Lilli. The problem is the price. Two hundred thousand.'

Schmidt was amazed at the amount. He stared at Dressler's massive profile.

The detective said, 'I can't get that kind of money.'

Schmidt considered the facts. Hands deep in their overcoat pockets, they were both stamping their feet, almost in slow motion. The giant detective towered over him. Schmidt thought: What an odd pair we must look. He trusted no-one *was* looking.

They were silent, stunned by the acuteness of the problem.

In that other world across the platz, beautifully-gowned women tossed perfect falls of hair, mimed exuberant dialogue, performed with body language as exaggerated as that of the quick-stepping waiters: a white shoulder lifted coquettishly here, a well-turned arm pointed imperiously there. Uniformed escorts danced attendance, hemmed them in with attentions. A blue haze of cigarette smoke seemed to romanticise the figures quarantined behind the distant thick glass.

Schmidt stared at the scene, the antithesis of his own deadly rendezvous. Suddenly he was thinking along concrete lines. 'Are you sure this Jew is reliable?'

'More reliable than most men you meet today.'

Schmidt continued his thinking, which was becoming complicated.

The detective said, 'Nothing's assured. But well-known Jews have escaped this way. I've hopes that it might be easier for … a secretary, an unknown person, and cost less. If some money could be found, perhaps my services pledged.'

What kind of pledge could he make? To whom? Schmidt wondered. Dressler watched his front as he'd watched all those years ago across no-man's-land. Air whistled in his lungs, his vast gully of a throat.

Schmidt's thinking had reached a destination. He re-examined it carefully. Amazing! It *might* be done. His mind had glided into a superdangerous realm, easily as a knife into butter. Now he was thinking only of the technical problems. It was the kind of progression that Helga had feared.

He said quietly, 'The money can probably be obtained. Please make your arrangements with this Jew. I'll be here tomorrow night, 6.30. I will have it.'

In wondering silence, Dressler accepted this. He didn't look at the pocket-sized bank auditor who, for an obscure reason, might, amazingly, provide the means to save his daughter. Erratic gifts from Providence didn't repay analysis. A survivor's life had taught him this.

'Thank you, Herr Schmidt,' the detective said. 'I must return to duty. The Nazis have not eradicated ordinary crime.' Schmidt lifted his head at the hint of irony. He saw that the detective hadn't intended it. An even more bitter wind scythed the platz. But Dressler hadn't finished. 'My contact in the Gestapo said that Dietrich is behind Lilli's downfall. Of course, we knew that. He's been relentless in his pursuit. He submitted a damning affidavit to the court. The animal –' his voice choked. He breathed heavily, went on '– has an unusual background. For six months in 1937 he was an instructor at Marienburg – one of the Nazis' secret Order Fortresses. Prior

to that, he was posted to the Reich embassy in Washington –'
The detective stopped. Even in the dark he'd caught the auditor's reaction. 'Herr Schmidt?'

Schmidt was already half-frozen, but the information had driven a new icy wedge into him. He could hardly take in the proposition. Unbelievable! First von Streck, now Dietrich – connected to the Order! And this very night the Nazi'd revealed that he knew of Schmidt's studies at the Municipal Library. It was a shadow-dance.

An idea had come. If the detective had found out this about Dietrich ... he made a decision. 'Herr Dressler, there's a high Nazi functionary called von Streck, described as a special plenipotentiary ...' He went on for a minute, asking the detective if he would make inquiries.

After they'd parted, Schmidt's mind remained focused on Dietrich and the Order. Boarding his tram shortly after seven, he still couldn't believe the connection.

By chance, Herr Dorf was working a late shift. Few passengers were aboard during the dinner hour. After a polite greeting the conductor swayed to the front where, hanging on two straps, head ducked forward, he mournfully watched the boarded-up shops drift past. It was rumoured that two hundred Jews were committing suicide each day in his native Vienna. The synagogue Schmidt had seen ablaze passed in the darkness. The site was to be cleared for a car park, so they said, its former worshippers co-opted for the work.

Maria had his dinner ready and he ate it quickly, immersed in his thoughts. He complimented her on the meal; nothing had been said about the family's changed situation, but she must be worrying. First, he had to deal with the problem of his mother's apartment, nervy Frau Bertha still in situ.

What stone cell, iron bars, was Lilli staring at? That came like a splinter of glass into flesh. He couldn't picture her circumstances. He'd a good visual imagination, but like a horse

baulking at a jump it failed him now. Instead, he concentrated
on the plan which might save her. Travelling home, eating his
dinner, drinking his coffee, it had been evolving in his head
like the most complex audit program he'd ever worked on.

He thought on it as he retired to the bathroom and began
the chore which he'd been postponing. He took saline solution
and a small bowl from the cabinet, and laid a thick bath towel
over the handbasin. He applied pressure under his eye. The
prothesis shot out and he caught it deftly. He washed it in the
solution, laid it on a clean handkerchief. He poured more of
the solution into an eye-cup and bathed the socket. Then he
positioned it in his fingers, and reinserted it. The suction took
in half his eyelashes as well; painstakingly he sorted that out.
He sighed; the nerves in the socket would ache for a day or
two.

He stood in the door of Trudi's room. A few dolls had
been taken; most waited on the shelves. He'd have Maria pack
a box for Dresden. All her treasures to the little one. He closed
off that thinking, went to his study, shut the door and sat down
at his desk.

The Dürer engraving was behind him, but the detail was
engraved in his brain. The knight was riding out stern-faced
on his quest, dogged by demons. Dürer had engraved him in
1513 — two hundred years after Schmidt's forebear had gone
with the Grand Master to Marienburg. What had happened
there? His father's archives were a blank on that period of the
knight's life. He'd next turned up in 1319 at Torun — docu-
mented fact. Then the family fable took over: he'd gone into
a city on the Vistula River in disguise, subverted the city's
leaders, sabotaged the defences. Fact: the Order had taken
this city. The mayor and corporation had been flung from
the battlements, tethered at their necks. How had that group
of widows lived afterwards? The perturbation of that age had
faded to silence. As would these times, one day.

The paragraph in de Sales' book he'd kept to think about, too occupied for its complexity. He took out the copy he'd made and scanned it. The Order had assumed a military character in 1198, and towards the end of the crusades had left Palestine forever. In 1211 the first European enterprise had begun in Hungary when they'd colonised the Transylvanian borderlands. The Hungarian king had granted the knights extensive autonomy, but when their demands became excessive had expelled them in 1225. They'd moved to Poland. A Polish duke had needed their help against the pagan Prussians. The knights had wiped out most of the native Prussian population. Bloody conquest and cruel subjugation of the eastern Baltic lands followed, a mailed heel on a wide territory of vassal states, the population treated as slaves. In 1263 the Pope had allowed the knights to become traders, relieving them of their vow of poverty. Then − the salient information − the brief chronicle of a knight of the Order, in the period 1310–1315, who'd intrigued to become a high administrator, one of a group of knights opposed to the strategy of conquest, the cruelties, the greed for treasure and power. He'd begun to plot against the Order from within, a man who kept his counsel, who'd diverted wealth, scattered assets to counteract some of the evil, weakened it immeasurably ... in 1315, unmasked, tortured, and killed.

A knight called Erik Streck.

And now a *Nazi* called von Streck had appeared in the special reading room. What did it mean? A brittle thread reaching down the centuries? A meteor of fate heading earthwards through the cosmos, programmed to reach its destination at the point when his and the Nazi's destinies were poised to move into the ascendant? He knew what Helga would think of such ideas.

Herr Goebbels had said of the Fuehrer, 'You are like a meteor before our astonished eyes ...'

Schmidt sat perfectly still. The obscure connections vibrated around him. He put the paper aside, and deliberately corrected the course of his thinking.

He'd said to Dressler, 'I will have it.' Two hundred thousand. In the platz the nucleus of the plan had come like a dart of light.

And that's where it stood – work in progress, but already an illuminated page set out with stylised capitals, and rich-coloured illustrations. And with it Wagner's excitable face, as though the deputy foreign manager knew he was the key. A workable plan in its first phase with Wagner's co-operation. In the second, as it stood – suicidal.

Schmidt looked at his watch: 8.35 pm. He rang the exchange. Were they intercepting Wagner's calls? Another risk to be run, but now he felt the steel in him; in his brain, in his heart, as though a sword, never previously unsheathed, had been drawn.

22

'WELL, WELL, MY friend. A meeting here? At this hour? What's got into you?' Wagner grinned slyly over the rim of his glass. 'Is my auditing colleague peeling off as do our brave aviators, into a fearless dive!' He studied Schmidt curiously. What was really on his mind were the events surrounding his colleague's imbroglio with the general-director's secretary. How in hell had he stayed out of the clutches of the Gestapo? Poor Fräulein Cream Cakes. There was no derision in the use of his private nickname for her; it came only with a sentimental feeling. A sad, sad, business.

Schmidt winced at the beerhall noise, at his colleague's flippancy. Though what mood was Wagner really in? And what did he really think about this summons? He glanced around the huge hall, at the riot in progress. He'd chosen this place because of its uproarious crowds.

It *was* a reversal of their usual roles. The late-night beer-drinking session was Wagner's homeground. In a moment, his attitude was going to change when he heard why he'd been called here. His unkempt hair was sprayed out, cigarette going, eyes drooping against the smoke. Despite his night-owl reputation he looked most vulnerable at night.

Behind these observations Schmidt was ordering his thoughts. Time was short. He said, 'Today Herr Dietrich warned me against you. Have you been opposing him by any chance?'

Wagner stirred. 'Aha! We haven't crossed swords directly. You can put it down to my old political affiliations. No doubt he's briefed himself on that through his contacts in those gangster agencies watching over your intemperate colleague. Though, I did have a run-in with Otto the other night that seemed to fascinate Herr Health and Sunshine. Otto was blind drunk. Unedifying sight.'

'That's the kind of situation you should be wary of. Dietrich's a trained watcher. He's watching all of us for clues to fill in the picture he's building up. Who knows what his instructions are from Berlin.' And he knows about me and the Order, he thought. But how much? He continued, 'He's a man with multiple objectives.'

Wagner shrugged. 'I agree they're devious bastards, but you're making that Nazi sound more interesting than he is. Franz, with your record are you really the fellow to be telling me to take care?' He glanced at the auditor with nervy amusement.

Schmidt ignored that. He wasn't quite ready. He said, 'A dose of excitement today?'

'The Field-Marshal?' Wagner struck a match and lit a cigarette. 'The million that slippery crook banked with us doesn't belong to him. Have you heard the story? A lunatic at the Reichsbank wrote out a cheque for a million and sent it to him. The Reichsbank's moving heaven and earth to get it back, but he's not letting go. Absolute thievery!' He laughed sardonically. 'Aided and abetted by the respected old house of Wertheim & Co.'

Schmidt stared at his colleague. He was in touch with his auditing counterparts at the Reichsbank, but hadn't heard a whisper about this. Wagner grinned. Everything was coming out the way he'd predicted. 'This morning at any moment I

felt Dietrich might've disappeared up the Field-Marshal's arse.'
Schmidt frowned his distaste. 'Sorry,' Wagner chuckled.

They were sitting side by side on a pew-like seat. *Now.*
Decisively Schmidt turned his head, began to speak into Wagner's ear. Calmly, he communicated Lilli's situation, her father's
efforts, his own. Wagner's eyes had sprung open.

'I require two hundred thousand, at least.'

Wagner drew in his breath sharply. 'God Almighty!' He
laid down his cigarette.

'Careful.'

Wagner was shaking his head, disbelievingly. Like many at
Wertheims he'd been fascinated by the revelation of the Franz
Schmidt–Fräulein Dressler imbroglio. He'd guessed more
would be going on, but was staggered by this. He pushed his
thin shoulders back against the pew. '*No* more lectures from
you, Franz ... two hundred thousand! What kind of wonderman is this Jew?'

'It doesn't matter. I must take him at face value, accept
Dressler's judgement.'

'Yes?' Wagner stared down the barn-like hall, as though
trying to penetrate a smoky battlefield.

'I've undertaken to find the money.' Wagner's stare shot
back to his colleague. The hubbub washed around them like
surf swirling through rocks, their talk as lost as a tiny mollusc
tossed about in foaming seawater. As Schmidt had calculated. 'I
need to get into the Party's safe.'

Beneath an iron circle impregnated with coloured electric
lights crudely imitating candles, a group of middle-aged workers raucously burst into a marching song from the Great War.
In rough time, they thumped their steins on the boarded table.
Had Wagner heard him? From a side-room, SA men gathered
in a storm centre, abruptly launched into competition with the
veterans, roaring out the 'Horst Wessel' song.

Oblivious to the uproar, the deputy foreign manager

turned to Schmidt. 'Herr Chief Auditor, I've been seriously misjudging you. I don't know whether to laugh or cry about that.'

Schmidt waited. Neither response was required, but he understood. He said, 'I need your safe combination.'

'You do, indeed. And my dear Franz, I remind you, one other.'

'That's not a problem.'

Wagner remembered his beer, and took a long draught. He laughed is disbelief.

'Will you do it?'

The vehement competition between the marching song and the Nazi folk anthem had crashed to a stop. Wagner's eyes gleamed. He leaned forward, guarded, out of character. 'The Nazis have my number because of the Social Democratic membership. The Gestapo are watching my flat – though, I think, not tonight. Dietrich, I suspect, smells some kind of rat about me. And you propose I help thieve a large portion of the hard-won funds of the NSDAP to assist a Jewess, interesting lady though she is, flee our country! Am I a lunatic? Are *you* mad?' His eyes shone with half-horrified amusement. Schmidt shrugged. Wagner was putting on one of his acts. 'Of course I'll do it my dear Franz. What else do I have to do with my life?'

Schmidt relaxed his shoulders. 'Neither of us fancies suicide. Beyond the act a plan is needed to give us cover. I've the glimmer of an idea on that.' It was conceivable that he might find such a plan.

'Franz, I hope you come up with something. Everywhere I look in my department I see your green-inked fingerprints. Best use gloves for this little adventure.'

Through a corridor in the drifting tobacco smoke, Schmidt was looking straight into the eyes of Herr von Streck.

'*My God!*' he exclaimed softly. Suddenly his eye was stinging, the Nazi's face blurring.

'What?' Wagner's head had jerked around.

'*Don't look now.* The man across the room, in the astrakhan coat. I know him. He's a high Nazi functionary.'

Wagner swore. 'Not a lip-reader, I trust.'

A large blond man was with the Nazi, and they were both staring at Schmidt. He thought rapidly: Is this a coincidence? He'd omitted von Streck from his diatribe to Wagner. Had his phone – Wagner's – been tapped? The two Nazis were getting up, plainly coming towards them, the plenipotentiary looming broader and broader. Wagner was fumbling for cigarettes. They arrived at the bankers' table. Schmidt stood up, and felt the full weight of the ironical eyes. The big blond man, head and shoulders over von Streck, stood back, hard eyes switching from Schmidt to Wagner.

'Well, well, Herr Schmidt! You drink beer?' The mole stood out like a beacon on his cheek, the homburg was held lightly in his beringed, hairy fingers.

'On occasion, mein herr.'

'And tonight is one such.' He looked at Wagner.

'May I introduce my colleague, Herr Wagner ... Herr von Streck.'

The Nazi examined Wagner, nodded, slow and deliberate. 'So this is Herr Wagner, deputy foreign manager.'

Wagner bowed slightly. He'd become dead pale.

Von Streck smiled coldly. 'Gentlemen, have a good evening.'

The Nazi duo, massive in their individual ways, left.

'Thanks for introducing me,' Wagner muttered, as they disappeared. 'How in hell does he know me? And how do you know him?'

'We met at the Municipal Library.' Wagner stared incredulously. 'I don't know how he knows you.'

'I don't like this,' Wagner growled.

Schmidt was silent, also disturbed. It'd been a shock. He

came back on track. 'Tomorrow evening at six, in the vault?'

Wagner nodded, spat out a shred of tobacco, and stuck the cigarette back between his lips. Schmidt said, 'At short notice, could you find an excuse to go to Zurich?'

§ § §

Until this point in the evening, it had seemed to Otto that the good ship *Wertheim* had been loafing along through a rather placid and boring sea. Now, there was tension on the bridge – as though the deck officers had observed the barometer plunge.

This transformation had been brought about by the senior of two Ruhr industrialists who were dining at the bank, putting aside polite conversation, and in a thick Swabian accent, getting down to tintacks. Using his blunt hands, as though assembling a structure before their eyes, he'd explained the project, the assistance they sought from the bank. The man's milk-white face moved attractively as he spoke. When he stopped, it appeared as grave as a preacher reflecting on his just-delivered sermon. Herr Wertheim, seated next to his nephew, was reminded of a Lutheran pastor he'd disliked.

The Wertheims, Dietrich, the other visitor, had watched the capable hands shaping elevations. The man's firm wouldn't normally have come within the bank's ambit. However, he'd powerful connections in the NSDAP, and in the letter of introduction which he'd brought it was intimated that the Party's private bankers should extend him every courtesy.

He lifted his round eyes to Herr Wertheim. 'We'll be buying this business for a quarter of its true value. The Finance Ministry will see to that. We'll be acting in tune with government policy. Government contracts for the output will follow.' He sat back, shrugged, as though such strokes of good fortune were as predictable as night following day.

Herr Wertheim smiled blandly. The man's cold-blooded detachment didn't surprise him. Discussions at this level concerning money usually ignored questions of morality. Though Wertheims hadn't been involved, he was perfectly familiar with the new policy, which rested on the expropriation of Jewish businesses at ludicrously undervalued prices.

'We await the finance,' the industrialist said, spreading his hands.

Herr Wertheim said, 'We'll study your proposal with great care.'

'And *very* positively,' Dietrich interposed. The letter of introduction was from SS Fuehrer Himmler.

'*Naturally,*' Otto agreed with a smile.

The general-director said with the faintest hint of steel, 'As I said, it will have the bank's diligent consideration.'

Alone, he stood at his window and watched the visitors depart. A black limousine drew up at the bank, a black-uniformed SS driver held open its door. The car drifted off quietly along the darkened street. The general-director gave a cold smile.

The unusual nocturnal appointment fitted the nature of the business. He'd known that, along with their profitable accounts, the acquisition of the Nazis' business would bring the bank face-to-face with their more grotesque strategies. The sea into which the bank was heading was skeined with different currents: for example, the one that'd brought the Field-Marshal through their doors this morning.

His thinking turned to Lilli Dressler. Her arrest had shocked him, immobilised him for a brief period. Then the startling events encompassing Herr Schmidt, his mother and the fräulein, had come like a bombshell. The chief auditor had tried to get her away! Who would've believed it? What would be the consequences? Schmidt must be on very thin ice – though all was strangely quiet. With Dietrich lurking in the wings, Wertheim had decided not to question the auditor, and had merely written his condolences. They'd wait and see.

For the moment, a curtain had dropped on her fate. He'd been fully occupied all day, anyway, had not chosen to make inquiries. His phone tapped, the triumphant blackmailing attitude of Dietrich … but he would find a way. Perhaps the sentimental employer could request favoured treatment, an earlier release? As for Dietrich – ultimately, there'd be a way to deal with him.

Always he'd been confident in his power and influence; in the past days he'd felt it bending under a strain. It didn't daunt him. He'd no regrets at stepping into the Nazi world. The strange new rhythms sifting in his brain had driven him in that direction. Had driven him to buy *The Eye*. And where would they take him next? In what direction would he steer the *Wertheim*? With his heart condition he didn't have much time. He'd been rereading Nietzsche: 'Believe me! The secret of reaping the greatest fruitfulness and the greatest enjoyment from life is to live dangerously!' Herr Wertheim thought that the great poet's words might well sum up the way he saw Wertheims these days – and the world at large.

He'd have a glass of champagne before he left. Fräulein Dressler had loved champagne.

23

SCHMIDT SAT ON the edge of his bed trying to bring an eerie dizziness under control. For a few seconds, still entangled in his last dream, he was puzzled by Helga's absence. Then he remembered the beerhall, and the stark fear on Wagner's face as von Streck and his blond companion had disappeared into the night. He stared across the bedroom, now seeing only that vivid image.

After breakfast he gave Maria instructions about Trudi's toys, and regretted the maid's dismayed look. A good girl – Helga'd left him in capable hands. He went to the bank. Breeze from the west; acrid factory smells drifting in from the outskirts; no fog, but dark and drizzling. Through the tramcar's blurry windows the city was impressionistic.

Watching the passing streets he felt let down from the drama of the recent days, as though things were finished. Clearly it was a deceptive sensation; the flow of danger had merely fallen back to a slower tempo, like a footballer varying his pace to confuse the defence on the point of attack. He *must* find time to deal with his mother's affairs. The unpublished cantatas were the foremost concern; in today's world, in the midst of his difficulties, what to do with them?

At the bank, he opened the post, sorted it, and sent it on its way. Yesterday, between events, he'd concentrated on bringing his work up to date. Today, feigning normality, he continued in the same vein, treading a wheel towards 6.30 pm.

§ § §

Under Director Schloss's penetrating gaze Otto had never been at ease, and this interview was no different. He resettled his ample backside in the chair, and nervously but stubbornly continued the 'pitch' – as Dietrich termed it – to his superior.

'It's worth looking at. I mean, here we have seventeen million of the Party's funds sitting in our safe in Reich bonds earning a mere 3 per cent – or in the cash accounts earning peanuts. Why not place them in foreign currencies, invest in these bargain Jewish businesses? Make some real money. Bring in a more *aggressive* strategy.'

For Otto, the meeting with the Ruhr industrialists had been an eye-opener. His ambition suddenly rampant, excited by a newfound creative energy, he'd decided that if he were the agent to introduce Aryanisation business into the bank and into Party investments, rewards would follow. But he'd have to work hard. He suspected his uncle was going to be a stumbling-block.

'More aggressive?' Schloss tapped huge blunt fingers softly on his desk. He thought: Peanuts! God save us. After a long pause, he added: *'Foreign currencies?'*

Even Otto detected the irony, and blinked quickly. 'Yes. I've no doubt the Party would instruct the Reichsbank on the approvals.' He spoke defensively, cursing inwardly. Such a prickly bastard. Ingrained with outmoded ethics. By God! Wait till *he* was in charge!

'You haven't by any chance overlooked Wertheims' responsibility as a member of the Reich Loan Consortium, have you? Or the chronic shortage of foreign exchange for *essential* purposes? Even our esteemed account-holder might baulk at the anti-patriotic proposal of retaining such for speculation. You know they imprison people these days for foreign currency transgressions?'

His sarcasm cleaved the air.

Otto said warily, 'Whatever the Party does is for the greater good of the Reich.' He'd a minor imagination, but he'd come to equate Schloss's eyes with the freezing Baltic which abutted the man's wretched Rostock. He stared in fascination at the long white duelling scar – from beneath his left eye, to the corner of his mouth. Inwardly, he shuddered.

Schloss smiled, as though he'd heard something both inept and ridiculous, but from this source predictable.

'I'm certain Herr Dietrich would be in favour.' Otto regretted this immediately. He was finding it impossible to detect where Dietrich stood on anything.

'I suggest to you, mein herr, that it's not the Wertheim way – regardless of what our account-holder may, or may not think.'

'The Wertheim way's changing,' the younger director muttered sullenly. God! What a struggle this was!

Schloss was silent. With the same precision that he applied to a balance sheet, he examined Otto's flaccid face, the unsavoury bags under his eyes, the broken capillaries high on his cheeks ... the Nazi Party badge. Unfortunately, here was the next general-director. Hopefully, not for many a year yet. Though God knows what was going on in the mind of his uncle. Recently the G–D seemed to be trying to walk a tight-wire. It was incomprehensible. Wertheims was Schloss's life and the big director was extremely worried about it. At last he said, 'I can't support any of that.'

'May I bring it up, informally, with my uncle?'

'By all means,' Schloss said acidly.

Otto withdrew, relieved, but cursing under his breath in

the hall. The staff said Schloss marched through these corridors as though to the beat of a drum. One day, he'd put an end to that damned parade.

§ § §

Dressler was abroad on a burglary case, but as he went through the streets his mind was ranging further. The atmosphere at his station wasn't pleasant. He was circumspect in his relations with his colleagues, who were mainly younger. Aloof, they considered it. His stolid performance, the trauma of his war experiences never articulated, set him apart. 'Nose to the grindstone. A big dopey bear with a piece of steel in his head,' they said suspiciously. He'd never involved himself in the politics played out in the state police; he ignored the 'new' variety under the shadow of the SS, which was consolidating the Reich police forces.

However, he wasn't oblivious to the further distancing that'd been going on. This morning when he'd arrived for duty the detective signing off had been stiff and embarrassed. Of course, his problem was all over the station. But it wasn't only that: his arrest of the two SA rapists had raised dust, as had their cracked skulls.

So what? He shrugged massively, shedding the station atmosphere, welcoming the street. A change of this nature was the least of his worries. He transferred scraps of paper from his left overcoat pocket to the right. From the in-tray to the out. He didn't believe in deskwork, spent hardly any time at the station. Did his paperwork on the zinc bars of coffee houses.

He stopped at a phone booth, looked in his notebook, and dialled the number of the man in touch with Herr Rubinstein. Guardedly, he made his request. Call back in an hour.

Into the Jewish streets he went, swaying from side to side with his distinctive gait. The boarded-up shops reinforced the bankrupt atmosphere. With the chronic shortage of glass, would they ever look like shops again? These incidental thoughts drifted in his mind, like the mist loitering at the ends of alleys.

He entered another phone box. Herr Rubinstein would see them at 7.00 pm, but at a different address. Quite understandable. The eyes of Gestapo informers were every-where. He knew precisely where some were. Surreptitiously, they unearthed the leads for their masters' missions. Now, it was up to Herr Schmidt. He re-examined the street, continued on his way to the scenes of the string of overnight burglaries. He knew the identity of the perpetrator already: the modus operandi matched up with an index card in his brain.

§ § §

Otto's lustful inclinations were notorious within Wertheims – had been whispered about for a decade behind the hands of typists. Periodically, the family had removed young female staff from his reach. Generous settlements had always bought silence. To Otto's chagrin and frustration, Fräulein Dressler had outmanoeuvred him, but her successor looked like easier pickings. A simple country girl, ripe and juicy for his attention, he'd decided on the morning of her arrival. He'd gone to the general-director's anteroom for the express purpose of viewing her. From the door, his eyes had narrowed as they'd glazed with lust. Otto couldn't conceal his sexual reactions. Having made his judgement on her type, he'd turned on his heel and left.

After his interview with Schloss, he came upon Fräulein Blum, statuesque but ill at ease in the unfamiliar surroundings. A corridor of the fourth floor. He was surprised to encounter her here but his brain, facile in such matters, made a quick calculation: his uncle wouldn't come to the bank until lunch-time today. But caution was needed: the general-director's secretary wasn't to be compared with a typist from one of the departments. He blocked her path.

'Heil Hitler!' He'd adopted this salute with a calculated enthusiasm. 'Fräulein, this is *very* convenient. I require assistance in locating a file in the archive. Come with me, please.'

He led the way around a corner, and opened a frosted glass door into a long room jammed with high shelving, stacked with chipped, gilt-lettered ledgers, and neat brown paper packages. Outsiders might've recoiled from this graveyard of financial and social history, of Wertheim & Co's past endeavours; or, might've been fascinated by the potential of its secrets. Otto was oblivious to such nuances. He threaded his way to a remote corner.

Fräulein Blum, surprised, flustered, blushing, followed obediently.

'Here we are,' Otto said. He leaned negligently against a shelf marked 1921, and through half-closed eyes arrogantly inspected her body, causing her eyes to widen. 'You know, fräulein, I'm a director of the bank *and* a member of the Party.' He used his throaty, overbearing voice.

'What do you wish of me, Herr Director?'

He was gratified at her quick breathing. He grinned, and his fleshy lips drew back, displaying gold-rimmed front teeth. 'This.' He moved his rotund body adroitly forward, forcing her into the corner. His teeth clashed against hers, his tongue forced its way into her mouth. They were exactly the same height. The transition from arrogant repose to arrogant action was seamless. His lips and tongue were working vigorously, filling her mouth. His hands dropped to roam roughly around her waist, went under her sweater, plucked blouse out from skirt. She gasped as they got to her warm flesh, then again, as his fingers slid under her brassiere, burst it off, and began kneading her breasts.

'Fat, Munich pig!' he hissed, quickly out of breath,

dribbling saliva into her gasping mouth. His erection throbbed painfully against his trouser flies. He was overwhelmed now by his lust to penetrate; to reduce this Amazon to a suppliant, mewling victim. To make good his losses with the Dressler bitch! He ripped open his flies, spraying buttons on the floor, baring his genitals. His left hand pinioned her to the wall by one of her breasts, which overspilled his flabby fingers. He thrust his right hand under her skirt, tore down her bloomers. Expertly, two more flabby fingers found her declivity.

'Aha! You big *wet* pig!'

He stiffened in shock. Her large nail-polished hand had shot out and seized his testicles in an unbreakable grip, was kneading them as fiercely as he'd worked on her breasts. Fiercer! Herr Otto's firmament came ablaze with wheeling lights; through his every fibre, paroxysms of pain and pleasure rippled. His raucous groans filled the room. His trousers fell down. His penis was free, jagging awkwardly, uncontrolled, straining for that place. Her long, muscular legs came horizontally out from the wall, and trapped his arse.

Her hand had gripped it. *'Oh God, fräulein!'* What'd happened to the woman?! *'Gently!'* Her pelvis had descended on it, muscles like oscillating steel bands had taken it, were dragging it in, were going to tear it out by the roots! 'Agony!' he cried, fighting to withdraw, the drive to ejaculate gone. Thank God! He crashed back against the shelves, his chest heaving, his penis burning, but free of that churning, mince-meat-making vice. He was dazed, in shock, his trousers and underpants tangled around his ankles.

Fräulein Blum quickly, efficiently, was straightening her stockings, thwacking her garters into place. With a nervy gesture she pushed her blonde hair back. 'Herr Director, you did *not* satisfy me,' she said succinctly. Her lips enunciated this with an exaggerated twist. Her mouth drooped disdainfully.

Stunned, his eyes protruding, Otto looking over his

shoulder watched her leave. The pain! The air froze his podgy, defeated-looking arse. His heart was bounding in his chest like a hammer. This Munich pig had thrown his directorship, his Nazi Party membership – *his manhood* – back in his face like a handful of chickenfeed. Otto couldn't believe it. The Dressler bitch was responsible for this! Gingerly he felt his testicles, and groaned afresh to the Wertheim records.

24

A N HOUR TO wait; Schmidt slipped into meditation. The day had evaporated. Though he'd been half-listening for it, the sound of the bank shutting down took him unawares. Chesty coughs, footsteps, faded away in the corridor leaving a pregnant silence. The scene's being set, he thought. Another ten minutes ...

His thinking picked up speed. Until last night's rendezvous with Dressler, he'd been adrift in the convoluted passage of events, reacting on impulse. Through following his conscience, following his heart, he'd moved to Lilli Dressler's side; just doing it. But *failure*. Then the plan had come, out of the new necessity; a mad, dangerous plan. But a thing of concrete, putting his previous fumbling to shame. *The Nazi Party's bonds would finance her release and escape from Germany!* As he'd stood with her father at the cathedral, the knight implanted in him had ridden out of the mists, and lowered his lance to the point. They'd exchanged comradely greetings. *Not a fantasy.* Not to him. And the knight had the humanistic character of Dürer's, not of his ruthless ancestor of the Teutonic Order.

Sitting, waiting, immobile with his thoughts, in the deep silence of the closed bank, he realised that the hold of the Teutonic Knights on him had gone; that he'd been moving towards this moment as he understood more and more how the Order had been debased by greed and the lust for power.

For twenty years, his research had been like water dripping on a rock; suddenly the rock had cracked.

Someone walked quietly along the corridor. He listened to the sound die, took up his thoughts again. It was a catharsis. But immediately it'd been outshone by what he'd realised about his father: the surgeon had arrived at the identical destination. His father had said nothing about *his* catharsis. He'd left Schmidt to find his way to his own. Why had it taken so long? The classic case of the auditor with his nose too close to the grindstone? So his father had given him Dürer's knight. Left him this symbol of knightly virtue. In waiting.

He became aware of the Wertheim grade three clock, his grade at the bank, ticking away. He glanced at it: 5.33 pm.

After returning from the beerhall, in the grip of a slow burn of excitement and fear, he'd concentrated on that glimmer of an idea; the lifeline he'd spoken of to Wagner. He'd moved it around in his mind. How to cover up the theft; to save their lives. He'd had the weird notion that von Streck might've been sitting in the corner, a sardonic smile on his lips.

He was still turning it over in his mind.

This morning several envelopes imprinted with the Nazi insignia had arrived. He'd placed them in the confidential pouch for the G-D, wondering about their tidings. He stroked his lips with his fingers. More crucial to the moment, how was Wagner bearing up?

Five forty: time to begin, but he allowed himself a minute. Not a faltering of will; more like a parachutist pausing to check the quick release lock on his harness before the jump. Go! He flexed his shoulders, took out an unopened packet of quarto-sized paper, inserted it in a large expandable envelope used for safe-custody items, and sealed the adhesive flap. Carefully he wrote the words certifying to a face value of ten million, to match the envelope in the vault.

What he did next he'd spent some time practising. From

a drawer he took out tracing paper, and from two pieces of memoranda in his in-tray traced the signatures of Dietrich and Herr Otto on the envelope beneath the certificate. Quickly, confidently, he wrote over them in ink. He studied the result. Satisfactory. From his safe he took the bank's official metal seal, then from his desk drawer, sealing-wax and a piece of string. He lit a match, coaxed the string alight, and held it to the shiny red bar, which began to drip into a pool on the envelope's flap. When the quantity was sufficient, he pressed the seal into the wax. He locked the seal away, and placed the envelope in his attaché case. Then he destroyed the tracings.

A fading clue to the clandestine act lingered: the acrid smell of the liquefied wax.

At three minutes to six, carrying the case, he went into the corridor. As expected, he saw no-one. Otto Wertheim's office was on the same floor but on the far side; the light-shaft, black as a coal-pit, lay between. On each floor corridors formed a square upon which opened the doors of rooms and departments.

Quietly Schmidt traversed the deserted building. The light was burning in Otto's anteroom. The auditor walked in, excuses prepared, in case … a glance told him that the director's secretary, a fiftyish, Wertheim veteran, hand-picked for the job by the elder Wertheim, had left for the night.

He knocked on the connecting door, and went in. Otto's office was messy; presumably he was still around. Schmidt crossed to the handsome carved oak desk inherited from the director's paternal grandfather, slid open a drawer, and sighed, with both relief and regret. The latter emotion pertained to Otto's unforgivable transgression. A mere employee would have been dismissed on the spot. The three numbers, 4, 14, 44, were on the scrap of paper stuck to the side of the drawer. Schmidt committed them to memory, quietly closed the drawer, and listened.

The aroma of brandy was all that he picked up. He glanced at the cupboard door behind which Otto's liquor bottles were concealed.

§ § §

Dietrich strode vigorously along the corridor to the chief auditor's office and burst in – on the empty room. He pulled up, his ready-made grin fading. Schmidt's hat and coat hung on the peg. The Nazi meditated on them for a moment, sniffed the air at a slight odour, and glanced at the clock: 5.59 pm. He stroked his chin, changed his mind and went out. He stood thoughtfully in the corridor rocking on the balls of his feet.

This was annoying: he'd a particular reason for wanting to see the auditor tonight. He would drop in on Otto, return here later. Ha! Herr Otto! Dietrich bared his yellowish teeth in a private grin. As though he'd taken off one coat and put on another, he prowled away to his left.

§ § §

Schmidt didn't retrace his steps but, following pre-planned moves, went left when he came out of Otto's anteroom, and reached the corner at its west end, seconds before Dietrich arrived at the east end. He didn't return to his room but went to the lift which was situated on the north side. With its customary clunk and whirring, it began its descent.

Wagner was waiting in the basement's foyer, a sardonic expression on his face. He wore his overcoat against the bone-numbing chill.

'All set,' Schmidt said as he entered.

The deputy foreign manager nodded tersely.

Schmidt gave his colleague a measuring look, and unlocked the grille door. They entered the vault and walked through one room into another. The Party's safe with its three combination tumblers faced them. Wagner stepped forward, brushed his hair from his eyes, twirled the centre one to the start-point, and removed his combination. Schmidt removed his own. Then, pausing for an instant to bring the numbers into his mind, he addressed the top tumbler, Herr Otto's. Precisely, he revolved it onto each mark. On the last, he paused for a second, then turned it back. Like a train hitting a buffer it stopped dead. The safe was open.

They glanced at each other. Schmidt swung open the door, took the sealed envelope from his attaché case, exchanged it with the similar sealed envelope in the safe, and put the latter in his case. He closed the door, and spun each tumbler to reset the combinations.

Each had been listening and now they gave the silence their undivided attention. The bank was as deeply quiet as a mausoleum. Wagner, as ever, seemed careless of the occasion. But his face was gaunt.

The auditor said quietly, 'Thank you, my friend. Could you come to my apartment tomorrow night – say at seven? The next step … '

The deputy foreign manager nodded.

'Good. Let's leave quickly, you by the lift, me, the stairs.' He looked up – as though his single vision could pierce the floors above, and reveal where enemies might lurk. He perceived danger pulsing in the air.

§ § §

Dietrich paused as he heard the abomination of a lift start up on the northern corridor, from where he'd just come. Now that was strange. He slanted his head, and pursed his lips; the floor had seemed deserted. Descending. The sound faded away, the pervading Wertheim after-hours' silence moved back in.

He went on. He entered Otto's anteroom, then the inner room. He studied the desk, smelt the brandy. A toast to absent friends – or enemies? The thought was more irritated than incisive. Tonight undercurrents of mysteriousness seemed to be flowing through these empty corridors and rooms. Frowning, he returned to the corridor, and abruptly increased his pace.

§ § §

'What is it Otto, at this time of day?'

On the first floor, Herr Wertheim regarded his nephew with polite scepticism. The young director had an unsettled air, though plainly he'd spruced himself up. The general-director scanned the sagging jowls, the Party badge, the staring blue eyes, caught the faint aroma of brandy, and once more wondered whether he'd imposed sufficient checks and balances on his kinsman. Indubitably, he'd dived head first into the Nazi pool.

Breathlessly, Otto said, 'I've been speaking to Herr Schloss about the NSDAP account. About a more productive investment strategy. Seventeen million marks are sitting there earning a mere 3 per cent or less. And daily the money flows in.' He blinked rapidly, nervously, at his uncle. 'He agreed I should mention it to you.'

The elder Wertheim doubted it and gazed down the room to the painting. He fully understood any reservations Herr Schloss might have in dealing with Otto.

'Yes? What have you in mind?'

In the hard-back chair his uncle had directed him to, Otto shifted forward the large posterior which, two hours before, had been imprisoned by Fräulein Blum's muscular legs.

He said, 'A good portion to be reinvested in foreign currencies *and* Aryanisation opportunities. I thought the Ruhr people were most informative.'

Wertheim interlaced his fingers and, put them to rest on the desk. A family trait: the elderly male Wertheims had fingers that looked as fragile as sticks of chalk. On them the gold bands glinted.

What a fascinating picture! He felt it had X-ray powers, was seeing deep into his brain. He must meet the artist. One day. He withdrew his gaze, and reappraised Otto. His nephew's intellectual qualities were mediocre, but he did possess a native cunning which, occasionally, enabled him to hit the mark. He must have received *something* from their ancestors' genes. On the other hand, Schloss's character and intellect were admirable, though a lifetime of private banking had rendered him ultraconservative.

'My dear Otto, you might have something. But foreign currencies – no. Political dynamite, I would think. The Reich's gold and currency reserves are practically exhausted. The other – yes, possibly.'

He'd been considering what to do about the Ruhr industrialist's loan application with its special purpose. Despite the sea change in him, the general-director still understood banking as well as he ever had. The banks were being prostituted in respect of the Aryanisation business. Doubtless other customers were going to require such loans. Why not the Nazis? Did he really have a choice in the matter?

Otto said earnestly, 'The Party's above politics. What it wishes to do, it can do.'

'Perhaps I meant, public relations.' Face-to-face, Herr Wertheim had been surprised by the Field-Marshal's extravagant uniform and persona. A mixture of egocentricity and circus showmanship. He'd been amazed to see something of his own self in the man.

His nephew shrugged, and blinked again, nervously. He'd waited until that bitch had gone home to come to his uncle's office. His stunned confusion following their encounter had settled into a bruised anxiety, was changing into a brooding anger. Tonight he'd seek solace at an establishment as removed from his uncle's world as Mars.

'I'll speak to Herr Schloss.'

Otto nodded respectfully, hauled himself up and withdrew from his uncle's presence, with gratification, and the usual relief.

§ § §

Ablaze with electric light – unlike the dim corridors with their low-power bulbs – Schmidt's office seemed to await his next move. One could compare it to a chessboard at a tournament left overnight, the pieces in place, the next moves in a sealed envelope. This kind of thinking smoothed his nerves.

He paused, and continued to listen. Quietly he pushed the door almost shut, sat down at his desk, took a rubber thumbstall, slipped it on, removed the sealed envelope from his attaché case, slit it, lifted the bonds out, squared them adroitly, and began to count them off.

Working fast, he inserted five certificates each for 100,000 Reichmarks into a fresh envelope and placed it in his attaché case; he was allowing plenty of margin. The remainder – for 9,500,000 marks – he returned to the original envelope and carried it to the safe. He revolved the tumbler to lock it, straightened up, and turned around.

He was looking straight into Dietrich's cold blue eyes. The Nazi stood in the doorway watching with an acute, inquiring expression. Schmidt's heart froze; he'd not heard the door move – not heard a thing.

The Nazi smiled. 'What is this? Working late, Herr Auditor?'

Schmidt nodded; a desperate reflex action. How long had he been in the doorway?

'I've been looking for you – came in earlier, but you were not here.'

'I've been out, Herr Director,' Schmidt said. 'Calm down,' he intoned to himself. He walked back to his desk, reassembling his composure with each step – each breath.

'Ah ... out!' Dietrich tilted his head, as though weighing the possibilities of 'out', his gaze unwavering. 'But now in.' He lifted his scrutiny smoothly from Schmidt's face, then to the photograph of the Wertheim building. 'The building's deserted yet I feel people are around – lying low. Isn't that strange? Never mind.' He pointed to the safe. 'I'm curious. How does the system work? If you're unable to attend the bank, say in the case of a personal disaster, how do they open the safe?'

Schmidt felt he was wearing his calm with the ineffectiveness of a threadbare coat, veteran of too many winters. 'As with everyone, Herr Director, my combination is in a sealed envelope at our clearing bankers – available on the signature of two directors.'

'I see. How interesting. Is everything going well? No problems?'

'Everything is proceeding as normal.'

'Good. I've told you, even in the rosiest apple there's sometimes a vile worm. Be vigilant, my friend.'

Schmidt nodded. His concealed breathlessness was abating.

Dietrich grinned. 'Naturally, one hopes nothing will happen to you my dear Schmidt.'

He came and sat on the desk-edge, brought out his cigarettes. Schmidt sat down too, and they both lit up. Swinging his leg back and forth, the Nazi smoked away companionably, while Schmidt measured out the moments.

'Nothing to go home to, my friend?'

'On the contrary, I was about to leave. My dinner will be waiting.' Deliberately, Schmidt kept his eye from the attaché case which lay beside the Nazi's splayed left hand. It was strange to think of that old case, his father's, as a potential death warrant.

'No medieval history tonight at the Municipal Library?'

'No, mein herr.' To Schmidt's hyperactive nerves, it was another loaded question. Then came yet another:

'Your family's returned suddenly and unexpectedly to Dresden. My dear Franz, I hope no problems?'

Schmidt couldn't conceal his surprise. Dietrich's face was intent now – as though straining for a confirmation. And – *My Dear Franz?*

The auditor said, 'Normal family movements.'

So they were watching his family. The contents of his stomach turned over – audibly. Beyond the Nazi's head the clock showed 6.15 pm. A different current of pressure came. How long could Dressler wait?

The Nazi exhaled blue smoke, and smiled indulgently. 'The Gestapo are still interested in you following the Dressler affair. Twice now you've featured in the Party's files. They're like hounds on the scent, hard to whip off it. It cost me a lot to get you off that. But don't worry. They're not short of other work. And you're not going to make any more mistakes, are you?'

'No. I owe you my thanks for that, Herr Dietrich.'

The Nazi beamed, almost embarrassed, opening up a crack in his controlled personality. Schmidt smoked, watched and waited.

'I've a high regard for you. For your work, for you personally. I considered it a worthwhile investment. Why don't you join me one night soon for an intimate little dinner, a little champagne. We'll get to know each other better. Off-duty, you will find me a very pleasant fellow.'

Schmidt's heart and mind had moved into a synchronisation with the ticking of the clock. A subtle kind of gearshift. This last proposal came as a jolt. The Nazi was in the grip of some strong emotion. The yellowish teeth flashed, but nervously. Instinctively, Schmidt felt that they'd arrived at the crux of this episode.

'I would be honoured, Herr Director.' Would he ever leave?

Dietrich relaxed visibly. 'I mustn't detain you, my dear Franz. Shall we say – soon?'

The auditor glanced at his hat, his coat, and the Nazi's gaze alighted on the attaché case. He frowned. Schmidt's heartbeats bounded. Abruptly, Dietrich left his perch. Back in command, he grinned. 'Goodnight, Herr Auditor.' From the door he gave Schmidt a look as if to say that the auditor's thoughts were a road-map he could see clearly.

Schmidt sat rigid, the cigarette burning to a column of ash in his fingers, the taste of metal in his mouth. By God! What was tonight?

Outside the door Dietrich paused, also analysing the interview.

25

THE INVESTIGATORS FROM the Gestapo central office drove out to the Dresden suburb as night fell. Catching up on the run, the man in the passenger seat, with the aid of the car's interior light, read a teletype aloud. When they arrived at the turn-of-the-century house in its acre of wooded garden, they were fully briefed.

'Come on,' the senior said as they climbed out, 'we can be back in town to eat – with or without this woman, as the case may be.'

Helga opened the door: on the porch two faces floated in the dark like dabs of cream. Behind them in the trees an owl called. She heard it as a warning, but thought: *What small men for policemen. And: Oh, Franz!*

She was surprised how calm she felt as she peered at the official card. With a slight gesture, she bade them step into the hall. Her mother was upstairs in bed, Trudi was with her, colouring-in a book. The childish voice sounded, a thin plaint in the stairwell. She could hear her sister preparing the meal in the kitchen. The simple sounds of domestic life. And here in the dark-panelled hall nuances of Franz, his mysterious world, the steely cadences of the State.

Can I cope with this?

'What is it you want?' she said politely, her head tilted, arms clasped under her breasts. She kept the men standing, drawing the line of intrusion.

'We have questions about your husband, Frau Schmidt,' the senior said. 'A few questions, soon answered, I would hope.' He considered the light and warmth of the living room beyond glass doors. 'However, I warn you to think carefully before answering.'

'Yes? Please go on.'

'Has your husband ever been a member of a political party?'

'Never.' The answer was automatic, accurate.

'Who are his chief friends and associates?'

This was harder. Franz's interests were circumscribed by the bank, his family, and his solitary esoteric hobby. She frowned, exhibiting her concentration, fighting to hold back this nightmare.

'My husband is devoted to the bank. His colleagues there make up his friends and associates.' She spoke quietly, again with accuracy.

'Including Herr Wagner?'

'Of course, they've been colleagues for many years.'

'Who else is he close to at the bank?'

Helga thought methodically, decided boldly. 'Herr Dietrich. He's closely associated with him.'

They dwelt on this for a moment.

'Has your husband taken trips away? Especially abroad?'

'No.'

The three of them were silent, as though they were players on a stage who'd lost the thread of a scene. The team leader's face was expressionless. He reconsidered two paragraphs in the teletype: the incident with the SA three years ago, the recent death of the man's mother during an investigation by colleagues involving a Jewish woman: two dramatic incidents sitting damned strangely in such an uneventful life.

'Why have you returned to Dresden?'

Helga had lowered her chin, now she brought it up and tossed back her blonde hair. 'My mother continues to need my support.' Doubtless they'd know about the operation.

'Yes? But you've a sister here.'

Deliberately, she moistened her lips. Was it the right time to make the revelation? Perhaps the perfect opportunity. Her heart was beating much faster.

'There is a private reason. I've decided to divorce my husband. I will not be returning home.'

A flicker of animation passed over their faces. 'Uhuh?' the leader grunted. 'What's the reason for this sudden decision?'

'It's not sudden. We're no longer compatible in the married state.' In her ears, her voice sounded like someone else's.

The leader sucked at his teeth, as though retasting his last meal. 'You're disturbed by his actions, his opinions? Isn't that so?'

'No, that is *not* correct. I've told you the reason.' She stared at them, willing them to go. Then she'd think about what such questions meant for Franz. Contact him. She presumed they'd not yet questioned him. Why hadn't they? But perhaps they had ...

The men looked at each other, the leather coats crackled, electrically alive. She thought: In tune with their thoughts.

'We won't detain you longer, Frau Schmidt,' the leader said. They turned their backs and went down the porch steps.

Helga listened for the sound of their car but heard nothing. All her fears had been well founded. That the situation had crystallised here − tonight − was inexplicable. An idea came: Perhaps it was Wagner they were interested in. It was a straw to clutch at. Her heart was really pounding now. *'Dear Franz − it's a device − not the end for us.'* She whispered the fervent explanation out to where the owl sat, searching the darkness for telltale movement.

The leader sat in the passenger seat assessing the house

and grounds. The huge, dim oaks which hemmed in the house didn't impress him. The suburban streetlights failed to penetrate the massed trunks.

'That woman's either honest, or cunning. See? Even in a routine job like this, our work's no fucking picnic.' He sounded as if he were clinching an old argument.

'A bit of work on her can fix that,' the other grunted.

'Don't count on it.'

'*Has* he gone off the rails?'

The leader shrugged. 'Maybe. Let's go, I hate this fucking suburb, it stinks of the bourgeois.'

The engine started, and gravel crunched under the tyres. In the hall, Helga slowly let out her breath.

§ § §

Schmidt hurried to the cathedral. Again, the giant detective wasn't there. The stone embrasure was empty. Schmidt surveyed the platz. Six forty-five pm. Was he too late? At a loss, he gripped the attaché case and stared across to the ever-present, incandescent café-life. The intervening motor traffic latticed headlights across the platz.

What now? He felt exposed, the attaché case a deadly liability.

A touch on the shoulder. God! He whipped around. Dressler loomed above him – like a statue displaced from the public gardens; a mobile statue which'd stepped out of a pool of darkness, and approached silently on thick rubber.

Schmidt exhaled his tension, gasped: 'My apologies.'

'I went to look the neighbourhood over. Also to see if you're being followed. It doesn't appear so. Now Herr Schmidt, we must get a move on. The people we're to meet have the nerves of wild deer. *They* won't wait.'

They walked into a dark district. Breezes sang softly in

the alleys: sighs of despair. Did Dressler feel this atmosphere?
Schmidt had to break into a run to keep up, which spurred
his thinking. Beside him, Dressler's breathing whistled in the
dark. They turned under an arch. A touch of life: a violin was
playing deep in an interior. Congratulations to the player.
Schmidt tripped, plunged out of control into a black abyss.
Dressler's giant hand shot out and plucked him back, steadied
him.

'Careful, Herr Schmidt. This isn't like *your* suburb. The
municipality doesn't spend money here.'

The detective slowed, inspecting doorways. They stood
under a portico, heard a bell resound in the interior. Schmidt
was vaguely aware of masonry columns on either side. A house
of large proportions. A scratching came at the door; like a rat
going at ceiling wiring.

Three men waited in a library. Rubinstein, his hat
removed on this occasion, gestured to chairs set at a vast table
gleaming like a mirror. Schmidt was dazzled; a surfeit of electricity here.

A greater surprise was the short, barrel-chested, white-
moustached man, his massive head on one side as if it were a
burden. He stood apart. The famous Jewish banker watched
them with a speculative air, smiled slightly at Schmidt's sign
of recognition. The man had dropped from public view. The
auditor bowed formally, took his place beside Dressler at the
table.

Rubinstein studied Schmidt. He said, 'May I ask what
value you've brought, and in what form?'

Schmidt welcomed the absence of preliminaries. He
silently drew in a breath. 'I have 500,000 marks of Reich
bonds − in denominations of 100,000. As I understand the
situation, the 200,000 − is it? − necessary for Fräulein Dressler's
case, and 300,000 to be used at your discretion.' He spoke rapidly, in a meticulous tone.

A younger man with black, glued-down hair looked up quickly from the tabletop. They considered the figures stated.

Rubinstein said, 'A generous proposal. However, you'll understand we give no guarantees. Circumstances are variable, sometimes we succeed, sometimes not. The persons we deal with can be trusted only to the degree their self-interest is satisfied. They're not people of honour. And the influence they have today may be gone tomorrow. The Nazi leadership, as much as they can, keep things on the move.' His hands made gestures, massaging his words. 'The fact that she's in detention is a complication.'

Schmidt glanced at Dressler. He opened the attaché case, passed the packet across the desk. Rubinstein examined the Wertheim & Co identification, and regarded the auditor with curiosity. Schmidt thought: Everything isn't known. The ex-judge passed the packet to the younger man, who opened it, examined the top document, held it up to the light, inspected watermarks with an eye-glass, put on a rubber thumb-stall and counted with the same facility Schmidt had shown earlier in the evening. Then he examined the other bonds. They watched in silence.

The banker had moved to watch the young man over his shoulder. His eyes downcast, he said deeply out of that chest, 'These will be fed onto the markets in Berlin, Frankfurt, Hamburg over several days. However, they're numbered, of course, and it would not be impossible to trace individual bonds back to source – should an investigation commence, and the investigators have enough power, skill, and luck. And if records have been kept. I presume it's inevitable they'll be found missing at some point.'

He'd spoken in a relaxed tone. He looked directly at Schmidt. 'Doubtless you've taken that factor into account.'

Dressler sat erect, huge and silent at the table, as though he were a non-combatant watching a barrage going up. The flick, flick of the count, the stiff rustle of the security paper, was beyond his experience.

Back in the street Schmidt wondered at the detective's thoughts. Then he wondered at the force within himself which had impelled him on this strange odyssey.

'Thank you, Herr Schmidt.' Dressler's voice unexpectedly vibrated with emotion, as though he, too, was thinking about Schmidt's conduct. 'Now, let us get away from here.'

26

AT 7.30 am the next day the doorbell shattered the bachelor-silence. At the breakfast table, Schmidt froze. Who ...? Maria went into the hall. The auditor waited, breathing suspended, coffee cup held in mid-air. He thought: *Gestapo*. He heard muffled voices.

Maria returned, and gave him a curious look. 'A gentleman to see you, Herr Schmidt.'

Schmidt got up, feeling he might be going to meet his fate. Though, one man ...

An obese man waited in the hall, exuding an air of reluctance to be there. He had faded blue eyes as clear as glass; many chins. He wore a provincial-looking overcoat, and the ringed fingers of his left hand clutched a homburg. He bowed minimally, and held out an envelope. Up close this visitor smelled of cigars. He stared at the auditor with a kind of alarm.

'Herr Schmidt? Herr Fischer. From Dresden. A neighbour of your mother-in-law. As I was coming here, your wife asked me to bring this letter to you.' Schmidt took the letter. 'Thank you, mein herr. Some coffee?'

'I'm afraid I'm late for an appointment.' The stranger's chins vibrated. He edged towards the door. Schmidt moved to hold it open, and somehow they shook hands.

'Of course, again our thanks.'

The man from Dresden left. Schmidt was sure of a sigh

of relief from the stairwell. An appointment at 7.30 am.? He returned to the breakfast table. The messenger had impressed as a fortunate survivor of the Inflation; one who'd bought assets as others had sold.

He read Helga's letter quickly, then reread it. When he'd finished he sat with the pages in his hand, and felt loneliness creep from the corners of the flat into his heart. Abruptly, he went into his study and burnt the letter – as she'd requested.

'*Hugs and kisses from Trudi.*' The phrase stood in his mind after the pages were ashes. Dear Helga, pragmatic in the face of disaster. '*In the interests of Trudi, my family, myself …*' Always, totally honest. His vision blurred with tears. He stared blindly across the room. The Gestapo were still in the picture. Dietrich might have less influence than he believed. Or was working with them, watching him for a false move. Maybe they'd observed his meetings with Dressler. His mouth had gone dry, and his hands were sweating. He got up and paced the room. He and Wagner could already be finished. He steadied himself. *That is not the message I'm getting from Dietrich.*

'*God willing we will come through this, be together again, my dearest one,*' she'd written as she moved to her separate planet. They could no longer trust the phone, the post, or meet. She'd made an appointment with her mother's lawyer, to begin divorce proceedings.

Schmidt stared at Dürer's knight on his wary ride past the unattainable castle. He went to the window, and looked down into the street. Wintry sunlight. An illusion of easy normality, lulling the unwary spirit into lowering its guard.

Fervently, he prayed that the Gestapo had finished with his family.

He heard them coming, despite the double-glazing. Twenty Brownshirts marched into view, singing, jackboots stamping, each holding aloft a red-and-black swastika on a brass-tipped pole – identical to the one which had hoicked out his eye.

Had the Dresden messenger, with super-sensitive hearing, heard them?

With a sense of urgency, he turned away.

An hour later, at the bank, he considered more tangible matters. Lilli had vanished into 'protective custody'. He speculated on the channels Rubinstein would be following. It would be a highwire walk, dealing with corrupt Nazis. How long would they have to wait for news?

He drank coffee, and gazed at his safe as though he'd X-ray vision and could see the remaining 9,500,000 marks worth of bonds. He felt keyed-up, but no fear. 'My phlegmatic colleague,' Wagner had called him. The possibility of torture chambers, broken bones, bloodied faces, assaulted genitals – as whispered by the knowledgeable – seemed to be circulating around him. The world of von Streck and Dietrich – now his world. It was true, he felt no fear for himself ... instead, a strong sense of predestination. He smiled thinly. It seemed Wagner's Calvinism had shifted subtly into his bloodstream.

Wagner? The deputy foreign manager shouldn't come to his flat tonight; he'd use his mother's. Anxiously he settled down to reconsider the vital unresolved second stage of his plan. The internal phone on his desk rang.

'Herr Auditor? Come to my office, please.'

The corridors are a degree or so colder each day, he thought. 'Healthy,' Herr Wertheim reportedly told the directors. 'Coming out of overheated rooms into fresh air stimulates the brain.' And, 'Better higher salaries than higher heating costs.' This slogan amused the general-director, and irritated his co-directors, as salaries were fixed by the government. Had the G-D calculated the point when the water pipes would freeze up?

Deliberately he carried these routine thoughts to Dietrich's door.

Dietrich had nothing on his desk but his coffee cup – and the auditor's latest report. The ice-blue eyes transfixed Schmidt. 'There you are! Just a moment of your valuable time, Schmidt.' Grinning, the Nazi gestured towards a chair. 'By the way, have you looked out of the window lately, and observed the wonderful progress the Fuehrer is making in the Czechoslovakia negotiations?'

Dietrich's tone was ironic. A gibe against the introverted Wertheim world. 'Never mind. The auditing sphere may be boring to my more mercurial mind, but it's a valid function. Please feel relaxed about that.'

The Nazi's window faced the street, but Schmidt had never seen *him* look out. His dealings with the world were by phone. He appeared to spend much of each day with that instrument glued to his ear. Now he assumed seriousness. 'I re-emphasise something, Schmidt. Don't make another mistake in your personal relations. You will keep clear of Deputy Foreign Manager Wagner. That man is *not* of the right calibre. Are you listening, Herr Schmidt?'

Schmidt gazed at the Nazi, thinking: *Listening? I'm listening and watching you with the kind of attention you'd hardly credit.*

Another warning about Wagner. He felt the worry turn over in him. What did Dietrich know about Wagner's future? Did he have him in the same sights he'd brought to bear on Lilli? Wagner was so careless with his slanders of the Party – a criminal offence. But, what else? His own doubts about his colleague surfaced again.

'Herr Director, I do have duties to discuss with Herr Wagner on a regular basis.'

Dietrich raised his hands. 'I said *personal* relations. I could hardly have missed that you're a walking repository of discretion. Use it.'

The auditor nodded.

'Another matter. How much unused safe-custody space

do we have in the vault?'

'For what purpose, Herr Director?'

Dietrich worked his lips over his teeth. 'For gold bullion. Let us say, for thirty or forty millions.'

Schmidt blinked. 'Space can be made.'

'Good. I'm looking ahead, my friend. I mentioned Czechoslovakia. Now I'm mentioning the Czechoslovak National Bank – and its gold reserves. Need I say more? Of course, your lips are strictly sealed.'

Schmidt did not show surprise, though it had given him a solid jolt. The idea seemed ridiculous. The Nazi was smiling again.

'Does it worry you, my dear Franz – your eye?'

'I'm used to it.'

'Good! Now, our little dinner.'

His voice had dropped. He leaned forward intimately, suddenly at his most personable. 'Tomorrow night, my apartment. Seven o'clock. Here's the address. You're going to enjoy this, my friend. Have no doubt.'

Politely, Schmidt indicated pleasurable anticipation.

The phone rang; reluctantly the Nazi withdrew from further preview of the golden occasion, and gave an airy wave of dismissal.

Schmidt returned to his office. In terms of what he had on his plate, tomorrow night seemed an age away.

§ § §

Otto Wertheim passed through the general-director's anteroom with a feeling of acute discomfort. Under the appraising eyes of Else Blum, his usual self-important swagger deteriorated to a hasty waddle. It made him angry, but he felt powerless. By a laborious mental process, he'd decided that her innocent demeanour was a mask for a huntress type. How else to explain it? Her cunt was made of Krupp steel! He was still sore, and rigorously avoided eye contact.

'Herr Director, please advise when you again need special assistance in the archives,' she said earnestly.

He nodded tersely, eyes rigidly ahead, missing the gleam in her eye. His face was hot. Last night he'd visited his favourite club to soothe his bruised ego with a woman who'd cooed and melted beneath him like butter. With indignant relief, he closed the door of his uncle's room behind him.

'Yes, Otto?'

'Our recent talk ... I've done some research. The Dortmund's pipe and blast furnace company is to be Aryanised. I think we could get it for a million. Its net worth is six, at least. We can easily fund it from the Party's balance of Reich bonds. Would you agree to me working on it with Herr Dietrich?'

He stopped, out of breath, apprehensive for this opportunity. That Blum pig had shaken his confidence.

Herr Wertheim stared at the soul-searching *Eye*. Otto had really been burning the midnight oil, though what else had he been up to? He'd that uneasy air which had accompanied several of his past escapades. Well, no doubt he'd find out about it. Heinrich Dortmund's sober face appeared in his mind's eye. He'd known the Jewish capitalist for thirty years, served alongside him on several committees. He could hear his slow, thick, kindly voice laying down the building blocks of civic life.

His mind seemed to blink – the image vanished like baggage thrown off a train; he was seeing the *Eye* again. The die was cast for the Dortmunds, and some banker was going to be involved in the end of their business empire. If it were Wertheims, perhaps he could temper the ill wind. Yesterday, the bank had approved the loan for the Ruhr industrialist and his Aryanisation project.

Was he, or was he not, in control of Wertheims, its destiny?

What stimulation he felt from the danger which lurked in such a fundamental doubt! How revitalised – if not always clear – he felt in his mind!

He switched his gaze to his nephew and smiled. 'Why not, Otto? Keep me advised.'

§ § §

Meet me 5.00 pm usual place. D.

The note had been put on Schmidt's desk, mid-afternoon, during his brief absence. So Dressler had someone inside Wertheims. Schmidt stared at the printed words. How many secret cabals existed in this rabbit-warren of a building? Where was the *Nazi* cell lurking? They were supposed to be springing up like black fungi in all institutions. Six months ago he'd have found the notion ludicrous; today it merely moved through his mind as another grim current.

The stone embrasure was empty, and freezing. However, on past experience the municipal detective would turn up. But what news would he bring? Fervently, Schmidt hoped that it'd be positive. Above his head, a crowd of carved stone figures, amazingly entwined, struggled ever upwards into the gloom. He stamped his feet, and commenced a solo watch on the café-life as though warmth, illumination – even hope – might be gleaned from there. He'd no expectation it would be found behind him. A few pedestrians passed, ten metres distant. None glanced towards the freezing repository of a myriad sung masses.

The detective came out of the darkness, and his great white hand flashed near his waist, and swallowed Schmidt's. His breath whistled eerily into the auditor's face, smelt of cabbage and pickles; a meal and digestion on the run.

The policeman moved into the embrasure. He was still

holding the auditor's hand, as though he'd forgotten to release it. He seemed bereft of words. Schmidt felt the giant frame shaking. *'Herr Dressler?'*

A long, fierce sigh.

'Yes, Herr Schmidt. Please, allow me a moment.' He released the auditor's hand. His shoulders shook in a frightening spasm. Schmidt was alarmed. 'My dear Lilli died on the 16th ... Herr Rubinstein found out ... pneumonia.' His voice choked.

Schmidt's brain and body swooped away as the vertigo gripped him. It lasted for a few seconds. He tried to speak. Tried again. 'My deepest condolences,' he heard himself say, then his throat closed up.

The detective's great head was moving back and forth. His massive shoulders shook violently. He whispered: 'My dearest only child. I'm to receive her ashes.'

Schmidt put his hand on the giant arm. He still couldn't speak but his mind was clearing. He stared at the detective's face. The café lights laid gleams on the tears in the eyes above the moustache. Schmidt thought: *It's over. She was a strong, healthy woman.* In his memory he looked into the considering eyes, caught the sad, puzzled defeat of a woman who'd specialised in solving problems, who'd always got things done with her small stabs of humour, saw her walking away in the Wertheim corridor. His heart beat in rythmic thumps, as it walked with her.

'You did more than I, anyone, could expect,' Dressler said brokenly.

'No father could have done more.' Useless, efforts at consolation – pitiful in the face of such evil, such misfortune. A flurry of wind whirled bits of rubbish across the platz into their hiding hole.

'I slept too long. Was paralysed. The war dulled me, scrambled my brain. Some days I cannot think at all.' The detective blinked rapidly, shedding diamond-like gleams.

Schmidt dabbed at his own weeping eye. What could he do, tonight, with the heart-broken man? What was it *best* to do? He wondered at himself – at the calmness which had settled in him. Feeling seemed to be draining from him day by day, leaving the reasoning core, shadowing that evil, getting on terms with it. Or was he deceiving himself, playing a futile game, his own crash waiting its time?

Dressler brushed at his eyes, said, 'Rubinstein has offered to return part of the bonds.'

'Let him keep them,' Schmidt said.

The detective nodded.

'Will you come home with me, Herr Dressler?'

'No. Thank you. I'm on duty.' The detective had his ready-made solution to hand.

Schmidt thought: *Yes, the best place.*

In a voice which had become flat, Dressler said, 'Your Nazi, Dietrich, is no different from most of them ... but to me he is a special case.'

Schmidt was silent. Dietrich's face had loomed up in his mind. The Nazi had entered their lives like a deadly virus. He glanced at the detective. 'A special case.' There'd been something in that totally flat delivery. Dressler's breath whistled, and subsided in his throat. He shook his shoulders, forcing his mind to this: 'I've not found out much about von Streck. Except he was in the Ministry of Economics. He's an office at Party headquarters. I couldn't find out where he fits into the Party. He's a man without much of a past, though that's balls. My contact said he could be one of those who answer only to the top ... but guesswork.'

The giant detective sighed heavily, felt for Schmidt's hand, and squeezed it. As he walked away, the wind attacked his overcoat, flapping its skirts wildly as though even the elements could tell when a man was down, and were moving in on him.

27

HIS MOTHER'S APARTMENT was as 'quiet as a mouse' – as Trudi had recently learned to say. Little Trudi of his old life. He'd dreamt last night that he'd been on a pier from which a ship was departing with his family; his wife had flung a streamer, he'd grabbed for it, felt it slip through his fingers.

Frau Bertha had left after disposing of his mother's wardrobe; already the furniture had a coat of dust. He sat in his father's study, in the surgeon's chair, in a stand-off with the silence. He pondered its density; saturated with his father's thousands of hours of brooding on the Order. On its demise. He sensed it moving past him like a draught of air. In 1408 the rebellion in Poland and Lithuania had begun the rot. In 1410, the knights had been defeated at Grunwald. Thereafter their authority and wealth declined. In 1525 their rule in Prussia ended; in 1558 the Livonian territory was lost, and in 1580 the land in the Low Countries. In 1801 they'd been stripped of their German possessions. Napoleon had proclaimed the Order dissolved in 1809.

It'd all been blown away like chaff in a wind. Schmidt raised his eyes and stared down the room at the past. His life had been dominated by his ancestors – on both sides of the family. He nodded to himself.

Seven nights ago he'd been here with Lilli and her father

planning her survival! Then he'd hurried with the father through the streets to that Jewish house with his attaché case of the Party's bonds. It was *all* the stuff of dreams – no, a ridiculous farce! Lilli had already been bound to her fate. Dietrich had shut all the doors, watertight as a submarine's compartments. Why? Efficiency? A favourable notation in a dossier? Or some malignant, deep-seated antipathy?

To Lilli it was now immaterial. He and Wagner must deal with the aftermath. If they were to survive in the short term, the missing bonds must be covered up. As for the long term ... He started and tensed at a faint sound, back in the depths of the apartment. ... A single fact had been hovering above his musing: Dietrich knew of his connection to the Order. He'd been looking into it. But another mysterious fact: the attitude of von Streck to Wagner when they'd met at the beerhall – a kind of knowingness. Perhaps not mysterious to Wagner!

A farce? To this point, perhaps. But as he continued to sit in his father's chair a vista opened up, becoming wider and wider. What had been maturing in the subconscious stepped forward with a flourish, presented itself like a woman turning, showing the pleasing fall of a skirt. He sat up in the chair. A plan! He nodded wonderingly. Amazing! It went far beyond any protective cover-up. It went like a dagger into Dietrich's heart. Excitement burned in him. The *perfect* plan!

It occurred to him that the thoughts now going through his mind were those of a complete stranger.

The deputy foreign manager slouched watchfully through the streets to 178 Frederickstrasse. Though Wagner's habitual attitude was cavalier and cynical, he wasn't without some instinct of self-preservation. Last night he'd burned his Social Democratic Party papers. Up in smoke – like the party. The snake had slipped its old skin.

They'd taken to following him in the street – the same pattern as the watch on his flat: occasionally, and inefficiently. To them, his life must seem a ragbag of suspicious ingredients. Fervently he hoped the totality of it was proving confusing; that no man's intelligence had penetrated to the core. Tonight he'd been especially careful.

'All quiet?' he said to Schmidt as he was admitted at the tradesman's door at 7.00 pm in a whiff of fog and tobacco. He was referring to the stolen bonds. Hatless as usual, his hair was brittle and frosty.

Schmidt said, 'Come through to the salon.' He led the way. In the room, keeping his face calm, he turned. 'Heinrich, I'm afraid – very bad news. Lilli Dressler is dead.'

Wagner staggered.

'God Almighty!' he whispered. He was stricken. His face sagged. Sympathetically, Schmidt watched this sequence of emotions. A human response. His own shock and grief were sunk deep by the pressure of events.

He cleared his throat. 'Herr Dressler told me an hour ago – had it from Rubinstein, who found it out when he tried to open up negotiations.'

'How?'

'Pneumonia.'

Wagner sank down in a chair, his hands spreading bitter gestures. 'And they think that'll be believed?'

'To their minds it's like the bureaucratic filling-in of a space on a form. I've some experience.' With abject weariness Wagner shook his head. He understood that Schmidt was referring, obliquely, to the incident of his eye ... Things had been bad, now were much worse. Schmidt continued to observe the emotion in his colleague. He said, 'I feel deeply for Herr Dressler. But there's nothing more to be done. We tried, we failed.'

'We fooled ourselves – him – that there was a chance!' Wagner sneered.

The auditor accepted this, and kept silent. Wagner hunted for, found cigarettes, and savagely scratched a match alight.

Schmidt said, 'Tragically, it's all over for her. For him. For us, another matter. We're dangerously exposed. Until the next stage is put in place.'

Wagner exhaled a gust of smoke. 'Ah yes, the next stage.' He looked at the auditor as though seeing him anew. Suddenly he sensed the excitement in him. 'You know, Franz, you're surprising me more each day. I always knew you were cautious – and, with respect, cold-minded. Now, obviously more cold-minded than cautious. It's a wonder ...'

Schmidt shrugged. It was his friend's character that interested him. Despite his familiarity with Wagner's opinions concerning the Nazis, and his bouts of recklessness, he'd been surprised himself at his colleague's prompt consent to step into the zone of extreme danger. Wagner was a complicated individual, and Schmidt now feared that his past political affiliation might be ticking away like a time bomb. Maybe not an ideal accomplice. But he must press on.

'For the second time, Dietrich has warned me against you.'

Wagner shrugged helplessly. 'What can I do? As I've said, it's to do with my old political life.'

'I think they'd pull you in if they had solid grounds. They're watching so many on speculation. That reassures me.'

But Schmidt wasn't reassured.

Wagner blew smoke into the room where Schmidt's mother had forbidden smoking. 'Could you get the bonds back, return them to the safe?'

'I don't intend to do that. Anyway, some have been sold. I hope you agree.'

'Of course. Foolish to ask.'

'The next stage ... Heinrich, could you go to Zurich tomorrow night?'

The foreign manager's expression didn't change. Clinically, he inspected Frau Schmidt's antique furniture – as though he'd come there for that express purpose. 'The answer's yes. I'm overdue to see our Swiss correspondents, a visit's been set up. I can leave at a moment's notice. If the Gestapo permits.'

Schmidt studied him acutely. 'Excellent. When I asked you about Zurich before, I was examining ideas, searching for the way to cover up our little operation. Now, I've a plan.'

Wagner watched the auditor, thinking: *insert 'theft' for 'operation'. It must've really gone against the grain.* But his upright colleague had changed dramatically. Perhaps here was the real man. A plan ...

'A plan which goes further than I originally intended. A long way further.'

'You're sounding very mysterious, my friend.'

Schmidt looked away, apparently changing the subject. 'It's distressing to see what's happening to Wertheims.'

Wagner laughed bitterly. 'Distressing? I told you from the beginning, old Wertheim's sailing the ship into dangerous waters. What's he really up to? I await his next act of senility with bated breath. It's worse even than I imagined. I think he's developed a taste for danger. Not for greed – just danger.'

'Hardly logical.'

'His mind's no longer *logical*. Witness those damned paintings. And the reek of Nazism in our venerable edifice. Dietrich's spreading the infection. But it's invading us through every crack in the damned place. I suggest to you none of our colleagues can be trusted.'

Schmidt brooded on a handsome silver chalice that had belonged to his mother's father; safe in his grave.

'Dietrich ...'

'Yes,' Wagner said. 'Didn't our famous Goethe say: "For all guilt is punished on earth." What do you think, Franz?'

The auditor had no comment. He'd turned over the Nazi's black-edged page in his mind. It was spattered with blood. Dietrich's reckoning was going to come – if he had the wit and the nerve to implement this plan. Wagner was going to get another shock.

Schmidt said, 'Otto's working on Aryanisation projects, he's targeted the Dortmunds. He'll strip their wealth and the authorities will kick them out, or worse. They'll be paid about twenty per cent of what their company's worth, and after the twenty-five per cent Flight Capital Tax on that amount, they'll have only peanuts left. Isn't that how Dietrich puts it?'

Wagner shrugged elaborately. '*That* farting, fornicating bastard, Otto. Finally, he's found his true metier. I thought he'd peaked as the rapist of the archives' room, the polluter of corridors, but he continues to develop.'

Schmidt scarcely listened. 'From our point of view, this is quite alarming. They'll need to sell Reich bonds from the working stock to pay for it. Sooner rather than later.'

After a pause, Wagner almost whispered, 'And the cupboard is bare.'

Schmidt smiled thinly. 'Not quite.'

'Poor Lilli Dressler,' Wagner murmured, 'to run into someone like him.' He held his right hand before his eyes. It was shaking. 'Look at that,' he said disgustedly. 'You know, Franz, the whole of my life's been littered with errors and omissions. I lie in bed at night, look back and feel deeply embarrassed for my mistakes. That's my life ...' His face broke into a desperate grin. 'Why am I confiding this depressing information to you?'

Was Wagner going to crack? Schmidt considered consolations. Better a change of pace. He left his chair and went to a cabinet: third drawer on the left. He took a key from his pocket, unlocked it. Matter-of-factly, he put the manuscripts he'd retrieved from the cabinet into Wagner's hands. His colleague glanced at him in puzzlement, then began to turn over the sheets of music.

Another facial spasm. He straightened in his chair, and quickly began to flick through them. 'My God!' he breathed, then looked further, as though he couldn't believe what he was seeing. 'My God!' He came back to the first sheet. His head jerked up to stare at Schmidt. 'J.S. Bach! *Unpublished manuscripts – from him! It's the find of the century!*'

'My mother, her forebears, wouldn't publish them – because the Great Man hadn't. It's fortunate they weren't destroyed – by someone along the line. They've been hidden from the world in a sacred trust. A strange family tradition!'

Wagner was mesmerised. 'What will *you* do?'

Schmidt smiled slightly. It was clear that in the past weeks the leadership relationship between them had been reversed. Again in a matter-of-fact tone he said, 'The plan I speak of requires you to take the 9,500,000 of bonds still in my safe to the Swiss Bank, Zurich. You might take these along, too.'

§ § §

Rubinstein, overcoated, hatted, apparently a visitor in his own house, stood at the top of his cellar steps and meditated on the ruinous scene. Herr Dressler stood beside him.

'In a world of shortages, such a waste,' the Jew said.

'The act of criminals – and fools.' Herr Dressler wasn't present in his official capacity. The floor of the cellar was a glutinous, multi-coloured morass of preserved fruits and pickles, several centimetres deep, impregnated with the glass of smashed containers. A sweet odour laced the air. Upstairs, the faces of family portraits had been slashed. The canvases hung in ribbons between the ornate frames. Turkish rugs were despoiled.

'Thank God, my family were away. I'll have it cleaned

up before they return ... I am sorry about your daughter. Beside *that*, this is nothing.'

Dressler lowered his head onto his chest in acknowledgement. He'd thanked the the ex-judge, for his efforts, for his courageous intervention. Though he still appeared to meditate on the scene, Rubinstein's mind had shifted. 'The auditor, Schmidt – a strange man. In the courts one sees many types passing through. Criminals who've the appearance of innocent citizens. Innocent citizens who've the appearance of criminals. Of course, you've seen this phenomenon, Herr Dressler.' The detective acknowledged that he had. 'I don't mean to infer that Herr Schmidt falls into either type. There are others, of course. However, I admit if I had to make a quick judgement, I'd err on the side of the first.'

'He is a good man.'

'None of us is wholly good. His colleague, Herr Wagner, whom I happen to know something about, is another strange individual.' He looked at Dressler to examine his reaction. The detective showed none. However, as he left the despoiled house, close to midnight, Dressler wondered what the Jew knew of this Herr Wagner. Something, obviously. But he let it go, and strode across the city with his grief. Dietrich's face, which he'd never seen in the flesh, appeared in his mind's eye. He wondered whether the Nazi Party photo, in his pocket, was a good enough likeness. The old colleague who'd got it for him didn't know about that.

28

COULD HE GET it out in one short speech? Schmidt drew in breath.

'Herr Dietrich, this is the mandate for the Party's new account in Zurich. Our investment department anticipates Swiss-related transactions, and asks that this be opened. Yourself, Herr Otto, are recommended as signatories. If you agree, please sign where I've marked.'

Dietrich's eyes flicked to it, then away. He leaned back in his chair, and smiled broadly. 'Well, Franz, looking forward to our little dinner?'

Schmidt bowed affirmatively, and thought: *Why didn't you get those teeth cleaned?* An anxious Dr Bernstein had reported only an examination − during which the Nazi had silently examined him, and his premises.

'Good! You will enjoy it.' Becoming briskly businesslike, Dietrich turned his attention to the form. 'Now what's this about a Swiss account? Surely the bank already has one?'

'Yes, Herr Director − several. But this is to be a sub-account specifically for the Party's business. Under the approval of the Reichsbank, the bank opens such facilities as needed. Of course, any request of you to append your signature for *withdrawals*, would be submitted with full supporting documentation.'

Gravely projecting his years of auditing probity, holding

down his nerves, Schmidt eyed the destroyer of Lilli Dressler, and waited. Did the bastard know she was dead?

'This is a blank form, Schmidt?'

'The investment department will complete it. I'll personally verify that it's in order.'

'A blank cheque?' The Nazi grinned, pulled the form to him and signed. 'Explanation accepted! Knowing you, I'm sure you will see to the paperwork as appropriate.' Schmidt smiled politely, and withdrew from the Nazi's room. Again he committed his nerves and his cold resolve to the corridors, and traversed them to Otto's rooms. He sighed on the way, to reduce his tension. The Nazi's last comment had been weighted with an amused sarcasm. But he'd signed.

God! How boring we breed them, Otto thought, listening to the long-serving auditor with his grey-toned personality commence his speech. If I permit it he'll stand there for an hour talking like this. With an irritated gesture he cut Schmidt off. 'Spare me the details, Schmidt. I do understand these matters. Just give me the form. I've got *important* affairs on my plate this morning.' He signed with a flourish and negligently tossed it back. 'Today I'll need to withdraw Reich bonds from the Party's safe. Make sure you and Wagner are available.'

He waved Schmidt out.

Otto, having dismissed the auditor from his office, did so from his mind. He was excited – even exalted. He'd made a killing. Ambitious thoughts cartwheeled in his head. With the support of the local Nazi authorities, who twice in one day had remitted the agreement for renegotiation at terms less favourable to the Dortmunds, he'd got their business for 1.3 million. A ludicrous price! A splendid deal for the Party, and a splendid commission and accolade for Wertheim & Co! It might've been a million, except for his uncle's intervention ensuring that the price was set at one point three. Ready for signing today, the final documentation lay under his soft hands.

He'd demanded the lawyers work through the night. And by God, it's only the beginning! he thought.

Schmidt returned to his office. Otto's demand gleamed in his mind like a steel chisel. *Today!* With an effort he pushed it away and concentrated on the mandates just signed. From his desk he took the paper he needed, and carefully traced on it each signature. He put this aside, and taking the mandates to the typewriter used for confidential reports to the board, typed in the blanks, and put the forms in a leather pouch embossed with the name of Bankhaus Wertheim & Co AG. Crossing to the door, he listened. The corridor was steeped in silence. He hurried to the safe, took off his combination, and removed the large envelope with the remainder of the bonds. He put this in the pouch, too.

With a rigour which sought to detect any nuance of danger in the atmosphere, he listened again. Wertheims seemed to have stopped all engines, to be wallowing in a swell. Back to work. His throat was dry, his heart racing. Quickly he brought out different forms. Going over the tracings on the paper he'd taken from his desk, he traced the two signatures on a form. Taking up a pen he went over them. This time it took several attempts before he had two forms which satisfied him. Tensely he thought: Getting expert! He burnt the trial runs in his waste tin. On the typewriter, he tapped words into the blanks on these forms; each was Wertheim's instruction to its clearing banker to either release or accept for safekeeping a sealed envelope.

Five minutes later, the first instruction form, requesting the release of the sealed envelopes containing Wagner's and his combinations to the Party's safe, was on its way to their clearing bank via a messenger.

Wagner glanced up warily, as Schmidt entered his office and precisely closed the door.

'We might have a problem,' the auditor said quietly. 'Sometime today Herr Otto requires to withdraw bonds from the Party's safe.' Schmidt sat down, keeping his manner low-key. Wagner's nerves had to be respected. He observed that the deputy foreign manager had had a rough shave, and he smelt of body odour.

Wagner's eyes blinked in a nervous spasm. 'I'd expunge *might.*'

'I estimated we would have more time, but he's put together the Dortmund Aryanisation surprisingly quickly. I've been keeping a watch on its progress. I calculate he'll need up to 1,300,000, for the settlement.'

Wagner laughed mirthlessly, and tensely lit a cigarette. 'And there's 1,200,000 remaining in the unsealed packet in the safe – and a sealed packet of blank paper? This, my friend, is going to be one of those days.'

'May I suggest you keep your voice down?' the auditor said. He held the pouch he'd brought in his hands and regarded it, biting his lower lip. After a moment he said, 'Otto doesn't attend to detail. All he'll be interested in is having the amount he needs. If the bonds in the working stock are insufficient ... I'll add what's necessary, from here.' He tapped the pouch. 'It shouldn't take more than 100,000.'

'From here, Franz?'

Schmidt held open the Wertheim pouch holding the bonds to show his colleague the thick packet nestling there.

Wagner became even paler. 'And if it does?'

'Let's say I allow for 200,000, then.'

Wagner's face livened. 'Yes, Franz, it might save us. For the moment. Are you good at sleight of hand?' His hands were shaking, but his old mocking tone overrode the nerves.

'When we're in the vault I'll ask him how much he's

withdrawing. I'll take the unsealed envelope to the table, and count out the certificates in it. At that point, I'll need his attention diverted, while I amend any shortage.' Wagner clasped his hands under his chin and brooded, as though adjudicating on a recommended chain of book entries. Schmidt continued, 'Could *you* arrange the diversion?'

Wagner brought a hand to the cigarette, and exhaled. 'I'll have to, won't I? Perhaps if I stand on my head?' He grimaced at the ceiling.

'If we can create enough time for you to complete the arrangements in Zurich all will be well.'

Wagner watched Schmidt. Precisely how all would be well wasn't yet clear to him. Sooner rather than later the theft of the bonds would come to light. The trickery Schmidt was now proposing would only bridge the gap in the short term. After that? Franz hadn't revealed the innermost workings of his plan. These days his friend seemed absolutely certain of his destination. For his own part, it was sink or swim. For years he'd been too carelessly living his life on that basis … But it was time for him to know more. 'My friend, at the risk of stating the obvious, the time will arrive – assuming we survive till then – when the shortage is going to come to light. How does your brilliant plan cover that?'

Schmidt regarded his colleague patiently. 'I'm coming to that, Heinrich.' He reopened the pouch and laid the Swiss Bank mandates, signed by Dietrich and Otto, on the table.

Wagner examined them and gazed at the auditor, his eyes widening. They were for accounts in Dietrich's and Otto's own names. '*Christ,*' he breathed. '*What's this?*'

Schmidt said, 'You'll set up two accounts – one each in the *personal* names of these two.'

Wagner was silent. In a choked voice he said, 'You understand that their names'll vanish behind the numbers of their secret accounts?'

'Yes, Heinrich. In theory. When the Gestapo starts delving into it with their Swiss banking contacts what do you think will happen?'

Wagner's gaze was fixed on the mandates. Some Swiss were very sympathetic to the Third Reich. A lot of profitable business was being done, with much more in the offing. He said, 'They'll spill the beans.'

Schmidt nodded. 'So that's your job. You should apportion the bonds between each account. Is it clear, Heinrich?'

'Very clear. And, when the day comes to open that packet of blank paper ...?'

'The cupboard'll be empty. But who'll have emptied it? There are other arrangements in train which will point quite clearly to —'

'*My God!*' Wagner was stunned as he finally fully understood. He sucked in his breath. It was an act of revenge and retribution worthy of their opponents.

Schmidt was watching him intently. 'It's them or us,' he said quietly. 'However, there is today's little complication to get over.' He reopened the pouch, replaced the mandates in it, and without removing the envelope slipped from it two of the 100,000 bonds. He put them in his breast pocket, closed the pouch, and pushed it across the desk. 'Everything's there, Heinrich ... No, not quite.'

He laid a large buff envelope on the desk. 'Here's my family matter. It's to go to my cousin in Zurich at this address —'

'Ah ... one could say, the more important of the two. In terms of life's big picture,' Wagner murmured. Each considered the *Salzburg cantatas*. 'I take the five o'clock express, assuming we survive the interlude in the vault, and assuming the Gestapo permits my departure, and I'm not searched. Those risks hang over us, my friend. Explaining this pouch would test even my professional ingenuity to the maximum.'

They both knew its contents were unexplainable.

A slow smile came to Schmidt's face. 'We're locked into this path, Heinrich. All we can do is keep cool heads, play the cards as they come to us.'

'A card-player, too, Franz?' Wagner's mouth had twisted in a grin. 'And I thought *I* was the gambler.' He needed his caustic humour as much as his cigarettes. At this moment, he really needed it.

There was a final matter to consider. A rather difficult and unpalatable one. Schmidt had had it under consideration but hadn't made progress with it. Last night he'd put it aside. Now he came to a decision.

'Heinrich, if we bring this off, the bank and the Gestapo will rigorously look into *how* the bonds actually reached Zurich ...'

Wagner, watching his friend, thought: At which time, I am going to be in the soup. In the past minutes, the problem had loomed up in his own mind. He nodded slowly, and reached for a fresh cigarette.

'It's a loose end to the plan which leaves you in a bad situation.' Schmidt's voice was apologetic. He said decisively, 'You must leave Germany. You appear to have connections in Paris – could you go directly there from Zurich?'

They regarded each other in silence. Wagner turned away in his chair and stared at the wall. He sucked a shred of tobacco off his lip. Abruptly, he turned back to face Schmidt. 'No. I will go to Paris, but I'll need to return here briefly. There are matters I must finalise.'

Schmidt frowned, considering this. 'You'll need to be quick. Very quick.'

Wagner grimaced. 'I know that. Now, a little surprise for *you*. In case I don't return from this stimulating mission.' He produced a small brass key. 'Our mutual dentist, Dr Bernstein, has stairs going up to his surgery – as you'll recall. Under those stairs, beneath the fourth floorboard from the door, quite cunningly fitted, is a metal box. In that box … but I don't need to tell you that … a fellow of your startling ingenuity would know what to do. Have you got that? I have another key, and hopefully, I'll be able to deal with it myself.'

Schmidt nodded, assessing his colleague. He put the key in his pocket. A fraction more of Wagner's political past had emerged into the light. Not past, *present*, he corrected himself. God forbid that it wouldn't sabotage their mission.

The two trusted servants of Wertheim & Co shook hands and exchanged a long look.

When Schmidt had gone, Wagner contemplated, sitting there quietly, his own life, which appeared to be in a state of deconstruction – and his doubtful future. He gazed around his room. He felt stale with cigarettes, sticky from the day's tension and work. A slight headache had begun and he massaged his temples with both hands. Yes. It'd be certain death to hang around here. The time had come. If he returned safely he'd do that job and take off for Paris immediately.

29

BACK AT HIS desk, Schmidt was now waiting on Otto. He turned to his in-tray, hesitated, and took up the envelope that had arrived at his home this morning. A Dresden law firm's name was printed on the flap. Postponing opening it wouldn't delay the issue. He slit it neatly, and gazed at the papers. *Whereas Frau Helga Katharina Schmidt and Herr Franz Frederick Schmidt* … He replaced the divorce papers in the envelope, put it away, forced it from his mind.

Wagner was well respected in Zurich; he'd have no trouble opening the two accounts. The Gestapo, and customs at the frontier, were the dangerous factors. Wagner had been crossing the frontier for years on the bank's business, and had never been searched. They were counting on that, and he was counting on Wagner's nerves holding up.

He couldn't face his in-tray. His own nerves, which had been mainly quiescent, were no longer so. He looked at the phone, reassessing his plan step by step, his fitness to carry it out. A bead of perspiration formed on his upper lip. It all looked good but a complication could emerge without warning, and he thought of the enigma of von Streck.

The messenger's return from the clearing bank with the two sealed envelopes drove these thoughts from his mind. Wagner's, and his own, combinations to the Party's safe. Schmidt dismissed the man, broke the seals on the two envelopes, then resealed them with sealing wax in which he embossed the bank's seal, and inserted them in an envelope with the prepared lodgement form. The clearing bank's records were going to show: withdrawn am, re-lodged pm, this day, order of Directors Otto Wertheim and Frederick Dietrich.

§ § §

Herr Wertheim watched the young Amazon as she entered the inner sanctum, his eyes glinting with amusement. Such an intense, nervous young woman but quite capable, and definitely she had an earthy sexuality. She reminded him of his youth: of the cornfields in her native Bavaria in which the bare-footed, brown-skinned, muscular women swung their scythes, and their abundant hips. If only he were ten years younger! As he'd been when Lilli had arrived. He'd give a lot to relive those days. Though with his dicky heart, it would be living even more adventurously.

He dictated his letter. When he'd finished he said with his urbane consideration, 'I trust you're finding your way around our bank, fräulein, and settling in happily?'

'Oh yes, Herr Director-General, thank you.'

Her eyes, as blue and blank as a mid-summer sky, met his with a kind of counterfeit vacuity which he found amusing – and enchanting. As he watched her go out, the amusement moved from his eyes to his pale lips. It had occurred to him that she could easily have been the model for the statuesque woman of Commerce on his wall.

Otto's rapid consummation of the Dortmund project had been a surprise. The family's experience was that not much could be trusted in matters where Otto was involved. Too many promising starts had finished in tears. Still, on this occasion, aided by the Nazi authorities, he'd confounded his critics.

The G-D glanced down at a paper on his desk. Otto, unusually, was much in his mind this morning. He'd submitted a new target: a moderate-sized, profitable Jewish engineering concern, established for fifty years. Its owners had been keeping the lowest of profiles. But these Jewish businesses were doomed; in economic terms, an unsound strategy: the nation's commercial structure was being gutted, and unbalanced. As for ethics ... Herr Wertheim shrugged, and let the tortoiseshell-framed pince-nez fall into his hand; his gaze became abstracted. Pneumonia. Poor Lilli. He'd never known what was behind those luminous eyes; not even in the height of passion. Now, he never would. He couldn't open a file without feeling her presence rise up at him, catching a whiff of her fragrance, hearing her teasing him. So sad that it would fade. He'd written a letter of condolence to her father. He remembered the huge, silent man.

As for Dietrich ... Herr Wertheim tightened his lips. He looked up at the wall, into the unfaltering omniscient gaze. It was clear for an instant, then seemed to jump out of focus. Surprised, he rubbed his eyes.

§ § §

'You're looking a little tense, my friend,' Schmidt said in a quiet, reassuring tone to Wagner as they met in the vault.

'That is an accurate reading of my feelings,' his colleague said tersely. 'I'm not partial to any kind of waiting. As for risking my life –'

'Shush! You'll soon be on your way to Zurich.' Schmidt adjusted the position of the folder tucked under his left arm, and glanced sharply towards the door. *Those* footsteps! *Those* shoes!

'Good morning again, Herr Auditor!'

Dietrich loped into the chamber. Behind him, out of breath with keeping up, wheezed Otto.

The Nazi clapped his hands, setting up an ear-splitting reverberation in the vault. 'Well, well. This is very satisfactory. The Party's business is fairly humming along in the capable hands of Wertheims – and Herr Otto. All ready?'

Schmidt and Wagner had been converted to statues. Respectful, subservient statues. Otto assumed this as he swaggered towards the safe, a self-satisfied grin flickering on his face. Dietrich paused, sensing an atmosphere. He smiled at Schmidt, then frowned as his eyes alighted on Wagner. 'Son-of-a-bitch, this place's an ice box. Come on, let's do it, and get out.'

Otto addressed the safe first. He encountered his usual problem. His grin disappeared. After the third failure, Dietrich came to peer curiously over his shoulder. 'Are your fingers cold, Otto?' He turned his head, grinned at Schmidt. Otto flushed, muttered something, squared himself up for the fourth attempt and was successful. Wagner quickly took off his.

'*Come on*, Schmidt,' Otto said impatiently, as though the auditor was the one holding them up.

'You bankers love your little rituals, don't you,' Dietrich said.

'Yes, we do,' Schmidt agreed silently, 'though "love" is hardly the word.' He took off his combination, swung open the door, and reached for the unsealed packet. His heart was thumping. 'What value should I mark out of the register, Herr Otto?'

'One million, four hundred thousand.'

The auditor took the packet to the table, placed it beside the gilt-emblazoned register, laid his folder close to hand, sat down, put on a thumb-stall, and began to count off the certificates. Mentally he awarded Wagner an accolade: for his caution about the sum required. His throat felt tight and dry. His fingers numb.

Dietrich moved to stand behind him. It was the Nazi's obsession to stand close to people, to breathe in every odour, absorb every nuance of their condition. Schmidt felt it like a poised dagger, but he kept his face impassive. Wagner would have to excel himself.

Otto, alongside Wagner, disdainfully ignored the deputy foreign manager. This was old history; their recent evening encounter in the corridor had left no record in his memory. The faint rhythmic riffling of the thick security paper, the young director's breathing labouring in his over-ripe body, the squeak of Dietrich's shining new shoes, were the sum of sounds in the vault. The uncounted bonds dwindled under Schmidt's fingers.

'Herr Otto, you're a man of the world. Have *you* ever seen anything like this?'

Wagner spoke in a marginally respectful voice. He took two large photographs from his breast pocket; abruptly, he flourished one before the young director's face with the gesture of an illusionist.

Suspiciously, Otto took it; he peered at it, became seriously engaged; a high-pitched laugh erupted from him, turned throaty. This timbre of laugh, normally only heard by his late-night companions, was like pressure being slowly released from a valve.

'By God!' he spluttered, '*Look*-at-the-size-of-it! And she's going to get it *all* − right up to the balls!'

'And *this* one?' Wagner said.

Otto grabbed it. He roared with excited laughter. 'And by God she's taken it! To the last centimetre! But look at her *face!*'

He turned impulsively, eagerly, to Dietrich, who was observing this side-play with irritation. 'You must see this, Frederick,' he gasped.

Reluctantly the Nazi left his position behind Schmidt. He

examined each photograph for a long moment. He turned to Wagner and surveyed him with a threatening contempt. 'Utter filth!'

'It's the size of a torpedo!' Otto couldn't help himself; he wiped his eyes.

'Herr Otto!' Dietrich snarled.

Deflated, Otto subsided into a few titters, wiped his eyes again, his wet lips with the back of his hand. 'You have to admit, Frederick —' he began, but desisted at the Nazi's furious glance.

As a signal to Wagner, Schmidt dropped the register with a thump on the table. He produced a Wertheim pouch from a drawer and laid it beside the pile of bonds.

'Please count off the amount, Herr Otto, sign where I've bracketed the releases in the register.'

Trying to hold down his mirth, Otto scrawled his signature a couple of times. Wagner replaced the photographs in his breast pocket.

A few minutes later, crestfallen Otto, carrying the pouch, went up the stairs with a silent Dietrich. He'd aggressively twirled his combination: a rearguard act attempting to regain his dignity, reimpose his authority over that dumb steel box, and his subordinates. On the way out he whispered back to Wagner 'Copies?', then pushed on ahead.

'That's that,' Schmidt said quietly as they followed. 'Thank you, Heinrich.'

Wagner let his breath out in a rush. 'That Nazi might feel cold, I'm wet through. Thank God our fat director didn't check the numbers against the register.'

'Herr Otto's not a man for detail,' Schmidt repeated.

Wagner laughed tensely. 'No? Would you like to see those photographs?'

30

WAGNER WATCHED the outer suburbs slide past as the train began its journey to the south. Alone in a first-class compartment he sat quite still, recovering. The nerves which had locked up his throat as he'd walked past the Gestapo at the barrier were loosening their grip. He shifted his shoulders, and felt a drench of perspiration in his armpits. The dark world beyond the carriage seemed to be mocking his discomfiture. He gazed back at it, and sucked a jube to ease his throat.

Franz's objectives were becoming more devious, more complex, by the day; Wagner sensed that they were continuously expanding. He sucked away, and continued to gaze at the night. In an eye-blink, apartment buildings patchworked with lighted windows quick-marched out of the darkness, then, like battalions on parade falling out by numbers, wheeled one by one back into blackness. Flick–flick–flick. Gone. Like his life ... The chance of marriage, children, had passed him by. Once he'd been hopeful about that; no longer.

He lit a cigarette and settled back, controlling his tension. The second movement of Mozart's Piano Concerto 23 came drifting into his head, to his aid. But insistently, the image of the Nazi, von Streck, at the beerhall, shadowed it. At that meeting, it'd seemed that von Streck knew both his past and his present. If it was so, why hadn't the Nazi had him arrested?

The music had faded away; Wagner mopped his brow with a handkerchief.

Six fifteen pm. They were burrowing into the darkness, well set for the Swiss frontier, a diligent engineer hooting away to dispel unseen perils. Grits whirled in, though the window was closed. He brushed them off his overcoat.

Six twenty pm. In the corridor, two men in black leather coats swayed past like drunks; he didn't turn his head, but from the corner of his eye caught the blur of faces peering at him. His pulse raced. He'd company. Foolish to have thought otherwise. But why hadn't they stopped him at the station? Were they planning to trail him all the way to Zurich? 'Keep calm, Wagner.' He was perspiring even more but the coat, with its special pockets, stayed on. He glanced at his watch again: one hour to the frontier.

§ § §

Schmidt's thoughts were with Wagner as the taxi drove into the new estate. Now – he shook his head, took a deep breath, preparing himself. The Nazi was pacing the foyer. 'Franz! There you are!' Exuberantly, with a seeming relief, he smacked his hands together. 'I didn't know whether you could find your way to the outskirts. You're such an inner-city dweller! But, as reliable as ever.'

Schmidt bowed slightly. The taxi driver'd had no trouble.

Dietrich wore a white smoking jacket which harmonised brilliantly with the blond-wooded, white-walled entrance hall into which he led the auditor. With his blond hair, his milky face – in this blondish ambience – the Nazi, tonight, plainly had stepped out of his on-duty character.

Swaying tulips etched upon double doors of frosted glass greeted Schmidt. He stepped through these. The Nazi threw his big hand expansively at it all, and beamed his yellow grin. 'Different from the Wertheim morgue, eh?' Ablaze with electric light, the flat was more Schmidt's idea of a morgue than the Wertheim building. 'Come, take off your coat, sit down on this lounge. Real comfort. You must have champagne!'

His energy had a sharply nervous edge; that pacing of the foyer, the fumbling as he uncorked the bottle, the nervy grin at the significant *pop*. Yes, a different Dietrich. In the lounge, feeling suspended rather than seated, Schmidt watched the new version as carefully as the old. Many times he'd asked himself why the Nazi had interceded to save him from the Gestapo. His pragmatic mind couldn't quite accept it. And why was he invited here tonight? He took the foaming glass. The Nazi raised his own high, and, narrowing his eyes, fixed it with a searching blue gaze.

'Superb! We're quite alone tonight, Franz. My servant's prepared an excellent meal which requires only a little heating. You will enjoy! To *our* partnership at Bankhaus Wertheim & Co AG!'

Politely, Schmidt raised his glass and they clinked. The walls of the flat had no artwork. Dietrich, intent on his every expression, interpreted the look.

'Aha! No decadent *Eye* on these walls, Franz. Uncluttered − like my mind.' He grinned in mock self-effacement. 'When I can afford it, a single, fine painting. Something to the Fuehrer's taste.' Another grin. He perched on the edge of a chair, swung his thick leg to and fro. With utmost gravity, he said suddenly, 'My friend, you have your problems, I read it in your face.'

Schmidt sipped champagne. Which direction was the Nazi's mind going in now? Dietrich's mood had turned around completely. Here was seriousness and concern. That *anything* was apparent on his face was alarming.

'Divorce must be painful for a person of your sensitivity.'

'It is, Herr Dietrich. May I ask how you know of it?'

'Never mind, my friend. Nonetheless, a new start, isn't it?'

Schmidt admitted the possibility.

'And Franz, when we're off duty you must call me Frederick.'

'Thank you.'

Dietrich leapt from the chair, and hurried out. 'Now, dinner will be served.'

They ate Steak Diane with duchess potatoes and sauerkraut. The Nazi was attentive with the wine from a special estate on the Rhine – a gift, he said, from the city's Gauleiter, with whom he claimed intimacy. In another quicksilver change, he'd become fascinated by his guest's adolescence. Solemnly Schmidt parted with an edited version of his youthful life.

Dietrich stretched his athletic body back in his chair and gazed intently at the small, handsome man. He felt his emotions rising, nearing the surface. The cautionary restraint in him was less oppressive. He'd still not determined whether, primarily, he was confronting a puzzle with dangerous undertones, or an enchanting interlude with the promise of memorability. He felt himself languishing in a heady atmosphere, less and less concerned about the answer to the conundrum. One had the power to tidy up a mistake.

'Wasn't it good? You're a very quiet man, Franz, and that's what I like.' He lowered his eyes. 'And, as I said, sensitive. We share this, my friend.'

Schmidt sipped the brilliant Rhine wine, visualising Wagner racing through the night towards Switzerland.

'Wagner! You and I are a world away from that vulgarian. You didn't see those photographs?'

Schmidt shook his head.

'I thought not. I'm glad you weren't exposed to that

filth. Wagner's days are numbered, you might like to know
that.' He raised his finger warningly at the auditor. 'And we
must have no sentiment *there*, Franz! But forget the traitorous
bastard. I'll put on an Offenbach record, and we'll have more
champagne with our dessert.'

Traitorous! Schmidt was staggered. What was going on
with Wagner – and, was it in danger of short-circuiting the
plan? *He was still active in the outlawed Social Democrats.* It must
be that. But doing what? The foreign manager's instructions
about the box hidden under Bernstein's stairs slipped into his
mind.

He glanced at Dietrich. Fortunately the Nazi was smiling and gazing into space. Schmidt felt his face must have
showed everything in the past moments. Smoothly the Nazi
rose and crossed the room to a cabinet. He put a record on a
turntable. As the music began Schmidt, in his mind, was back
at the Wertheim concert, walking to Lilli's flat, hearing her
restrained breathing in the darkness.

'Offenbach was born in Berlin, you know,' the Nazi
announced. 'Some people, incorrectly, consider him French.
Of course he was a Jew, but about some things we should be
broad-minded. I got that from Herr Wertheim.' He grinned.

Dietrich ate his dessert and watched his guest. He felt his
heart thudding, his breathing becoming constricted. Steady-
ing his voice he said slowly: 'You'll have a free hand now in
joining the Party. However, we must wait for things to cool
down. Timing in all our endeavours is critical.' He smiled, and
stood up. 'You'll have noticed the *wonderful* central heating. I'm
going to take off my jacket, and you will too. Then we will sit
down, and relax. Absolutely!'

The pressure was building to a crescendo. He must have
that tight, beautiful arse tonight – or die.

Suddenly Schmidt understood. *Good God!* Abruptly, he
picked up his adolescent reminiscences: 'In '28, I went on a

camping trip to Weisenbaden ...'

'Uhuh.'

The Nazi stretched again, exuding his physical power. Schmidt felt he was treading water against a strong current, waiting for the turn of the tide. Dietrich, now beside him on the lounge, relishing the last of his champagne, the music, emitted gusty sighs of lustful anticipation. Schmidt was now receiving that as clear as a bell on midnight air. He doubted if the man selected targets at random, so what mysterious signals had he been giving out? Whatever they were, the Nazi's passion was about to erupt like a volcano.

He sipped the wine, inwardly amazed. Never in his life had he been in this situation, even imagined it. What else could he throw in to delay the issue? A tasty piece of information from the bank? But he knew the Nazi was no longer listening. Dietrich seized the champagne bottle, and emptied the last of it into their glasses. He insisted on them clinking. What a bizarre mixture the Nazi was, and how ridiculous he seemed at this moment. Roehm and half the SA leadership had been homosexuals, as reported in 1934 after their murders. Nothing much had been made of it, publicly at least, before that. But these days he was running a big risk. If Wagner got through, much bigger than he could ever have imagined.

A chill entered Schmidt. The Nazi was far from naive. It was hard to take this at face value. Could it be he was playing a game of deception which matched his own; running deep and silent. He was indisputably the tormenting type; was he paying out rope? Grimly, Schmidt stared across the room at the cavorting tulips. Should he get up and walk around?

Dietrich put down his champagne glass with deliberation. As fast as a snake striking, his fingers went to Schmidt's face, and lightly traced across his cheek.

'You have beautiful skin, Franz.'

His hand dropped abruptly to the auditor's chest, dexterously opened his shirt-front and began to caress his breast, tease at his nipple. Schmidt had turned to stone. Dietrich began to emit steady gasps; his eyes had dilated, the scent of champagne suffused the air. He moved his heavy body emphatically closer on the lounge. The weight, heat, of his thigh was overbearing to Schmidt.

'By God!' The Nazi groaned.

Schmidt felt paralysed. If this was a subterfuge, some plan of entrapment, the Nazi was the best actor in the Reich.

The thick lips came at Schmidt's mouth. Simultaneously the muscular arms clamped an unbreakable encirclement around his body. The speed and force engulfed Schmidt. The yellow teeth clashed with his, a vigorous tongue came forcing its way into his mouth. He was driven back in the lounge. Beyond his shock he was aware that the Nazi was tearing at his own flies. Schmidt pulled his mouth away, and struggled with sudden desperate energy in the powerful arms. The Nazi's head whipped back as though he'd touched hot metal, his grip loosened.

'Franz! What's wrong?'

Schmidt found himself free, staggered to his feet. He had to gasp out his breath. He reeled a few paces, his mind racing. 'A shock ... Frederick. Total shock! The first time.'

The Nazi stared at him in amazement, then, visibly reassembling his composure, straightened his position on the revered lounge, and regarded the small man searchingly. As though a button had been pushed, the hard planes of his face softened. He became magisterial. He devoured the auditor with an expression of proprietorship.

'Oh my God! Of course! My dear friend. I've been *far* too impetuous. I do understand. Your sensitivity! How delightful! The first time is such an experience for us all. I could feel your heart beating!'

He stood up, too, adjusting his clothing, brushing down his hair with his broad hand, while Schmidt marvelled. He was back under control, the mocking smile again moulded on his features.

'Never mind! The virgin shouldn't be pressed on the first occasion, must be humoured. On the second, such a dispensation can't be granted — but then neither is it wished!'

Dazedly Schmidt thought: Who's he picked up that piece of wisdom from?

The Nazi's eyes had narrowed. 'But remember Franz, you're under my protection. That's something I could take back like this.' The snap of his big fingers sounded in the room.

Fifteen minutes later Schmidt drove away. He'd been ordered to return for drinks at the weekend. By then, one way or the other, his and Dietrich's worlds would have rotated into other orbits.

The taxi driver half-turned as Schmidt gave a strange laugh. The auditor was startled to discover that the incident had left *him* with an erection. It all seemed like another dose of comic opera. He wished he could wash his mouth out.

31

WAGNER FELT TENSION crawling up his back. He waited on the platform as the immigration and customs queue crept forward. He was tense, but in command of himself. Each time he went abroad the Reich officials were more painstaking, though he'd never even had a suitcase opened. His official business, the letter of recommendation he carried from the Reichsbank, had always got him through. Tonight they must be searching many. He held his passport ready, felt the subtle drag in the low inside pockets of his heavy overcoat; not hidden pockets, although, unusually positioned. He stamped his feet, trying to work up some warmth, and breathed deeply.

The slim, elegant woman in front of him wore a silver fox fur around her shoulders. He took in her perfume with the frosty air. Her face turned to Wagner, but the brown eyes in the beautiful face didn't see him. Over her shoulder, the fox's amber-coloured glass eyes gleamed in the electric light, seemed to see into his soul. Pointed towards Switzerland in a cloud of steam, the engine hissed at the night. The two Gestapo men on the train had not reappeared. Shuffling forward, a faint hope aroused, he entered the station building.

They stood alone against a white wall. Their eyes were only for him. *Christ!* He kept his own gaze on the move. In front of him, the elegant woman was having her problems with a seated official; a terse exchange was in progress. Reluctantly, she opened her handbag, placed pieces of jewellery on the table one by one, as though saying farewell to each. A policeman took her by the arm to a room at the side, and a female official followed them in, pulling on a rubber glove.

Having dealt with Jewish wealth and beauty, the seated official now scrutinised Wagner's face, his passport photograph. Taking his time, he read the passport from cover to cover. He referred to a list.

'What is your business in Zurich, mein herr?'

'Banking business. I'm the deputy foreign manager for my bank. I'm visiting our correspondent banks.'

Wagner held out the letter of recommendation from the Reichsbank. The official took it, read it. Wagner waited, hatless, his fair hair gleaming in the blaze of electric light, his face blank, his attitude formal and patient. He needed a haircut badly. He wished he'd spruced himself up. Enhanced his respectability. The official laid the letter aside.

'I see. Step over to that table, please, and open your suitcase – and your attaché case.'

Wagner moved aside from the queue. His heart had begun to thump in his chest. Well, Franz, here we are. On the edge of the abyss. But Wagner! You have *never* been searched! You are *not* a person who will be searched!

A woman's scream came from the room where his elegant predecessor had been taken. *'You are hurting me!'* Not an elegant sound. The voice quivering with pain and outrage had sundered the sniffling, boot-scraping sounds in the hall. The long queue of regulated faces jerked in that direction as though yanked on strings, then anxiously resumed their fixed gazes. An incident of the Third Reich. And here's another in the making, Wagner thought, as he thumped his bags carelessly on the table; a dull fatalism was being released into his system.

The uniformed official's fingers went through the change

of clothing, then read Wagner's routine banking papers with
a studied thoroughness, as though awaiting a confessional
outburst. The two Gestapo men had shifted along the wall,
and stood behind the official. All quiet now from the other
room. At the bottom of the case the official found the buff
envelope. He held it up, looked at it, at Wagner. He picked up
a dagger, weighed it in his hand, looked again at the banker.
Slit it open.

The music for Mozart's Violin Concerto No. 5 was shaken
out on to the table. The official stared at it, turned the pages in
a mildly puzzled way. Was this banker going to Zurich to play
the violin? – his expression said.

'What is this?'

'I'm an amateur musician. I'm taking the music to friends
in Zurich. There may be a little time to play.'

The official pursed his lips, as though considering how a
man on official business, in the service of his bank, the Third
Reich, would have time to play the violin.

Wagner waited. Out of the corner of his eye he could see
the Gestapo agents still in position, watching and waiting. As
he was …

The official still brooded on Wagner's face: his mind
stuck on an image of the banker playing the violin at the
Swiss banks. Abruptly, he turned over a page – and stopped.
He stared at the first loose-leaf manuscript sheet for a long
moment. He lifted his eyes to Wagner's.

'And what, mein herr, is *this?*' Accusation and shock
vibrated in his voice.

Wagner stared at him, mesmerised. Had he run into a
musicologist? The expression on the official's face suggested he
understood what he held in his hands. Wagner said tensely, 'My
friend, I think you know very well what it is.'

The official, seeming hardly to take this in, sat down
behind the table. He extracted Bach's manuscript sheet by

sheet from behind the violin concerto sheets, scrutinising each as he did. The queue behind Wagner fidgeted down its length.

'Don't call me "my friend", mein herr. I'm not your friend — and please answer my question.'

Had the man expected to find something else — was he thrown off balance by what he had found? The thought raced through Wagner's mind.

'I did not mean to be familiar, mein herr. It's an unpublished manuscript which has been in my family for many generations ... I inherited it from my parents.'

'Presuming this is true, why are you taking it to Zurich?'

'For years I've promised to bring it to show friends who are music-lovers.'

Wagner saw that the official was regarding him with total disbelief.

'This is part of our German heritage. The export of such works of art is a criminal offence.'

'With respect, mein herr, it's not an export. When I return in two days, I intend to bring the manuscript back with me. After all, it's a family heirloom ...' His throat had almost dried up. Yet, his Calvinistic convictions were resurfacing: it was all predestined.

'I will carry out a body-search,' the official said, his pale eyes now assessing Wagner's person. 'Please step this way.' Wagner hesitated. The immigration official said, sharply: 'Mein herr! *This way.*'

Wagner thought: *Well, Franz, what is the answer?* Suddenly he felt much duller. A kind of shutdown. He became aware of a black-uniformed SS officer stalking across the hall. Coming this way ...

Wagner felt a prickling on his back. The SS man was still coming — for him? The immigration official had not seen him yet, he was glowering at Wagner. *'Mein herr!'*

The SS man was tapping the immigration official on the

shoulder, surprising him out of his anger, taking him aside, speaking in his ear, ignoring Wagner. Something made Wagner look back along the SS man's route. His heart stopped. A short, hugely broad man in a homburg and an astrakhan-collared overcoat stood in a doorway, smoking a large cigar held in a black, leather-gloved hand. Herr von Streck of the beerhall! Wagner blinked in his amazement; in that instant the Nazi vanished.

The official was remonstrating with the officer, gesturing at the banker. The SS man leaned forward, stared into the man's eyes, and snarled words. The official stiffened to attention, like a person whose world was about to collapse. Wagner could go. Just waved out. With a thrill of deliverance, he saw that the Gestapo had vanished. The rear wall was as white and blank as an empty page. He carried his bags along the platform to rejoin the train.

Thirty minutes later, gazing into the Swiss night, indistinguishable from the German, he addressed this latest puzzle. His hands were shaking. Delayed shock. He could hardly light a cigarette. God, he was dying for a beer. Von Streck – inexplicably present – an angel of mercy in an astrakhan coat, smoking a cigar? A mystery. Whatever its implications, it'd allowed him to continue with the next stage of Franz's plan. And another's? This von Strech? That was something fresh to wonder at but suddenly he felt enlivened – able to order his thoughts to the task ahead.

One thing was indisputable. Bach's manuscript had saved him. Another minute or two and they would've had the contents of those two inside pockets out on the table. No man could've saved him then.

§ § §

Senior Detective Dressler drove the small black car into the forest of tower blocks. As his great hands turned the steering wheel, the chrome bird on the bonnet curved a seeming flight-path against a backdrop of brilliantly white façades.

He parked the car, and extricated himself from it with extreme difficulty; his head came within centimetres of its roof, and jammed behind the steering wheel, his knees were hard against its dashboard; he had to lever himself in and out with his arms, and did so now accompanied by stentorian breathing. He accepted this hardship stoically: Beggars couldn't be choosers.

When the door buzzer sounded, Dietrich, with a leaping heart, thought Franz had changed his mind. He sprinted to the door and flung it open. He was startled, then nonplussed, to find a solemn giant of a man standing there.

'Yes?' he said, frowning.

'Herr Dietrich?'

'Yes. Who are you?'

'I think I should come in to explain that.' Dressler placed a hand as big as a dinner plate flat on the Nazi's white shirt front, and without effort or show, pushed him back into the room. It was many years since anyone had laid a hand on Dietrich. Amazed, his face sagging, he went back without resistance. In the centre of his living room, the irresistible pressure on his chest was removed. His mouth agape, the Nazi stared up at the intruder's serious face, the luxuriant moustache. Somehow the man had managed to swing the door shut as he'd advanced through it. What did he have here, a thief – a madman?

As if a switch had been pulled, his face flooded with colour. In the absence of further aggression from the giant, who appeared to be methodically inspecting his every facial pore, anger flared in the Nazi. Good God! He wouldn't put up with this!

'Mein herr! If you know what's good for you, you will

leave this instant. Do you understand? You fool! I'm a captain in the SS!'

'Be quiet,' Dressler said, 'or I'll kill you now.' With surprising speed his hand shot out again, this time to shove the Nazi backwards into the lounge.

A deadly chill invaded Dietrich. He struggled to sit up. He was strong, athletic, but utterly powerless against this human mountain. His brain, slightly dulled by the champagne and wine, was swiftly shaking off its torpor. It came to him that anger and threats were inappropriate responses: that he was in deadly danger. Only his wits could save him. His Luger was in the top drawer of his desk four metres away. He took a breath and smelled menthol.

'Mein herr, I'm sure this is a mistake – but, how do you think I can help you?'

'You can't help me,' Dressler said dolorously. 'But you will answer my questions.'

The Nazi grimaced, nervously. 'Of course – if I can. I must have a cigarette.' He reached into his pocket and drew forth the packet, matches, and lit up. 'Now, I'm ready.'

'My name is Dressler. Senior Detective Klaus Dressler of the Municipal Police. Father of Fräulein Lilli Dressler, recently deceased, formerly secretary to General-Director Herr Wertheim, of Bankhaus Wertheim & Co.' He recited this with a deadly quiet formality, as though giving evidence to the court on an aggravated burglary charge – the most serious offence he usually dealt with. 'Doubtless, you remember her.'

Dietrich's face had changed again, drastically; the skin seemed to have shrunk against his cheekbones. But the puzzle was solved. He stared at the detective, his mind churning, grasping for a way out.

'Yes ...' Dressler said, nodding his head, confirming the Nazi's reaction. 'I wish to follow the workings of your mind – in the matter of my daughter. I know the criminal mind. But the *petty* category. It hasn't been my lot to come up against the more advanced type. Let alone a monster. So talk. And when you've satisfied me, I'll put a bullet through your brain. Grant you an easy death.'

In an afterthought, he reached inside his overcoat, and brought out his pistol. He worked the action, then dropped his arm to hang loosely by his side; the blue-metalled weapon had vanished into his fist as if by sleight of hand.

Dietrich's stomach had turned to water, moisture had pricked out on his brow, was running down his ribs from his armpits. This *infernal* central heating! For the second time that night, he sought to steady his voice. There was a key to every situation. To this deranged man's mind. The pragmatic lawyer in him was surfacing, the professionalism on which he'd built his life.

Into the silence, he said, 'I regret your daughter's death. A tragic outcome ... that wasn't my intention or wish. Surely, mein herr, you understand the situation? You're familiar with the laws of the Reich. Since 1934 it has been a criminal offence for her to be working at the bank. It couldn't be permitted to continue. Even if I'd not done my duty, in a short time others would have. You're a policeman – an upholder of our laws – an enforcer of them, I'm sure, without fear or favour. They *are* the laws and our duty as responsible, patriotic officials is quite clear. At this moment I look into my conscience, can't see any other way to act than I did. At your police station, you get your instructions, you do your job. We in the Party are no different. I did my duty – for the Fuehrer, for the nation. I regret the consequences, I could not foresee them.' He stopped abruptly, gasping for breath.

'The consequences? My daughter's death.'

Dressler's eyes had drooped as he'd listened to the speech, as if it both wearied and disgusted him. The steel splinter in his brain was angry tonight. The pain came in reddish waves, and the glaring light in this white hell of an apartment had joined forces with that sliver. The damned agony of it! He shook his head. What did he have here? The reasonable, yet unmerciful man? The ambitious man? The fanatic? But a deliberate, pre-meditating killer?

Sadly, Dressler, looking at the Nazi's tense face, knew what he believed in his heart. This type had broken out like an epidemic. Too many, for bullets to be a vaccine.

Dietrich, watching the detective, was calculating fever-ishly. 'If you kill me, you'll be murdering an official who did his duty, who'd only a tenuous responsibility for your daughter's death. Also, you'll be signing your own death warrant.' Drops of sweat from his face fell on his knees. As he uttered it, he realised the threat might be a mistake.

I've done that, anyway, the detective thought. This man was only slightly more brainwashed than the German masses. So many in the same boat. Possibly, he actually believed all the propaganda garbage. Felt himself a loyal German. Loved the Fuehrer. Should a man like himself who'd fought in the Great War, *really* given all that he had to give for the nation, bring himself down to the level of such a fool? Criminal, or not?

He said, soberly, 'You're a lucky man, for the moment. I don't trust you, or believe you. The lie is there hidden away. But you just might be a big enough fool to believe it.'

He brought the pistol up slowly, and holstered it. Then he turned and walked heavily but silently from the apartment. As he came out to the night air the whistling began in his throat, his nose, deep down in his lungs.

Dietrich sat absolutely still. For a long time he did not, could not, move a muscle. In 1934 he'd run a marathon in Munich, and had been as helpless as a baby after it. He was that way now. Eventually, he got to his feet and went to the phone, on legs that could hardly be trusted.

Later, still drained, he stood at the window facing the

other apartment blocks. In this light-blasted enclave night seemed to be perennially held at bay. Behind him the dirty dishes and glasses of the dinner party remained from the evening's first act; the smell of menthol, of his own fear, from the second. A *deeply* unsatisfactory evening; not at all what he'd planned. Yet, there was something to be salvaged. And by God, he'd see that it was!

32

FTER MIDNIGHT DRESSLER arrived at his block of flats and climbed the three exhausting flights of brass-rodded stairs, with their threadbare carpet. Halfway up, he gasped, 'Dressler! ... last time ... up the killer stairs.'

He'd made it home. Turning on the light he felt pleased that he had, pleased to be back in his small bastion. A few matters remained to be attended to. But what an effort! Shoulders leaning against the door, he gasped in air, whistled it out. *Murderous* stairs. Each time he returned from duty at evening or dawn, he thought his lungs were finished – though he'd been thinking it for eighteen years.

The flat seemed as frigid as the street and he kept his overcoat on, but took his hat off. The tiny kitchen which he entered, like his car, and his cubbyhole at the police station, fitted him as tightly. He, a giant, lived his life in a midget's environment; it'd never occurred to him.

He measured out and heated coffee on the gas burner, and watched it percolate. He carried a cup to his desk in the living room, smelt it, drank some, and felt warmth spread in his stomach. Two photographed faces in cheap frames watched him. He studied them for several minutes as though memorising every detail, then his giant fingers fumbled the pictures from the frames. Reverently, he placed them in the wastepaper basket, lit a match and set them alight. From a cold inner place, he watched them brown, curl, become ashes.

He opened a drawer, found his bank passbook and a withdrawal slip, took up his fountain pen, laboriously completed the slip for 4,000 marks – almost the balance – signed it, tucked it in the book and put it in his pocket. Hopefully, time for a trip upstairs. He looked at his watch: 12.32 am. From another drawer, he lifted a small official-looking box and tipped into the palm of his hand the Iron Cross First Class. In his hand, it looked like a miniature of the medal but was not. He rose from his chair, went to the window, opened it wide, phlegmatically accepting the icy blast, and threw the medal in a casual underhand throw across the rooftops. He heard it clank on tiles, listened to it slide until the sound ended. He closed the window. One day, some roof-climbing plumber would get a surprise.

He regarded the room: all that came back to him was the closed-up odour, a widower's silence, and the atmosphere of a plain and frugal life. He said, 'Not much to attend to, Dressler. Not much needed to complete it. Though, it's been a long journey.'

He'd wanted to hear the sound of his voice.

They'd not sent Lilli's ashes. Through his overcoat he patted the passbook. Now was the time to go upstairs to his neighbour …

A car crept into the street, lights off; its engine died, doors were shut quietly – but not quietly enough. He'd been listening for it, but so soon? A boot kicked a garbage can, and he nodded slowly. Gestapo. They were punctilious, if amateurish in their efforts; the police would've waited until dawn, at least, but what could be expected from a gang of convicted criminals and rejuvenated state political police? Previously, a warning phone call from a colleague might've come through, but not these days. Not for him.

He went back to his desk, took his pistol from its holster,

worked the action, laid it down, resumed his seat, his casual listening. He fell to dreaming. The outcome was certain, only the details were unclear, and not important. Gradually from the dim and far distance a dull resonance built in his eardrums: the muted, yet thunderous approach of the barrage creeping across no-man's-land, sending up great geysers of black earth. Soon, once more, hell would erupt all around him, but on a more human scale. Really, there was no comparison.

They took their time coming up the stairs, doubtless suffering that outlandish climb, and nervous of the general environment. He heard them labouring on the last flight. The pounding on the door came as a theatrical anti-climax. However, it would wake up the building.

Amateurs. He rose heavily and went to stand behind the door. Until this moment he'd not decided on a plan, but now, carelessly, he had one.

'What is it?' he said.

A silence. 'Open up! Geheime Staatspolizei!'

He waited. 'One moment, I'll get my dressing-gown.'

He did not move, but waited – as though he was back in the trenches awaiting the order to go over the top. The whistle blew in his head. He flung open the door, surged out. The two men in the midst of a whispered exchange received the pile-driving arms into their torsos, were launched into the air, became entangled in a flailing knot which landed halfway down that flight of the stairs with shuddering impact, somersaulted, kept going down.

A third man, on the landing, threw himself out of the way of the catastrophe hurtling down, brought up a pistol and fired twice. The second shot hit Dressler in the left shoulder. He flinched, and brought his own pistol out and up, aimed, and shot the man in the centre of the forehead. The dead agent fell back across his entangled colleagues, his eyes wide-open, his face exhibiting his final frantic miscalculation.

The gunshots were deafening and the stairwell reverberated from the concussions. Cautiously Dressler moved to the balustrade, and a fourth man fired several times at him from the hall, whining bullets off the walls, sending woodchips from the balustrade zinging. Where did they teach these men to shoot? With great concentration, the detective followed him with his gun barrel for a second or two. The man was now running back and forth in the hall like a panicked rat skittering across a barn. The senior detective squinted, squeezed off two shots, dropped this runner in his tracks, and watched him hammer out a frenetic tattoo with his heels.

The two on the landing below had untangled themselves, thrown off their dead colleague, and were getting out their weapons. One had a broken arm, Dressler noted. He was wearying of this; he shot them both.

He stared broodingly down at the shambles for a moment: an untidy heap of black leather, glimpses of white flesh, and emerging patches of blood, then went back into his flat, leaving the door open. One of those last shot was still moving, but it didn't interest him. Not a door had opened – even a crack. Quite understandable. The building seemed deserted but it wasn't, and everyone would be wide awake.

He returned to the kitchen to reheat the coffee. Then he sat in his chair behind the desk inherited from his father, laying his pistol down. He reached in his left pocket, and from the 'out' tray spilled a handful of brass bullets on his blotter. The blotter where he wrote his rare letters, and the odd report not done in a café with a black coffee standing at his elbow. His shoulder was becoming numb, a little blood was oozing through the overcoat's thick material. The next lot would come before too long, with a greater degree of preparation and forethought – if they could get their brains working. The pain glinted in his skull, not in his shoulder. He swallowed two pills. Coffee had become a main factor in his life, and he sipped this brew with dedication.

Five minutes of quiet, and meditation. Should've he killed Dietrich? The Nazi had been busy on the phone. No, he was quite comfortable with that decision. In the war, almost invariably, he'd seen cowards and malingerers, traitors and crooks, get their just deserts. In a world saturated with violence. A type of world that was coming back. In that respect, the wheel appeared to turn with certainty. All you had to be was patient. In his heavy, pragmatic way, he felt confident that the Nazi would get his. Herr Schmidt had come into his head: he stood in a street, his eye hanging out on his cheekbone. The detective wondered at the memory. Why hadn't he made that connection before? He shook his head slowly. The mind, and the memory, were strange. He'd been locked into his fear for Lilli, other matters had been passing him by. And it'd been years ago ...

Herr Dorf, his upstairs' neighbour, who was a conductor on the tramways and a veteran like himself, an ex-cavalryman, appeared in the doorway. Dressler had always respected the dexterity with which his neighbour, a largish man himself, moved on the building's steep stairs, and, went that extra flight. Doubtless, it was due to his experience with edgy horses and swaying tramcars. He was swathed in a dressing-gown.

'Is everything all right, Herr Dressler?'

Obviously, everything was not.

'Thank you, Herr Dorf. How is the cavalry this evening? Or, I should say, morning?'

His neighbour sadly eyed the spreading red patch. 'I don't complain. How is the infantry feeling?'

'Quite good, really. Certainly much better than those downstairs.'

He smiled, and Dorf reflected, with surprise, that it was the first time he'd ever seen the municipal detective do that. In the stairwell, the surviving Gestapo agent had begun to emit piteous groans.

'Could I call a doctor – for you?'

'No, thank you. But take this. I'll have no further need of it.'

Dressler took the passbook from his pocket. 'Go to the bank first thing in the morning. Withdraw the money, use it, with my best wishes. Your son's education …?'

Dressler, upright in his chair, offered his hand across the desk. 'Now … please return to your flat, and don't come out again on my account, on any account.'

The conductor shook his head sadly. 'These are bad times, Herr Dressler.'

'Yes,' Dressler agreed, 'bad times.'

33

HAD WAGNER got through? 'Has he?' he asked Helga's beloved Meissen coffee-pot. Each morning he used to talk to the coffee-pot for the amusement of Trudi. The attempt at levity did not alleviate the nervous tension that had settled in the pit of his stomach now. He wouldn't know until midday when Wagner was due to ring – unless bad news came earlier.

Seven thirty am. It was still almost dark. Schmidt stared out the window. His head felt a little heavy, though he'd been as careful with his intake of champagne, and wine, as Dietrich had permitted.

But last night seemed like a movie. Compared to his concern about the status of Wagner's mission, it was as past and petrified as the tulips on Dietrich's frosted glass doors. He'd had two dreams. The remembered essence of them was interweaved with his recall of the interlude with the Nazi. In the dark early-morning hours Trudi had come, soft and light as a breeze, through the flat to his bedside, laid her tiny hand on his, whispered: 'Papa.' That was all. The other: a bombastic explosion – big doors thrown open on a glittering assembly of the Nazi élite, a trumpet sounding, and he, Chief Auditor Franz Schmidt, being announced with this fanfare. He sat for several moments contemplating each. Now his throat was aching with nerves.

Lights on and bereft of passengers, the early tram waited in Bamberg Platz. Conductor Dorf seemed relieved to see someone emerge from the mist. While the auditor was folding his newspaper the Viennese came along the aisle opening his leather bag.

'Good morning, Herr Schmidt – another miserable day.'

Schmidt smiled a grim agreement, and handed over his money. The conductor punched a ticket and leaned above the auditor, a worried expression on his face. Depression of a communicable nature clung to him. Hanging on a strap, he dutifully scanned the platz for other approaching passengers, trying to penetrate the streamers of mist. He gave up, consulted his watch, and muttered, 'No-one wants to come out this morning.'

He turned his big, earnest eyes down to Schmidt, who was poised over his paper, and said confidentially, 'A terrible business last night at my flats. My neighbour was shot dead. And six others.' Though no-one else was present, he leaned closer and whispered, 'Gestapo. I saw the bodies carried out.'

Schmidt stared at the conductor. 'Dead?'

'Absolutely. A big gunfight. He was a police detective, a decorated veteran of the war, and clearly a very fine shot. Six of the Gestapo dead as mutton. The reason for it – I don't know But Herr Dressler was a good man.'

Schmidt looked down at his paper: it was spinning rapidly like newspapers seen at the beginning of newsreels. He felt ill. He became aware that the conductor was still standing over him.

'Excuse me –' Schmidt said.

Dorf regarded him sympathetically. This kind of event was a trial to all.

Something else was worrying the Viennese. He'd brought out a bank passbook, and held it as though it was a fragile heirloom. His hands were shaking. 'We were good neighbours.

Herr Dressler wanted me to have this – for my son's education. I don't know how to get it.'

The newspaper had fallen from Schmidt's hands; a sense of wonderment arose in him. What was happening to forge all these amazing connections in his life? He felt omnipresent – his mind was clearing, control returning. He took the passbook from the conductor, examined it and the enclosed slip. Dorf could have problems withdrawing the money from the savings bank. He would arrange it first thing, before the account was frozen; one more last small service to the doomed Dresslers.

He studied Dorf's strained face. 'Let me take it. I'll get the money for you.'

The big conductor smiled with immense relief and gratitude. 'I can't thank you enough, Herr Schmidt.'

The driver was signalling impatiently from the front, so Dorf pulled the bell, and they shuddered and clanked into motion. 'One minute late, my fault.' He clucked his tongue.

It was the first time Schmidt could remember being the only passenger from the terminus. It seemed an omen for the future.

He couldn't get Dressler out of his head. But after he'd attended to the post, Schmidt forced himself to examine his in-tray. The financial year-end was near and his work was falling behind. Whatever the exigencies in the wide world, despite personal crises, the bank's processes didn't falter. A confidential file of draft closing entries awaited his scrutiny. The bank ran two ledgers, one more or less public, the other strictly private. He grimaced. Depending on the outcome of today's events, someone else might have to deal with these intricacies.

After a while he put down his pen, took off his spectacles, and rubbed his good eye. Dressler's heavy, cautious face came to him. It merged into the imagined silent images of a grotesque gunfight; finally, to a giant, bloodied, bullet-riddled corpse. He shook his head as though to deny this. Another image came into his mind's eye: peeled of their black leather, six pink, also bloodied corpses. Harmless now as skinned rabbits. No regrets here.

He tried to steady himself. Nearly ten o'clock. No word from Dietrich. He checked and found that the director hadn't arrived. Was he sleeping off the champagne? Or had Party business taken him elsewhere? He did disappear frequently to mysterious meetings.

Sharply the thought came: *Had the Nazi been involved in Herr Dressler's death?* Had the Dresslers, *en famille*, become an obsession? He turned it over in his mind like a coin. His earlier amazement returned: Too much was interweaved in his life these days to dismiss anything. At ten he went out and collected Herr Dorf's 4,000 marks, and returned to the bank.

At 11.50 am the intercom phone rang and the Nazi's voice boomed painfully into his ear: 'What a night I've had Franz!' He laughed exuberantly – but confidentially. 'I'd counted on excitement but *not* the kind that turned up! I've spent this morning at Gestapo headquarters, sorting it out for them. It's something which will surprise and interest you. I'll tell you about it tomorrow evening, my friend. Be at my apartment at six. We'll have that drink.'

Schmidt felt his skin, his hair, prickling as he listened, as the line went dead. The Nazi had whirled to another sector of his existence, revelling in a new triumph. Forbiddingly, it seemed the connection had been established: in his mind's eye Dressler had appeared in a shadowed doorway, nodded significantly in confirmation. Dietrich again! The Nazi's evil hand was everywhere. Schmidt again had the feeling of speeding downhill in an out-of-control tramcar, his hand frozen on the shut-off lever. He moved his tense shoulders, seeking relief.

Nearly 12.00, he stared at the phone now. As the second hand of the wall clock swept past 12.00, it rang; the trunk-line operator announced a call from Zurich – a Herr Wagner – and the deputy foreign manager's familiar voice crackled down the line.

34

V ON STRECK WAS still unpacking a bag when Schmidt was shown into his room by the tall, blond resident of the outer office with the bulge beneath his armpit. It was 3.30 pm. The Nazi functionary had a scarf around his neck. His homburg rested on his desk. Here was the man of affairs, seemingly still on the move even as he came to rest. He'd peeled off the black leather gloves.

He waved the auditor to a seat, and continued arranging papers. The auditor sat neat and erect on the straight-backed chair in his overcoat, his own hat on his lap, and waited for attention. A portrait of the Fuehrer watched him with a melancholic expression highly charged with suspicion. He reflected: *Watches the whole population, down to the last railway ticket clerk. In my case, as to suspicion – quite appropriate.* These brooding portraits were almost as prolific as the swastika flags – equally reviled by Wagner.

'Well, Herr Schmidt,' von Streck said, removing the scarf, 'this is a surprise. I presume you've something important to tell me about the Party's banking affairs.'

'Yes, Herr Minister, unfortunately, I do.'

Now seated in his leather swivel chair, the short, powerfully-built man raised an eyebrow, pursed his lips, settled himself more comfortably.

'I see. "Unfortunately"? I've a feeling I'm not going to

like what you're about to tell me, but proceed.'

Schmidt edged his body forward. Uneasiness had begun to run in him like sand through an hourglass; something was in the air which he couldn't fathom, something not quite right; but he was committed now.

'Your instructions in mind, Herr Minister, I've been watching over the Party's business with special care. In any event, that's my duty ...' Though he'd rehearsed for this interview, suddenly he felt an imperative to take even greater care with his words. The Nazi's eyes were bright, but expressionless, his face unreadable, his manner uncommunicative. Different from the Municipal Library. He'd no choice but to go on. 'I believe ... fear, a substantial amount of the Party's Reich bonds may have been misappropriated.'

Von Streck gazed unresponsively at the auditor's face, specifically his artificial eye, making Schmidt wonder if he'd taken in the dramatic revelation. His disquiet was growing; this wasn't an auspicious atmosphere for his plan to bear fruit. Perhaps if I told him the Fuehrer's going to be shot?

'"Believe", you say ...?' The Nazi frowned. 'No matter – we'll pass that over for the moment. Go on.'

Schmidt studied the functionary. Where had he been? Had his journey been so long and wearisome? He'd carefully planned the sequence of his revelations; however, there was a major gap which required filling: how the bonds had got to Zurich. Wagner must have time to do whatever he had to do, and get out to France. Presuming he survived Zurich. It was a point of danger, but waiting for it to be resolved was also very dangerous.

The Nazi official had turned to stone: stone arteries tracing into a stone heart, all animation sealed in. So judged Schmidt. But, unaccountably, something was encouraging him to feel that the missing link in his chain of deception might be safely ignored.

'With great regret, it's my duty to inform you the persons I suspect are Herr Dietrich and Herr Otto Wertheim.' Von Streck's eyes had flickered. 'I suspect both gentlemen have opened Swiss bank accounts. I've evidence that the combinations to the NSDAP safe of the two custodians other than Herr Otto Wertheim – that is myself and Herr Wagner – were obtained from the bank holding them on the signatures of those gentlemen.' He paused. 'I fear what an audit will reveal.'

In the street below, a tram clanged its bell. Abruptly, the heating pipes gurgled in the room.

'"Misappropriated"? What does that mean, precisely?'

'I suspect the bonds may've been removed to Switzerland.'

'Why do you suspect that?'

'I happened to observe Swiss bank account mandates on Herr Dietrich's desk. I can't think of any reason why he'd have such forms.'

The lie fell easily from Schmidt's lips, but his fingers tightened on the brim of his hat.

The Nazi, still expressionless, gazed at the auditor. 'Have you disclosed your suspicions to anyone else?'

'No, Herr Minister.'

Schmidt did not know if he was a Minister; where he fitted into the Nazi machine.

'*If* what you say is true – how could these *gentlemen* expect to get away with it?'

'Sir, the bonds surplus to a working balance are sealed under their joint control. A deficiency might go undetected for a good while.'

'But ultimately, it would be?'

'Funds come in each day to build up the working balance. The sealed envelope in their joint names might not need to be disturbed for some time. I can't imagine what is in their minds as to the ultimate situation.'

'What use are German bonds to them in Switzerland? I fail to see what their plan might be.'

With his one eye Schmidt stared steadily at the Nazi. Friend or foe? The question echoed in his head. 'There are people who run clandestine discount markets in all European bearer securities. It's a matter of smuggling them back to source. Swiss nationals are crossing our borders every day. German businessmen, too. As to their plan ...' He shrugged the slightest of shrugs.

Von Streck's glance flicked along the edge of his desk, shot to the auditor's face. 'By what means could they've got the bonds to Switzerland? Opened these accounts?'

Schmidt pursed his lips: an earnest man seeking an elusive explanation. Von Streck had found his gap, the gap that any court or Party tribunal would surely run up against. Strangely, he still had that 'all clear' feeling.

'I don't know, sir.'

Von Streck brooded on framed photographs of the Nuremberg Rally of 1937, a slight, cynical smile now on his lips. 'An outside audit could open up this imbroglio – if it is such?'

'Yes.'

'Presumably these accounts would be numbered – to keep the account-holders' identities secret.'

'I'm afraid do.'

The Nazi brooded on this, and then abruptly spun his chair to survey another part of the room. Without looking at the auditor he said, 'I find this unbelievable, Schmidt. That those men would act in such a way.'

Schmidt stared steadily at the Nazi's profile. 'The fraudulent acts of trusted officials are always "unbelievable", mein herr.' He paused. 'I should report, also, that Herr Dietrich has instructed that 500 marks be paid to him each month from the Party's Number Four cash account. He calls it a commission. I believe this was also his practice in Berlin.'

He spoke in the tone which he used when addressing the board. This was minor and makeweight – yet it added another bad odour.

'A commission,' the Nazi repeated.

'He demanded I take an amount for myself but I have not, for obvious reasons.'

Von Streck raised his eyebrows again and softly cracked his knuckles. He abruptly swivelled his chair again to face the auditor. Were these intimations of excitement? This process was like tapping brass nails into a coffin. Schmidt selected another nail. 'Herr Dietrich is a homosexual. He's made that very clear to me.'

The Nazi's face suddenly showed animation. 'What an interesting experience the gathering of all this knowledge – that, in particular – must've been for you, Schmidt?'

Schmidt didn't respond; sat there, the steadfast auditor grounded in his professionalism, at the minister's service.

'You've suspicions, and certain evidence of a *possible* crime, Herr Schmidt. Is that what you're saying? If it's factual, if a crime has been perpetrated, of course a criminal and grossly traitorous act. However, if upon investigation it can't be proved I trust you understand the consequences?' Schmidt nodded. 'All right, Herr Auditor. Your message has been received. Not one word to anyone else. You may go.'

Schmidt left, glad to be out. As he walked quickly away in the chilly afternoon from the nondescript building, he pondered what von Streck's reaction would have been if he'd dropped the words 'Teutonic Knights' into the interview. His instinct had held him back. Yet it had seemed close to the surface. Periscope depth, he thought. His mind was hyperactive after the interview. A vision came to him of a panorama of the nation viewed from the stratosphere, cities, towns, black and brown stained countryside, forest and fallow – or SS and SA, frozen under the season – and the march of history. He saw no sign of life. His eye began to weep copiously; routinely he padded his handkerchief to it, drawing the glances of passers-by, the sentimentally inclined of whom imagined they were witnesses to a personal tragedy.

§ § §

Now the father was dead. Herr Wertheim thought: *This affair of the Dresslers is like a Greek tragedy. But the performance has ended — nothing else can be done to them. An all-pervading fate beyond any control has ruled off their lives. 'Beyond any control?'* The question echoed in his mind — as did Lilli Dressler's voice in certain phrases which she'd commonly used as they'd worked side by side.

But always compensations; he felt empowered by his risk-taking, the new course for the *Wertheim* with battle flags up. Nothing seemed fixed or unchangeable in his mind. Even his precept to maintain the value of clients' capital was now a shadow of its former significance. Though — going into battle for whom? Right now he felt his brain to be as sharp as ever, yet there were phases of a confused nature. He admitted that.

Thus, it was Herr Wertheim's turn to gaze into the abyss. He did so by gazing at *The Eye*. Gradually his mind seemed to levitate, to be looking down on his life and times, miniaturised by distance. These days, his mind did shift gears unexpectedly. Slow down, pick up speed. And yes — the bank was forging ahead on well-oiled, well-tuned engines. Not only had the Aryanisation business given it a fresh impetus, but their old industrialist clients were thriving, and each week came windfalls of Jewish clients leaving the scores of Jewish private banks, which were being forced to close down. Given the Aryanisation deals which Otto was pursuing, the chickens rushing into the fox's den! He rubbed his hands to stimulate some warmth.

His room was as quiet as a cloister. He lifted his head from its gaze, to listen. The phone rang. 'Von Streck here, General-Director, please be at the bank tomorrow at eleven with all your directors. I wish to review certain aspects of the Party's business.'

The phone went dead. The briefest of exchanges. The G-D replaced the receiver. Did Dietrich know of this? *Von Streck*. A man with power which was the more formidable because of its mysterious nature. 'Certain aspects' – what was the nuance there?

He pondered the shadowy power of von Streck. Real power, though. He recalled their meeting at the Party's head-quarters in Berlin. He'd been in no doubt that von Streck was the key decision-maker in the transfer of the investment business. At one stage, he'd been high up in the Ministry of Economics …

'Who is master here?' Herr Wertheim realised that he'd spoken aloud to the painting.

He smiled, pleased by how often he was surprising himself lately.

§ § §

Schmidt sat in his study in an attitude of listening. Maria had finished the dinner dishes and gone to the cinema. In recent days he'd shut himself into a world concentrated on the devi-ous passage of events in which he was engaged. Tonight, he'd poured himself a brandy. Doubtless, the shock of Dressler's death, the day's tension …

Wagner was due back at noon tomorrow. In the brief, guarded phone conversation he'd reported 'the task at hand' completed. The deputy foreign manager's experiences on the mission would be narrated another time, and he'd sensed there was much to hear. But would he ever hear it?

What would von Streck do? The consummation was now in the hands of the Nazi functionary. The next move might be the Gestapo knocking on the door of Franz Schmidt.

'We'll see,' he said to the knight engraved in his perpetual patrol. Delineated with increasing clarity he could hear in his head the clatter of hooves, the creak and jingle of harness – 'and as he rode his armour rung'. His reservoir of the Order's history, of current dangerous events was continuously circulating in his mind. Circling back, he returned to von Streck. Had the Nazi, in directing him to the specific era of the Order's history, wherein the knight, Eric Streck, had struck at its evil and corrupt strategies from within, intended it as a guiding light? He sipped brandy. He was gambling that he had. Did the story run like this: *Von Streck, the insurgent, the speculator, casting his eye over the Party's banking affairs, had alighted on Schmidt in his new pivotal role, dredged this auditor's past – discovered the incident with the SA, and, above all, his connection with the Order?*

Had a man who *did not* love the Nazis found a tool to damage them? A tool of opportunity: himself! What if this was rubbish?! The product of his warped and wishful thinking? Tension crawled over him afresh; he'd lost his taste for the brandy. And Dietrich – at this moment? The thought scraped like a dead leaf blown over cobbles to a hidden corner. Did the Nazi suspect the forces running against him, was he engaged in counter-actions?

A sharp vision came, doubtless sponsored by innumerable newsreels, of the Fuehrer, quite alone, pacing back and forth in the shadowy great hall of the Berghof, his mind locked in fantastic thoughts. Schmidt felt he could reach out and tap him on the shoulder.

He cut this off and thought of Dresden, of Helga and Trudi. He glanced at his watch – pictured them in his mother-in-law's familiar house, storytime, bedtime. He heard his daughter's childish voice repeating her prayers.

35

NEXT MORNING IT was windless, with fog. Walking quickly around the bend in the street Schmidt's eye went to the two flags drooping from the flagstaffs. The bank looked becalmed, waiting for a breeze, maybe a new course. The head messenger's hacking cough echoed in the foyer's gilded cupola. The auditor said, 'You need medicine, Herr Berger.'

Berger nodded respectfully. 'I'm taking medicine, Herr Schmidt.' Breathlessly he proceeded Schmidt to the lift.

The usual stack of post, the usual quiet room, the customary atmosphere. He swiftly opened and sorted the post. He glanced up at the clock: 8.45 am; for him, tension vibrated in the air. For others? His inner calm seemed to be faltering.

If von Streck believed his story – *if* he chose to act – how long? The confidence he'd felt as he'd left the Nazi functionary's office had thinned. But hadn't the man sought him out for a watchdog role, presumably had his reasons for doing so? To this point, he'd given his plan a good chance of unfolding as it had, but everything now felt well beyond his control. In the hands of fate.

Was his nerve beginning to crack?

The morning stretched ahead. He went out into the corridors, and glanced in at Wagner's vacant room. Otto came out of his office and without a word or a look swaggered from sight. The younger Wertheim's mind was focused on 11.00 am, on the brilliant accolade which he expected to receive from the Nazi leader.

Schmidt smelled the peculiar odour which Otto, frequently, left in his wake: a touch of normality.

§ § §

Dietrich, shining with grooming and health, smoked a cigarette. Herr Health and Sunshine. The nickname hadn't reached his ears. The fingers of his right hand drummed softly on polished wood. The meeting at eleven was an enigma. Worriedly, he wondered why von Streck hadn't brought him into the picture. Von Streck's power-base was one of the Party's myriad secrets, but clearly formidable, given the fear which it generated. He'd heard he was a personal confidant of Himmler. That he was attached to the Chancellery of the Fuehrer. But one heard many things.

Still, he was lucky to be alive. That madman had killed six of the Gestapo, virtually wiped out the local post's operational group. His own standing must be enhanced by the way he'd dealt with the incident. Perhaps he was to be congratulated before the board; or Otto was, for his Aryanisation work. Otto would certainly be thinking along those lines. Perhaps they were both to be congratulated! *The Party moved in unpredictable ways.*

He smiled tensely: Its façade was steel-clad, inspirational, but behind that it was relentlessly the sum of its human parts. You had to be a little cynical about certain things, alert for your own self-interest. He was confident of the good work he'd done, that it was being noticed in the right quarters. And – he'd six o'clock this evening to look forward to! He felt a stirring in his loins. He visualised Franz's body, smooth skin, his intriguing, mysterious personality. He was going to bust that little virgin wide open in two ways. *Make him sing like a choir boy.*

§ § §

With the forcefulness of a gale coming onto the Baltic coast, von Streck, at the head of four black-uniformed SS men, boots clattering, strode into General-Director Wertheim's anteroom. The SS were a head taller than he, but his muscular body was broader than any of them. He glanced back, as if to confirm the aggressive suspicion set on their faces.

He swept past Fräulein Blum, who stood by her desk, gave her a grin, and arrived at the double doors at the precise instant that they sprang open, orchestrated by Dietrich, who'd been standing by.

Herr Wertheim to the fore, the directors stood in a crescent in the inner sanctum. They sprang to attention, startled at the velocity of the visitors' entrance. Von Streck pulled up, beaming.

'Heil Hitler!'

'Heil Hitler!' – a ragged chorus rang out.

'Good morning, gentlemen! Herr Wertheim a pleasure … Everyone may go – with the exception of yourself, Herr Otto Wertheim and Herr Dietrich.' Methodically, he stripped off the black gloves.

Wertheim showed polite surprise. Something *highly* unusual was in the air.

'Of course …' He turned to the other directors. 'Mein herren?' They took their cue and filed out with palpable relief, led by the formidable Director Schloss, who darted a concerned look at the G-D.

The doors swung shut. Von Streck, his olive features still wreathed in a smile, standing at the head of the SS, said, 'Now to business. I'm here to personally audit the Party's portfolio of bonds. Please make arrangements.'

Wertheim's surprise went up a notch; he tilted his head in a calculating way. After a moment's silence, he said, 'I assure you —'

'Immediately,' von Streck said, his eyes narrowing.

'Of course, if that is your wish.' The general-director turned to a stunned Otto.

'They're kept in the vault,' the younger director stammered, disappointment plain on his face.

'We'll go there,' von Streck said. He was a reasonable man again.

Otto advanced with sudden energy. 'I am a custodian, and I will summon our auditor. The third custodian is absent on duty, we've his safe-combination in a sealed envelope under double custody. I will get it.' He hurried out as though his commitment to this errand, this inexplicable situation, would win back his accolade.

Von Streck watched Otto leave, raised an eyebrow, glanced around the room. 'Mmm. You've an interesting taste in art, Herr Wertheim.' The G-D bowed slightly. He thought: Yes, I do. I doubt it has a high priority in your mind this morning. 'What is the architecture of your fine building. Baroque classicism?'

Wertheim nodded. He said, 'Shall we go to the vault?'

Searching his mind for a gleam of light, Dietrich had been a silent witness to these exchanges. He was staggered by the development, by its implications, though his face remained calm and he was keeping quiet. What, in God's name, was it all about? Whatever it was, it reflected disastrously on his supervisory status, his standing at the bank. He, the director seconded by the Party, totally ignorant of what was afoot! Grimly, he thought of enemies he'd made, felt his apprehension rising. *Yet, everything would be in order.*

The iron cage arrived with a clank and a shudder, and

politely Wertheim ushered von Streck and Dietrich into it.
Dismissively, the high Nazi signalled the SS to take the stairs.

'Quite an antique,' von Streck said, nodding benevolently
at the lift. He'd become an instant connoisseur of the Wertheim province; but the general-director detected a mocking
edge. His father had installed the lift in 1902, and to the despair
of the manufacturer's mechanics, he insisted on its preserva-
tion.

He bowed again, thought: *Yes, he's playing with us. But
which of us doesn't have our secret games?* He was impervious
to such tactics, found at some point he could often turn the
tables. Again he went over his knowledge of von Streck – but
abortively – much as Dietrich had done. Again that whiff of
mystery. *If* the Nazi had worked behind the scenes to effect the
transfer of the NSDAP business, what were the implications of
that? What suspicions had now been raised in his mind? The
bank's systems were as good as any for security, everything
would be in order.

Otto and Schmidt were waiting in the vault; the auditor
had placed the big ledger on the table. The party from the lift
entered and in a wind of body odour the SS came clattering
down the stairs.

Dietrich flicked his eyes at them, and continued to ana-
lyse the situation. Why did von Streck have the SS on hand?
Grounded in the party's ways he didn't like this one bit. He
glanced at sober-faced Schmidt, then stared at the safe.

At a stroke, Schmidt's overnight and early-morning
doubts had been swept away. His heart had soared when Otto
had burst into his room and demanded his presence in the
vault. Von Streck had acted! Now they stood before the safe
like an assemblage of city dignitaries at the unveiling of a
plaque.

The high-ranking Nazi, as he'd been shown in, ignored
the auditor, and didn't appear to notice the G-D's polite intro-

duction.

'Go ahead, gentlemen,' Wertheim said.

Breathing audibly, Otto stepped forward to the safe, peered hard at the calibrated marks, turned the tumbler. Success first time! His several chins were atremble as he stepped back from the ordeal. He produced a sealed envelope and presented it with a flourish to Schmidt. 'Herr Deputy Foreign Manager Wagner's combination,' he announced.

This seemed to amuse von Streck. Schmidt opened the envelope and extracted a sheet of paper. He read the numbers, removed Wagner's combination. He took off his own, and swung open the safe door.

He thought: *Now, we'll see what we'll see.* Behind his mechanical actions he was amazed how suddenly calm he felt. He retrieved the sealed packet and carried it to the table, obliging the SS to make two crab-like jumps, aside. One of them stepped to the table but von Streck waved him back airily.

'I'll do this myself,' he said. He consulted a notebook, produced a fountain pen, laid both on the table. 'According to yesterday's report, after the Dortmund settlement, Reich bonds to the face value of 10,000,000 marks should be in sealed custody. And – nothing as of last night in the working stock.'

Dietrich nodded, deferentially. The funds that had come in this morning by mail and remittance hadn't been processed by Schloss's department yet.

With the knowingness of an illusionist about to perform, von Streck examined the assembled faces. He studied the seal on the big envelope.

'This appears in order – sealed with the official seal, notated with a certificate for 10,000,000, signed by Herr Otto Wertheim and Herr Dietrich.' Dietrich and Otto exchanged confirmatory looks, relaxed perceptibly – though their attitudes said instantly: What was there to be worried about?

Von Streck looked up, caught this, smiled. He lifted the

envelope, examined the seal again, weighed it in his hand. He laid the packet down.

'All in order, Herr Minister,' Dietrich suggested, his confidence flooding back.

Schmidt's heart had frozen. If the envelope wasn't opened ... Von Streck didn't appear to hear Dietrich, seemed immersed in a complex calculation. Could *he* dare suggest it?

'Do you think so, Herr Dietrich?' the high Nazi said very quietly.

'Of course, Herr Minister!'

'As safe and sound as Fort Knox in the USA, Herr Dietrich?'

Dietrich smiled. 'Absolutely, Herr Minister!'

'Even as clear cut as a legal lecture at the Order Castle in Marienburg?'

Dietrich smiled again, more warily. He remembered his days at Marienburg. What in hell *was* this all about?

Herr Wertheim and Otto were observing this by-play with mystification; Schmidt was identifying the sadistic nuances, broadening his picture of von Streck.

The Nazi functionary turned to Schmidt. 'Herr Auditor, we'll open this packet and count the bonds.'

Thank God!

Schmidt stepped forward, took the envelope, and slit it open. He held the empty packet in one hand, and gazed at the thick sheaf of plain white paper which he held in the other. He looked up slowly, at the frozen tableau.

Thunderstruck, Otto's eyes were protruding, as if staring into a void; Dietrich's had narrowed to slits and his mouth had set involuntarily into its yellowish grin; the general-director had become deeply abstracted – as though he'd *The Eye* in his vision.

'Jesus!' Otto gasped, all the horror of the situation in the exclamation.

Von Streck took the sheaf of blank paper from Schmidt, let the sheets flick through his fingers. Otto tried to speak again, but produced only a strangled sound.

Von Streck surveyed everyone with hard, sardonic eyes. '*Who* is going to explain this to me? Much more importantly, to the Party?' Accustomed to observing persons in crisis he noted that the shock appeared genuine. Except for Chief Auditor Schmidt, whose face was as blank as the papers, and the senior Wertheim, who appeared to have gone to an elevated plane. The Nazi smiled thinly.

'Herr Minister, this is a great shock.' The old banker had recovered first. His tenor voice was perfectly controlled. His intimations had been right, von Streck had expected to find this. What was the fellow up to? Using his urbanity as though pouring oil on a storm-tossed sea, he said, 'Herr Minister, could you enlighten us as to how your suspicions were aroused?'

Von Streck had entered the Wertheim day with considerable velocity, then he'd changed the pace to a kind of amiably ironic event. In the crowded vault, another metamorphosis was under way: his deep-chested torso swelled, exuded its muscularity, the mole on his cheek was projected like a beacon. The olive skin had lightened – a strange, ominous effect; the brown eyes glittered menacingly.

All in the vault stared at the transformation.

'Bankhaus Wertheim & Co AG, reputedly a model of financial probity in the Reich, trusted by the Party, has played host to an act of criminal treason! – *and you, Herr Wertheim, speak as though champagne's been spilt!*'

The general-director winced. The Nazi had almost blown him over. His brain was quite clear this morning. A lifetime of weathering situations had left him resilient to the crises of the banking world; and, he was sure now that there was a lot more going on with von Streck than met the eye.

Von Streck had sent a spray of spittle over them, none

wiped it off, except the G-D who produced a linen handkerchief from his sleeve.

The high Nazi snarled, 'Fortunately, we don't have to
search for the criminals. They're right here!'

He raised his finger, levelled it at Dietrich, and then as
though moving a gunbarrel brought it around slowly to point
at Otto.

'*Preposterous,*' Herr Wertheim exclaimed. But his thoughts
were going down deep.

The two accused gazed at von Streck: a madman dropped
into their midst.

'What actors,' he sneered contemptuously. 'What a wonderful show of innocence. *You filth!*' he shouted and even the
SS flinched. 'Do you deny the Swiss bank accounts in your
names?' Last night he'd phoned a very senior man in the Swiss
central bank; a man who was very sympathetic to the Nazi
Party. 'Do you deny the fraudulent obtainment of the combinations of the auditor, the deputy foreign manager, to this
safe? Do you, Dietrich, deny your depravations on the Party's
Number Four account? *Well?*'

'Herr Minister, there's been some terrible mistake,' Dietrich cried desperately. He stood transfixed, his teeth bared, the
whites of his eyes prominent. He'd the sensation, entangled
with others, that he was watching a back-street farce; that in
a moment this ridiculous scene would end and the rational
world would reappear.

'Yes this is the mistake,' von Streck said now in a dead-
quiet voice, holding up the sheaf of paper. 'We'll adjourn to
Gestapo headquarters, to further investigate it.'

Schmidt was spellbound by von Streck's performance – if
it were such. Here was an unbelievably effective consummation of his plan.

He looked at Dietrich and saw comprehension dawning
on the tortured no-longer-handsome face. *That blank form*

he'd signed! The Nazi's head rolled around as though it was on swivels, stopped at him with a jerk. Accusation blazed in his eyes. His face had become suffused − like a man suffering a seizure. His neck was corded, the muscles working. He was trying to utter.

'*Christ Almighty! There is the perpetrator!*'

He launched himself at the auditor but the black-uniformed bodies blocked his rush, applied armlocks. He was incoherent, shaking with passion. All heads swung to stare at Schmidt.

Von Streck roared into contemptuous laughter. He stepped up to Dietrich, a head shorter, but appreciably wider. 'You vile traitor,' he hissed. 'I've the strongest evidence of your crimes. Like all your corrupt, unintelligent, miserable kind, when cornered you seek to divert the blame elsewhere. We'll look into your perverted private life, too − you bum-fucker.' He gestured to the SS: 'Take them away.'

Dietrich's face was demented. He shook off the hands on him as though they were nothing. 'Hands off!' he shouted. '*What evidence?* I'm a captain in the SS! *I tell you that man is the criminal!*' His slicked-back hair had fallen on his brow. His eyes burned with rage, and fear.

Two of the SS laid big, work-roughened hands on him afresh, and dragged him out the doorway. He struggled powerfully in a desperate silence. At the foot of the stairs they smashed his face once, twice against the Wertheim wall, and everyone heard the chink-chink of the yellow teeth. Still he struggled, his mouth running blood like a drain. Halfway up the first flight, again they smashed his face into the wall, breaking his nose, releasing another red jet. As it sprayed their uniforms they swore like navvies unexpectedly striking a waterpipe. He began to scream like an animal injured in the steel jaws of a trap.

In a trance, Otto waddled behind this violent group, his

flabby biceps gripped by the remaining SS men.

Herr Wertheim studied these exits with a kind of supreme detachment which made Schmidt wonder whether the shock had at last disturbed his reason. Slowly, the silver head turned to von Streck, then to Schmidt. The auditor met his eyes. It was his turn to receive a shock: he was being gazed at with fascination – when he might have expected horror – as though a kind of Frankenstein creation was being viewed. Then the general-director turned away without a word, and followed von Streck towards the lift. The high Nazi seemed to have forgotten the auditor's existence.

36

'WHO OR WHAT do they hope to see?' – Helga asked herself. 'What are they waiting for?' The Gestapo agents had not attempted to conceal their surveillance. They'd not interviewed her again. Did they expect Franz to come? That was futile. Each night, like her mother in the morning, she watched the cigarettes glowing in the darkness and pondered these questions.

Day by day tension had accumulated in the household; even Trudi had absorbed it, become quiet, watchful of the adults' faces. Each morning when they left the house the car with the two Gestapo men was waiting to follow.

Frau Seibert, still convalescent, did not go out but peered anxiously through the front windows at the sinister black vehicle stationed, semi-permanently, at the end of the drive. Helga and her sister had become short with each other – the latter resentful of this frightening ordeal, Helga with a sense of guilt at bringing home the insidious, nerve-chilling danger. Her sister had nearly died the night the two Gestapo had come to the door.

But this noon: No car, no watchers! She stood with her market basket, holding her breath, and peered at the street. She'd lost weight and an acute tension was manifest in her movements, her posture, even in repose. But now something had changed and gradually she felt an oppressive weight lifting from her heart.

§ § §

If the *Wertheim* had seemed becalmed when Schmidt had arrived, now it was wallowing, rudderless. The auditor couldn't quite accept the fact that Dietrich's voice wasn't going to come booming down the line, or his large figure appear in the door and hoist himself onto the desk.

At 4.30 pm, the building's lighting was feeble. Beyond his window the darkness was thick and impenetrable. Today, dawn to dusk, had been a mere seven-hour sprint. But what a sprint!

After the drama in the vault, he'd not left his room, but the calamitous atmosphere which had descended on Wertheims had filtered to him through the building's conduits, via the nervy messengers doing their rounds. He'd pictured the shocked cleaners wonderingly scrubbing away the grisly trail of blood, broken teeth, and vomit which Dietrich had left up the stairs and into the front foyer. Had there been a more dramatic exit in the bank's history? He thought: *At this moment I'm rudderless myself.* He felt no elation, no relief, no warmth of retribution exacted — just a sense of another step completed, a temporary exhaustion. The game was still in play. The *final* consummation was up to von Streck. If it went to court, or a Party tribunal, the flaws in the case could become evident and a dissection of the evidence, his own questioning, could throw a spotlight back on to his actions and motives, into that gap: the smuggling of the bonds to Zurich. On to Wagner!

Wagner must go immediately to Paris! *Today.* Must get out.

But where was Wagner? His colleague hadn't returned at noon. He'd rung the deputy foreign manager's flat; his maid hadn't heard a word. The foreign department had confirmed he was overdue. He wouldn't leave the office until he'd tracked him down. The persons in his life were alternately emerging into the light, stepping back into the shadows, in tune with a melody which he couldn't quite pick up. So it seemed. He was waiting for Wagner to come out again into the light. For God's sake Wagner, don't delay. Nervously, Schmidt pattered his fingertips on his desktop.

The bank's situation regarding the NSDAP had changed drastically. He'd been half-expecting a summons from Herr Wertheim, but a steel shutter of silence had come down on the first floor. What could they say to each other? Outrage on one side; his regretful, lying testimony on the other? He couldn't get out of his mind the G-D's astonishing demeanour, that last look.

He picked up the phone and called Wagner's maid again. No news.

At 6.10 pm a summons did come. The Gestapo. He was shocked. He'd expected that when the moment for questioning arrived, it would've been under the auspices of von Streck – if the Nazi functionary's involvement was to make sense. That didn't appear to be the case. The voice of the man he'd just spoken to had infused in him a chilling doubt. Transfixed by a thought, he stood in his room. *Dietrich had been protecting him from the Gestapo and Dietrich himself was now under arrest.* He put on his overcoat and hat and went down in the lift.

§ § §

On the first floor.

'Would you stay a little later, tonight, fräulein?' Herr Wertheim smiled. 'Ask my man to bring up a bottle of champagne, and caviar – immediately. Thank you.'

Two glasses had been brought: one was in the fragile fingers of Wertheim, the other in the large, shapely hand of a surprised, blushing Else Blum. She'd not guessed that she was to be a participant. The champagne was poured, caviar heaped on a plate, and small silver spoons were on the desk.

'A day of momentous events, my dear fräulein,' the G-D said. 'One we will always remember.' He picked up his glass, studied the colour of the champagne. 'Have you heard of the saying: Every cloud has a silver lining? Today's events can be considered in that light.'

She watched him over the thin rim of her own glass. What did he mean? It certainly had been a day – even from the perspective of her limited experience. What a scene with Herr Dietrich! As for that Herr Otto! And he doesn't seem worried about it! Does the old boy want to play? If he does, it's all right. He's a good enough sort.

'You know, fräulein, I liken our venerable old bank to a ship. Have you picked that up yet? You and I – and others, such as Herr Auditor Schmidt – are the crew. We're on an interesting voyage – not without its dangers, and sometimes crew-members are washed overboard. *Some* might think that today we took a torpedo.' He leaned forward and scooped up caviar, conveyed it to his mouth, ate it slowly. 'Very good. Help yourself, my dear.'

Fräulein Blum tasted the caviar with slight suspicion, found she liked it. … Ships, crew, torpedoes? Wertheim refilled their glasses. 'I mentioned Auditor Schmidt. You might find our Herr Schmidt … a strange person. A little beyond your experi-ence, at this stage. In fact, I should admit, a little beyond my own. One might think that institutions like Wertheims breed and nourish this kind of individual. Up to a point. It's always surprised me that while they go home at night, they leave their *main* world … simmering away here. That said, Herr Schmidt is a remarkable case.' He admired the colour again. 'A unique case. Remember I told you that, Fräulein Blum.'

She drank her champagne. Schmidt had been pleasant enough, though there was something about him – the way he appeared, the way he watched – that gave her a touch of the creeps.

The G-D said, 'There are some things one leaves too late. If one is lucky a little lost time can be made up.' She did not understand this either, except that it was important to him.

Wertheim's thoughts had gone back to what she'd told him three days ago. Two of his cousins from Dusseldorf had arrived at the bank when he was absent. Most unusual. He supposed Herr Schloss had sent for them, for according to the fräulein, they'd spent an hour closeted with the big director. The two, twin brothers in their fifties, only ever turned up at the bank for the shareholders' meeting, with their hands out for their dividend cheques. They'd asked to see his room, and had paid particular attention to the new art on the walls.

His lips formed an enigmatic smile. 'Like spies,' he murmured.

Fräulein Blum looked at him sharply. Instinctively, she knew what he was referring to. The short, ruddy-faced men had gazed at the two pictures, and finally stood in front of *The Eye* as though mesmerised. Not quite knowing if she was doing the right thing in letting them into the inner sanctum, she'd hovered in the room. Casting her looks, they'd whispered together. *'He's cracked!'* – she'd caught the worried exclamation.

Herr Wertheim had moved his chair closer to hers. Without embarrassment, he put his hand under her skirt and pushed it up until it lay between the rich, soft warmth of her thighs. She smiled slightly, continued to sip her champagne. His hand was warm, which was surprising.

After a moment, Wertheim withdrew his slender bluish hand. 'My dear, I felt very comfortable doing that. But now you should run on home to your dinner.'

Fräulein Blum straightened her skirt, rose gracefully to stand above him. 'Should I clear this away, Herr General-Director?'

'No, my dear. But you might call Herr Director Schloss for me, and ask him to step in here.'

She looked doubtfully at the clock.

'He will be there, waiting for my call. He's been waiting for some months, and will be very relieved to receive it. You might be good enough to bring another glass.'

'Thank you for including me in your celebration,' Fräulein Blum said earnestly, blushing again, and went out. In the ante-room she heard the lift descending.

Celebration? The heat of her thighs. What a lovely young woman: a combination of nervous self-consciousness, and overwhelming sexual assurance. What an interesting experience to plumb her depths! He smiled his most languid smile, lay back in his cushioned chair, steepled his fingers and rotated to confront *The Eye*. He was surprised that he couldn't see it. Or the rest of the room. Suddenly it had appeared to fill up with fog.

37

A BLACKED-OUT CAR waited beside the bank's entrance. Its rear door swung open as Schmidt appeared. A shadowy figure leaned across, motioned to him. He climbed in and was in the company of the Gestapo.

Klaxon shrieking, they accelerated away, following the street's long curve. Schmidt thought: It smells of cabbage, leather, the pressure of state business, obdurate, deadly power. He ticked them off and considered whether his winning run was about to end. Very soon they swerved under an archway into a weedy, wet courtyard. A rusted machine of indeterminate purpose sat in a corner. The car doors banged. Gesturing to him to follow, one of them led the way into a stone-flagged, soul-freezing corridor. Not just the cold, Schmidt thought. But why don't I feel *more* anxiety? Have I, in fact, put on a kind of armour?

He blinked as he entered a white-painted room ablaze with electric light.

Wagner was slumped over a table, the side of his head flat against its surface, his face turned towards the door, his eyes staring, his mouth a red-rimmed, black hole hanging open. Flung down as if to tell a tale, teeth lay on the table. Blood shone stickily, starkly reminding Schmidt of a butcher's block. Reminding him of ...

He gazed at the scene in horror, his recent detachment

shattered. He looked up into the amused, assessing face of a man who sat negligently astride a reversed chair, smoking a cigarette. Another, in a worn, black suit, also smoking, leaned against a wall as though resting. Both seemed to have stepped aside from their work to concentrate on his reaction. The man against the wall gave two short, sharp barks of a cough.

The seated man exhaled smoke luxuriously. 'So you are Schmidt?'

'Yes. I am Herr Schmidt.' The muscles in the auditor's face had become rigid. He gazed at the Nazi. Since the incident of his eye it appeared to be his destiny to continuously enlarge his knowledge of the Party's prototypes. He said, 'Why is Herr Wagner here, and in this condition? He is my colleague, a respected senior official of Bankhaus Wertheim & Co.'

'Colleague ... Wertheim & Co,' the man repeated. 'We know all that, and more. Especially about his political activities, his courier-running of foreign currencies. In past months he's been in Paris, Brussels, and Amsterdam smuggling out funds, salting them away ... liaising with that den of criminals the SPD. We know about his opposition to the Party, his criminal defamations of our leaders. What we don't know – yet – but will soon, is precisely why he went to *Zurich*. To save him further hardship, perhaps *you* could help us on this point?'

Schmidt watched the speaker carefully as though reading his lips. On this bloody table, Wagner's secret life was exposed. It was as he'd feared. His colleague's chancey, double-game had been found out ... A great pity – a tragedy. But he'd been on borrowed time.

Zurich was still unexplained. *If* they got to the bottom of it ... but they hadn't. Their interest in Wagner clearly had its own life. He, Schmidt, had been brought here because he was a colleague and/or his name had come up in the Gestapo files.

The seated agent's face had an expression of mock inquiry.

The auditor's lips were clamped tight. He'd assumed von Streck's power to be absolute, though unexplained, the functionary's agenda similar to his own. This rested on the 'all clear' he'd been receiving as he'd dealt with him. And the connection with the Order. *That wasn't a figment of his imagination.* And surely it'd been validated by the events this morning at the bank.

Suddenly, the Nazi blew a smoke ring.

He must speak.

'I hope I can help you.' Wagner was watching him. He realised this. The eyes in the brutalised face were fixed on his own. 'Herr Wagner was sent by the bank to Zurich to confer with our Swiss correspondent banks. It's his duty to do so – as with such banks in other countries. Relations with Swiss banks are of vital importance to the Reich. Herr Wagner's a key man for this. He is highly regarded at the Reichsbank.'

His heart was thudding. But he spoke with gravity and civility and precise enunciation, going down the line he'd used on Dietrich, hoping to strike a civilised note in the lethal atmosphere – soliciting a turn of events which would enable him to extract himself, his plan, from this debacle. Wagner, his SPD activities exposed, was a lost cause, unless von Streck ...

'How remarkable,' the seated smoker said. 'The same story we heard from him. Could it be the truth?'

'Those are the facts,' Schmidt said. Could he drop von Streck's name in?

'I don't believe you, Schmidt. But there's hardly anyone I do believe. You've been a lucky man so far. But that bastard Dietrich can't protect you now. We've not forgotten your connection to the Dressler affair. That's extremely fresh in our minds.'

Schmidt kept his face expressionless. Doubtless, in that final remark he was referring to Dressler's decimation of the local Gestapo.

'However, you may go. For the present.'

'And Herr Wagner?'

The Nazi laughed.

Unexpectedly, Wagner spoke – a slurry of barely recognisable words. 'I'm afraid ... not ... going t'enjoy ... dinner tonight ... Franz ... beer ... might be possible.'

The man against the wall said, conversationally, 'You've drunk your last beer.'

Schmidt put his hand on Wagner's arm. 'I will do something, Heinrich,' he said.

'*Get away from him,*' the seated man said. 'You can do *nothing*. Do you wish to help an enemy of the Reich?'

Barely audible, Wagner muttered, 'No more mistakes ... for me ... my friend.' Then with a major effort, quite clearly, 'Fat man ... was here ... Bach.'

'Shut up arsehole,' the seated Nazi said, grinding out his cigarette.

Schmidt found himself alone in the courtyard; alone in the fresh, damp air; then in a drab street overhung by old-style warehouses. Delayed shock. He'd trouble getting his bearings, walked two dark blocks in a daze, found streetlights, familiar territory, and a taxi.

He went to von Streck's office, a five-minute drive. It was his only point of reference for the Nazi functionary. The building was another abject study in darkness and desertion, but breathing out frosty breaths he kept pressing the bell.

The clash of unlocking came. An elderly man with red-rimmed eyes, in a municipal uniform, stood in the gap of the door still chewing his dinner. Schmidt showed the pass and the man beckoned him in, closed and barred the door, and limped back into the hall. With grotesque upward-reaching clutches he pulled two light-cords, and pointed to the stairs. He'd vanished when the auditor glanced back from the landing.

'He's here,' Schmidt told himself.

But he was wrong. A single light burned in the anteroom above the desk of the blond, wide-shouldered man, who looked up in surprise from his magazine at the tense-looking visitor who was blinking rapidly behind gold-rimmed spectacles.

'I wish to see Herr von Streck,' Schmidt said, showing the pass again.

He stared at the large pistol on the desk.

'Is this urgent?'

'Extremely urgent.'

'Very well.'

The blond man wrote on a piece of paper, and without rising pushed it across the desk. 'You will find him here.'

Schmidt let himself out, and hurried down corridors of hollow-sounding parquet floors. He'd noted on his previous visit the names gilded on the glass doors: the den of small import/export agencies.

The address was in the district of beerhalls. Another taxi ride. For Schmidt, his birthplace had metamorphosed to an artist's composition of areas which were blacked-out and devoid of life, and gaudily-lit and frenetically alive – one tract rooted in the past, the other whirling towards the future. Degenerate art? Even streets he'd known all his life looked unfamiliar. And dangerous.

This was the district where he'd met Wagner six nights ago – no, an age ago – where they'd encountered von Streck and the man he'd just spoken with. Though it throbbed with the sounds of convivial activity, the building he arrived at had an air of exclusivity.

He climbed stairs following directions and stood outside the oak door of a private room. From inside came raucous singing, the crash of steins on tabletops. Nothing exclusive about this.

Again Schmidt held out his pass with its street photograph. The uniformed SS man who came out, breathing beer, examined it, and frowned at the request the auditor shouted in his ear. He inspected the small, blond stranger with hard-eyed suspicion. But he went back in. Schmidt had a glimpse of red-faced, jacketless men bellowing their lungs out, and breathed in German life … the Teutonic ethos. The Third Reich.

Von Streck came out in his shirtsleeves, his astrakhan-collared overcoat slung over his shoulders against the cold in the corridor. His face showed alert good humour. Schmidt had worried about the condition the functionary would be in, but he was perfectly sober, standing there like a rock, suggestive of darkness and intrigue and ambivalence. He wondered at this man's participation in these drunken revels.

'I regret this intrusion, Herr Minister, but could I have a private word?'

'Why not Herr Schmidt, why not?' The Nazi assessed the auditor's face. 'We'll walk along the corridor.'

They proceeded to do so. Schmidt's heart was beating faster; three images were clear in his head: Wagner's broken-mouthed face; the Zurich scheme, set up like a house of cards, awaiting an interrogatory puff of breath from any inquiry to come; his own jeopardy. Given the apparent case against Wagner, could the Nazi functionary work a miracle and remove him from the clutches of the Gestapo before they beat the truth about Zurich out of him, before they killed him?

'My colleague at the bank, Herr Wagner. The Gestapo have arrested him, beaten him badly. He was on a mission to Zurich for the bank which has aroused their suspicions. The mission was routine, perfectly legitimate. However, it's alleged he's been involved in some political action.'

As he uttered these half-truths Schmidt had fresh doubts about how far he could go with this man. Von Streck had been in that torture-chamber! He must concentrate. His mind seemed to have missed a notch. Concentrate! What if von Streck's action in the Wertheim affair had simply been the aggressive reaction of a dedicated and ambitious functionary protecting the Party's interests, his own? His connection with the Order, merely a coincidence and a little side-game. *His* sense of the 'all clear' – a mirage. He seemed to have missed another notch. Was his mind going to plunge into free-fall?

Were all his assumptions about the Nazi functionary built on sand?

Suddenly Schmidt felt empty.

Von Streck stared straight ahead as they paced along the wide, timber-planked corridor, and seemed to weigh the auditor's utterance.

At last he said, 'Dietrich and the gross Otto Wertheim are fine actors. Most convincing in their protestations that they know nothing of the missing ten million. One might think they're truthful – if one didn't know better.' His throaty voice vibrated in the corridor. He smiled sardonically. 'They make bitter accusations against you, Schmidt. However, they've been prevailed upon to sign authorities on the Swiss bank to repatriate the bonds.'

Schmidt stared at him hard, pulling himself together, and said, 'Herr Wagner?'

'Cannot be released. This past half-hour he's signed a statement admitting his complicity with Dietrich and Wertheim in embezzling the bonds, smuggling them out. Admitted other matters. Of course, in the Swiss affair he was duped by those criminals. *That* must be a shock to you.'

He gave the auditor a dry look.

Schmidt stared back. Von Streck had moved to bridge the gap. Though how that pair could dupe Wagner on a financial matter was a fragile proposition. Von Streck was ahead of him! He'd felt that events were running out of his control, and now the dimensions were taking shape. Involuntarily, he'd stopped walking. Alone the Nazi paced on.

'I saved Wagner at the frontier on his way to Zurich,' the Nazi said. 'The Gestapo had his number.'

Schmidt's shoulders jerked with nerves. Von Streck had known of Wagner's journey even as he was telling him of Dietrich and Otto's criminal actions ... He moved forward. 'Why didn't you save him tonight?'

'The situation is complicated, Schmidt.' The Nazi brooded on the dark at the end of the passage. 'Also it has changed. At the frontier, I'd no precise knowledge of what you were up to. Except that something was in motion – and Wagner and you were as thick as thieves. I wished to observe the full scope of your machinations. A suitable description, I think. My congratulations and admiration. Since you came to my office with your revelation, since that stimulating interlude at the bank this morning, I've a very precise understanding of the affair – even as to your motives. Poor unfortunate Fräulein Dressler. Again – my admiration Schmidt.' He was smiling at the auditor. 'But don't ask for too much.'

Wagner was to be sacrificed. Schmidt stared to the dead-end of the corridor. With a sickening feeling, he knew that the foreign manager no longer had any part in whatever von Streck's plans were. Yet, the special plenipotentiary was anti-Nazi. The confirmation was plain in his words.

Von Streck had halted, and turned his bulky figure to look back at the auditor. His eyes glinted in the light. 'I pointed out the deficiency in the case to you, Schmidt, and now it's been rectified. Herr Wagner has quite admirably served the purpose. A few in the Gestapo have brains. Never forget it. How the bearer bonds got to Zurich would've been a burning question in their minds. That deficiency had to be rectified. It won't go to court. The Party will have a hearing. Affidavits are being prepared for your signature. I have an excellent man who's done wonders in the drafting. Dietrich and Wertheim will be tried, executed within the week. Good news, eh?'

Schmidt remained speechless. Chilled. In a flash he'd an image of Dietrich and Otto, standing against a prison wall staring at the firing squad. *And Wagner.* They paced back. Schmidt's mind was wrestling with monsters.

'One feels sorry for Wagner, though he's been imprudent in his *other* activities. But the greater need must have precedence.' This time he shot the auditor a speculative look.

Schmidt thought dully: *That gap, that loose end, could have finished up anywhere. Would've sabotaged the plan. Wagner had to be Dietrich's and Otto's co-conspirator. If only he'd not tried to return – gone from Zurich direct to Paris.*

In signing the confession he had sacrificed himself. That struck Schmidt so hard that he staggered.

The Nazi seized his arm. 'Steady, Schmidt ... in the Third Reich, shocks await us every hour, around every corner. Much is in the air. Many levers are being pulled. For instance, that old fox Wertheim could hardly believe it when the Party's business was landed in his lap. But who put it there?' He laughed quietly. 'Very little can be taken at face value.'

Even in his daze, Schmidt knew he'd received an insight. Suddenly von Streck said, looking at him, 'You're a very brave and competent man, Herr Schmidt. An individual with rare talent and a hero's precepts. Altogether, a man with extremely unusual and useful qualities, and I've great plans for you.' He nodded to himself. 'I must return to my colleagues. We'll meet again soon.'

Recovering, thinking hard, Schmidt said, 'Wagner's a good man. He should be saved. He could be very useful to you.'

'I'm sorry Herr Schmidt, that is no longer possible. For your sake, and for mine.'

In the frigid corridor, stock-still, Schmidt heard the shouts of reunion as the special plenipotentiary, apparently the star turn, rejoined his party.

The man's last phrase flashed in his brain. Dully, Schmidt

felt the horror subsiding, and a sense of fatalism taking him over. Still he stood motionless. It came to him, that this Wertheim episode was just the beginning.

He suddenly remembered he had a home to go to — if it could be described as such now.

However, he didn't go home. Wagner's small gold key was in his pocket. He must take care of this last piece of business for his friend and colleague. Grimly, obdurately, he moved into the streets.

Where Dr Bernstein had had his rooms was a ten-minute walk, and almost immediately he was in a depopulated, dingy district. The thin building looked abandoned. From the opposite corner, Schmidt scrutinised it. No lit windows, but some feeble illumination in the downstairs foyer. Narrow streets went away from him like spokes on a wheel. Street by street, shadowy doorway by doorway, he inspected them. No sign of humanity. The cold bored into his bones like steel screws were being turned into them.

He crossed the street and entered the foyer. It was lit by a single bulb. Ignoring the door under the stairs he went up two flights to Dr Bernstein's dark door. Stuck to the glass was a notice: *Closed down. For dental attention contact Dr Muller*, etc. He retraced his steps.

In the foyer, he listened, sorting out sounds: a distant train; a shutter banging on a wall; the wind in some kind of wires. He opened the door under the stairs. Fourth board from the entrance. Enough light came in. The board looked a fixture; he bent down and tried it with his fingers. Then he took out his pen-knife and slid it into the crack. It came up easily. A tin deed-box. He laid it at his feet. He listened again: timber-creaks in the old building. He had the key out; it inserted, turned easily. He lifted the lid.

The banded packages of mint banknotes filled it to the

brim. French francs. The crisp smell of new money saturated the tiny space. It figured. Dietrich's phrase. He closed it, picked it up, and edged out to the foyer. He shut the door and turned to leave.

Two figures stood in the street door. Schmidt couldn't move; stared at them like a hare caught in headlights.

'*Herr Schmidt!* What a surprise! Though, is it really? Under the stairs, four boards in from the door ...?' The second figure emitted three short barks, begun as a laugh, finishing as a cough. Wagner's interrogators! 'You bankers do work strange hours. And at suspicious locations. In your case, that is. Let me see that box, mein herr.'

'This box?'

The Gestapo man leapt forward, as did his colleague. But they were in flight, falling. Explosions. Two. Horrific. Bursting his eardrums, blowing his head off, blasting apart the rickety wooden balustrade of the stairs. All in a micro-second. He reeled back against the stairs, his ears ringing, a strange smell in the air. At his feet the two men had thudded down, converted to inanimate bundles.

Von Streck's blond colleague stepped in from the doorway, the large revolver hanging loosely from his hand, a wisp of smoke detaching from it. 'Two less,' he said calmly. He nodded to the door behind him. 'Please leave, mein herr. Quickly! I will take care of the box.'

Schmidt stepped over the corpses and went out to the street, where the breeze sang in telephone wires. No lights had come on in the windows; no curtain was lifted. This was Germany. He was two streets away, and calming down, when the thoughts began to roll in his brain: the blond man must have followed him; von Streck was as thorough at tidying up loose ends as he was ruthless. He stopped and stared at his blacked-out city. He, Franz Schmidt, was now irreversibly in orbit around the special plenipotentiary's star. Wherever it was going.

EPILOGUE

SCHMIDT WAITED IN an anteroom. The atmosphere was reminiscent of being at his dentist, though Doctor Bernstein's waiting room couldn't be compared to this opulence. The French settees looked uncomfortable to his eye, but this wasn't an occasion to sit down. So he paced up and down the honey-coloured parquet floor, spruce from his barbering that afternoon, handsome in his new, well-cut suit – in its lapel the Party badge exhibiting his empathy with the times.

Von Streck had made him a special offer. He'd understood it was one he couldn't refuse. But then, he hadn't wanted to. Also, von Streck had returned to him his famous ancestor's *Salzburg cantatas*. Poor Wagner couldn't risk not bringing them back into Germany.

So here he was. He considered recent events in the banking world. Herr Wertheim had been diagnosed with a brain tumour, and had retired from the bank and gone into seclusion at his country estate, taking Fräulein Blum with him as an assistant for the last months of his life. Wagner had been the first to detect the symptoms of the disease, though he'd never known their cause.

While Schmidt was pacing the corridor with von Streck at 11.00 pm that terrible night, the deputy foreign manager had died of his injuries.

Herr Schloss had been appointed general-director and had taken control to the relief of many; Schmidt had admired the rigorous efficiency with which he'd returned the *Wertheim* to port, and dry-dock – if not to safety. The Party had recovered the bonds from the Swiss bank and now the lawyers were arguing over the mysteriously missing amount of 500,000.

His footsteps were setting up echoes in the salon. The NSDAP investment business had returned to the Berlin bank. In retrospect, he identified an inevitability about this, even as he recalled Herr Wertheim's euphoria at the time of its acquisition. Certainly, the Berlin bankers had always thought so. They'd travelled to Wertheim & Co for the settlement, patronising triumph in their eyes.

Von Streck. Schmidt stopped pacing and turned his eye to the gleaming floor. Clearly the Nazi ranks were rotten with power-plays, ambition and greed. The slippery politics of it were always in sinuous motion. In moving the Party's investment funds to Wertheims the special plenipotentiary had been building his power-base. Subsequently surveying the Wertheim scene, he'd discovered Schmidt: a man who'd lost an eye to the SA in a quixotic act; a man with a deep family involvement with the Teutonic Knights; a man who'd attempted to save a Jewess in another hopeless, quixotic act. A man who could be a great asset to a cause. And, he supposed, it could be said: Ultimately, a man with a machiavellian mind. Schmidt couldn't be positive about all of this, but, it must be close to the mark.

He'd thought further about the incident in Dr Bernstein's old building and decided that von Streck's blond assassin had not been following him. He'd been on the tail of Wagner's Gestapo interrogators to clean up that loose end. Von Streck couldn't risk the Gestapo team, after interrogating Wagner, looking too closely into the antecedents of the Swiss affair. Despite the foreign manager's confession ...

He paused to better appreciate the gilded room. Had the

Party paid for all of this? He'd been dwelling in a claustro-phobic existence – it seemed that his horizons were about to widen to embrace this pomp and circumstance, a new life.

As if this were a cue, double doors at the end of the room sprang open. Von Streck stood there, beaming, his hand grandly extended. Behind him hovered a restless galaxy of colourful uniforms and superior civilian suiting. It immediately struck Schmidt that the key motif to this striking scene – on the walls, on sleeves – was the swastika. As the guests circulated, the sinister emblem seemed to flutter and dance. 'Without finesse,' Wagner would've sneered. So here I am, he thought, entering 'a corrupt and bogus world'. Who'd said that? Not Wagner.

'Come in, my dear fellow, I want to introduce you around.'

Schmidt marched down the anteroom to take von Streck's hand. Surely, that was the knight's trumpet in the far distance? Inside his head? Did von Streck hear it? Forty or so faces, pink and approving, reminding him of plump hams, had turned to regard him, the general conversation had died, as though someone had tapped a wine glass with a knife in the time-honoured way.

Von Streck stood inside this inner sanctum, and raised his soft, strangler's hands. Throttling the conversation, one might say. Schmidt asked himself if he could still risk this kind of thought any more.

'Gentlemen, I wish to introduce to you Herr Franz Schmidt, banker and auditor, who's rendered the Party a great service – uncovering a traitorous fraud against Party funds – and who I'm certain will render it many more. *I present Herr Schmidt!*' Schmidt watched those hands drop to the func-tionary's sides.

Applause rippled throughout the room. Von Streck led him forward to introduce him to individuals. 'Congratulations,' they said one by one.

A brown-uniformed official said, 'We'll expect great things from you now at the Ministry of Economics.'

Schmidt bowed, and glanced at his mentor. Von Streck replied with weighty yet exuberant authority. 'As the director of audit he'll have great scope for engaging in the nation's financial affairs. *Great* scope. He'll bring his superior intelligence to the task, you'll see!'

Schmidt could tell von Streck was in the highest spirits. Recently, the functionary had remarked, 'You and I, Schmidt, have a kind of telepathy going. There are things between us which don't need to be spoken of – bear that in mind.'

Now, in a confidential aside he said, 'One door closes, another opens. Exciting times my dear fellow – for those of us of the right calibre. Special opportunities, to make the difference! I could tell from the beginning you'd a rare talent. One might say that the Wertheim imbroglio was a trial run. Much more important game's afoot. The fulcrum of the Reich is money and the economy. Together, we can be a lever! Ah! … we must pay our respects to Admiral Canaris, and Colonel Oster. This is the circle you'll be moving in, Schmidt. One of rare and splendid birds indeed. Come.'

He followed the formidable passage of von Streck through the assembly. There appeared to be a sympathetic undercurrent between von Streck and Canaris. Yes, exciting, dangerous – but fertile – times to further investigate knightly precepts, though he'd never seen so many steely, calculating, and just plain wary eyes at one time. In quick succession he was passing from hand to hand – like being on the floor at an old-fashioned country dance. One man was introduced without show. 'Von Hase, from Hamburg,' von Streck said softly with an enigmatic smile, 'he's just taken up a key post in the chemical industry.' He added, 'The three of us share a particular interest.'

Momentarily, von Streck left him alone in an enclave.

Schmidt stood transfixed, enthralled at a thought. Von Streck was lighting *many* small fires in key strategic locations across the Reich. Suddenly that seemed as certain as the shining glass prothesis in his left eye-socket. A nervous smile fluttered on his lips.

The faces of the Dresslers flashed in his mind's eye. Lilli's face. It seemed an age since he'd been drawn into her doomed orbit. Now he had to put it behind him. No more slipping of notches! He had to pull himself up and out of that.

He turned, surveying the room. He'd entered the citadel! Gone into its iron heart. Had a convoluted journey begun the evening three years ago when they'd put out his eye? Or, had all of his life been an overture to this crusade? He felt he could quite properly use 'crusade'. Or was it all absolutely due to chance? One thing he felt surely within himself: Dürer's knight had ridden back into the mist, and his ruthless Teutonic ancestor, he of the treachery on the Vistula, had ridden out of it to his side.

'I do not know myself, and God forbid that I should.' – the immortal Goethe. Time for reflection was needed but wouldn't be granted. It was on to the next thing. And clearly, the Fuehrer had much in store for the Third Reich.

Outside, Berlin brooded in the winter night. Beyond the voices in the room, the walls, he felt that. He told himself that Helga and Trudi would be safe in Dresden while he undertook the valuable work for which he had the 'rare talent'. Their safety depended on a sharp and complete separation from him. The danger he'd been in at Wertheims was a pale shadow to that which he could now expect, deep in the heart of the anti-Nazi movement.

He felt a pang of sadness (time flees and he would miss his daughter's childhood), but also a rare exhilaration. Of course, as one historian had recorded: 'To be useful, to earn rewards, the trick is to survive.' That was something Dietrich,

and Otto, already mouldering in their unmarked graves, had
failed to achieve.

AUTHOR'S NOTE

I N THE EARLY 1930s, based on certain precepts of the
Order of Teutonic Knights, the Nazis established so-called
Order Castles as one of three types of school for the train-
ing of their élite. Only the most fanatical young National
Socialists were selected for the Order Castles, one of which
was established within the medieval walls of the Teutonic
Knights' castle at Marienburg in East Prussia.

In 1938 Admiral Wilhelm Canaris was head of the Intelligence Bureau of the German High Command. Colonel Hans
Oster was his chief assistant. From the early days of the regime,
both men were strong anti-Nazis and two of the key conspira-
tors in a plot to get rid of Hitler in the prelude to the conquest
of Czechoslovakia, and in other plots during the war.